READER REWARD

As the author of this work, I offer you, the reader, the opportunity to redeem a cash award for introducing this work to any literary agent, publisher or producer that offers an acceptable contract Richard Evans for this work. The reward offered is 10% of any initial book advance or option contract for film or television up to a maximum of AUD $10,000. Why am I offering a cash reward to readers?

- **Odds:** 98%+ of all works published today initially found their way to a publisher by introduction as opposed to arriving via "the slush pile" so the odds are better doing it this way.

- **Volume:** Writing is an inherently solitary endeavour and as an author I struggle (off the page) to network, mingle, and promote my own work. Offering readers, a reward to do it not only augments my inability but also multiplies the effort as each volume in the hands of reader starts diverse chains of discussion and introduction, one of which will lead to success.

- **Collaboration:** Reading is unique among all entertainment vehicles in that it requires effort from the reader: the author and reader collaborate to tell the story. Hearing what readers enjoy is exciting to any author and the collaboration of this reward program offers the reader a chance to help jump start the career of an author he/ she enjoys. Besides, publishers are much more interested in readers' likes vs. authors' offerings.

Suggestions:

Via this reward, our mutual goal is to introduce this work to literary and publishing professionals or producers. Many are likely familiar with the term *"six degrees of separation,"* the theory that anyone on the planet can be connected to any other person on the planet through a chain of acquaintances that has no more than five intermediaries. This is what I aim to accomplish here with your help.

- Think about who you know in publishing (literary agents, editors, readers, executives, etc.) and pass this volume on to them.
- Think about who you know and who they might know in publishing.
- Think about who you know that reads and would enjoy this book.

Send any leads, or opportunities, or introductions via the email link below.

rewards@richardevans-author.com
Thank you in advance for your help.

READERS TALK ABOUT RICHARD EVANS

Richard Evans' first book, Deceit, is a five-star thriller that brings the Australian political process to life. – *GOODREADS*

I absolutely loved it, couldn't put it down. I would love to see your book become a movie. – *IAN S., MELBOURNE*

Rich in ideas and provokes much thought about our parliamentary process, abuses of power, corruption, and the need, at times, for ordinary people to step up and take a stand in the name of honour and professional integrity. – *NADINE D., EDITOR*

'The Kill Bill has such a fascinating concept at its heart, and you brought the characters to life brilliantly.' – *C.dB, EDITOR*

This is an outstanding debut from Evans, and this terrific read comes highly recommended.' – *GOODREADS*

From former Federal MP Richard Evans comes this exceptional political thriller debut, which serves as the first part of his Democracy trilogy.' *CANBERRA WEEKLY*

I adored Gordon O'Brien. Straight as an arrow amongst those who are only in things for themselves, I couldn't help but cheer him on as he was like a dog with a bone, searching out the truth' *BJ'S BOOK BLOG*

Just finished reading *Deceit* and it was gripping; I could not put it down. It was brilliant. I just loved the book and can't wait to read *Duplicity*.' *FORMER CLERK OF VICTORIAN LEGISLATIVE COUNCIL*

I thoroughly enjoyed the book and did not want to put the book down, but neither did I want the story to end! Congratulations! – *TRINITY MARKETING*

OUT OF
MY HANDS

RICHARD EVANS

852
PRESS

852

PRESS

First published in 2021 by 852 Press,
an imprint of Corven Pty. Limited
Suite 208, 5-11 Cole Street, Williamstown Victoria 3016 Australia
www.852Press.com.au

10 9 8 7 6 5 4 3 2 1

National Library of Australia Cataloguing-in-Publication entry:

Author: Evans, Richard
Title: Out of My Hands / by Richard Evans
ISBN: 978-0-6452823-7-5 (Trade paperback)
ISBN: 978-0-6452823-8-2 (ebook)
ISBN: 978-0-6452823-9-9 (hardcover)
Fiction.

 A catalogue record for this book is available from the National Library of Australia

Cover Design: www.852Press.com.au
Internal design: www.852Press.com.au

For Bonnie

There will always be Dobson's.

Every human being that believes in capital punishment loves killing, and the only reason they believe in capital punishment is because they get a kick out of it. Nobody kills anyone for love unless they get over it temporarily or otherwise. But they kill the one they hate. And before you can get a trial to hang somebody or electrocute him, you first must hate him and have satisfaction over his death.

We teach people to kill, and the State is the one that teaches them. If the State wishes that its citizens respect human life. Then the State should stop killing. It can be done no other way, and it will perhaps not be fully done that way.

There are infinite reasons for killing. There are infinite circumstances under which there are more or less deaths. It never did depend and never can depend upon the severity of the punishment.

I am against it because I believe it is inhuman, because I believe that as the hearts of men have softened, they have gradually gotten rid of brutal punishment, because I believe that it will only be a few years until it will be banished forever from every civilized country—even New York; because I believe that it has no effect whatever to stop murder.

Clarence Darrow (1857-1938)
New York, 23 September 1924

As of 2021

- The death penalty remains a legal sentence in 27 US states, including California.
- 55 countries retain the penalty.

CHAPTER
1

Billy may come to resent ever knowing Max Roberts. He will if he survives the wild car ride. A journey he regretted the moment he slid into the back seat of the stolen Dodge.

Speed was not Billy Humphries' friend. He stiffened, clammy hands gripping his knees, eyes stretched as colors flashed past. The roar of the engine muted any sound. He panted, and his tongue worked hard to moisten his lips.

His pal Max, high on exuberance, buzzed the window down and a gusting breeze whipped their lank hair. Billy squeezed between him and Joe Capelli, the younger brother of Bo and Arnie up front. The musty tang of exhaust fumes churned through the cabin, adding to his discomfort. The gushing air only slightly relieving him. His heart pumped hard; he could feel it beat against his clothes. Unlike the others, he was not enjoying the jaunt.

"Max, I hate this," he wailed, clawing tangled hair from his face.

"Sit back and enjoy, buddy, this is friggin' great." The others paid no attention. "Faster Bo, faster," Max hollered, counting on the barn-like driver to crank the acceleration.

Billy dropped his head on the seat, closed his eyes, wishing the ordeal over. His mind tried to drift to images of happiness, but it would have none of that. The ear-splitting noise irritated his ears. High on adrenaline and wild from the speed, the others hooting, bouncing about, breaking traffic laws as they hurtled toward Coronado.

Billy squeezed his eyes harder, screwing up his face, trying to keep the noise out.

He remembered the first time that drove his fear of fast-moving objects. It was the fun park rollercoaster at Mission Beach. Pushed against his will into a bucket by a smiling mother and scowling attendant. Then towed up to an enormous height and thrown down with such force it felt as if his hamburger would revisit. Then chugged up and tossed down again. His five-year-old body thrust from side to side. He screamed; no one came.

Traumatized, he vowed never to go back. Now he was reliving his nightmare.

The Dodge powered along Silver Strand; the land peninsular connecting the mainland to Coronado Island. They were a notorious gang showing a total disregard for the law from the Otay Mesa district of San Diego. Arnie, a tough rogue, intent on destruction, the oldest and leader. He treated the others as foot soldiers to do whatever he signaled. He wore battle scars with honor, the biggest a whitened scar destroying the complexion on the side of his face. Caused when a victim of his violent largesse shoved a broken beer tumbler into it. He was their general in a war against authority. Max worshipped him. Billy hated him.

Billy felt the car slow, raising his head from the seat, opening his eyes. The roar of the engine reduced to a hum; the excitement waned.

"Where to?" asked Bo, keen to crank it up again.

"Do you want to stay on the Island or go back, Max?" asked Arnie.

"Let's go back," Billy said, hoping Max would pick up his anxiety.

"What's wrong with you? Ya fag."

Billy knew Arnie didn't like him. He reckoned Billy was always complaining and not wanting to join in and was too close to Max.

"Look, the car's still hot," Billy said. "I reckon we should go back, put it under wraps, then hit the local bar for a game of pool."

"Yeah, I'm with you B-B-Billy," said Joe, prompting a snarl from his older brother.

"I vote for pool," said Max. "But let's head up Mission Beach way."

"Why not stay around here?" challenged Arnie.

"We could get booze, go north and pick up some girls. There's got to be more pussy up that way. Let's go check it out. Too many sailors round here," Max said.

He wanted excitement away from their normal hangouts. The illegals and dead beats in Otay were exhausting, and he hankered for something new.

"Mission Beach it is. Head for the tollway, Bo."

Billy sighed, slumped his head back onto the seat, wishing he were elsewhere. Loyal to Max, but he hated the Capellis. They were trouble. He wasn't afraid of breaking the law, far from it, but the snowballing violence of the gang's activities intimidated him.

Billy and Max were typical of their breed in Otay. They didn't work, had little education, and relied on family, friends and crime to pay for heavy addictions to booze and bennies. Crime for kicks was a common occurrence in Otay.

Billy, a diminutive eighteen-year-old a touch taller than Max, topping five foot four, disheveled with a careless attitude to themselves. Smelly with unkempt hair and unshaven fluff of adolescent facial hair, adding to their motley look.

Years of neglect took all sparkle from Billy's eyes. The emptiness of their darkness was symbolic of a torrid and wasted life. Daily floggings from an abusive stepfather hardened him from life's normal affections. His mother tried to offer the love her son needed but spent most of her days in a prescription drug haze.

Billy and Max shared many things together, taking great pride in their matching tattoos; the homemade blue ink and hot sewing needle type, with letters of hate and scum tattooed across the fingers of each hand. The poor inked characters over their arms and legs showed they didn't see body decoration as an art-form. It was a sign of their bond, and unintentionally, their lack of respect for themselves.

"Snap out of it, Billy," said Max, punching Billy, arousing him.

"Christ, Max. Piss off. That friggin' hurt," Billy said, rubbing his arm, then whispering behind his hand. "What are we doing with these guys? You know they scare the hell outta me."

"Don't worry buddy. I promise you a hot honey tonight. I think a west coast babe may be better than gutter trash. Come on, snap out of it," said Max. "It'll be wild, man."

"That's crap," scoffed Billy. "No honey from up the coast is going to give us the time of day. Look, I've got weird feelings about this. The hairs are up on my neck."

"Relax brother, I'll look after you."

Billy cupped the back of his neck, giving it a reassuring rub.

The Dodge roared over the tollway, cruising through downtown before heading north past the airport, then onto Nimitz. Bo cranked up the speed. The boys responding, Billy groaned, dropping his head back.

"Give it the j-j-juice, Bo," Joe squawked.

Bo bit down on his lip, squinted, gripped the wheel, pushing his boot hard into the floor. Billy sweated in silence. They sped through a bend and the setting sun's brilliance blinded Bo. Instinctively, hitting the brakes.

"Christ."

Billy's greatest fear now upon him as Bo struggled with the flaying car. Arnie howled in encouragement. Max and Joe sat braced. The car came to a standstill in a pallor of smoking rubber and a stench of wasted money.

"You dumb friggin' bastard. What the hell do you think you're friggin' doing? Trying to kill us?" Billy shouted.

"Hey!" snarled Arnie, turning from the front with a waving clenched fist. "Keep ya cock suckin' mouth shut."

"Ease up Arnie," Max said. "We're okay. Anyways, we should hold it down now I reckon. We don't want the pigs onto us."

"He's got no right to call my brother dumb."

Arnie was almost over the seat. Billy cowered.

"Arnie? Hey? Are you kidding me? His name is Brett, for goddamn sake. Bo is his nickname... you know? As in Dumbo. Give the guy a break. He didn't mean nothin'." Max offered a timid chuckle.

Bo, a gentle giant who did what he was told. He had no right or wrong, just a sense of duty toward his brothers. Whatever they called for him to do, he did it. In return, they looked after him, getting the things he loved. Fast cars mostly.

"Yeah, but that don't mean he can call him dumb." Arnie settled back into his seat, glaring over his shoulder.

"No, you're right, Arnie. Say you're sorry, Billy."

"Ooh, for Christ's sake." Billy just needed it to end. "I'm sorry Bo, I didn't mean it. Can we slow down now? Please?"

"Sure thing, Billy." Bo smiled and got the car going again.

Now happier with a cut down speed, Billy sighed, gazing across at his pal. He smirked at the anticipatory grin on Max's face as he stared out into the passing scenery.

CHAPTER
2

It took the gang almost twenty minutes to reach Mission Beach. Billy passed a fretful glance at the fun park as they cruised by, and the traumatized memory touched him for a moment.

"We need gas, Arnie," Bo wheezed, his asthma building.

Billy turned his nose to the window, sniffed and picked up the unmistakable refreshing aroma of the seaside. The air seemed different to the southern suburbs, and he thought why. Perhaps it was the constant stench of industry shrouding air back home.

"We'll get a few beers into us, Bo," said Arnie. "Pull over when you see a bar. How much money you guys got?"

"Roughly thirty," replied Max.

"Me too," added Billy.

"Geezus! Do you boys do everything together?" Arnie said. "How's about you, Joey?"

"I've got f-f-forty."

"That'll do. Enough, I reckon, for shooters and a couple of beers. We may even get a game of pool in before we pick up gas. If we need any more, we'll just take it," said Arnie.

"A fat wallet is all we need," said Max, laughing.

"Come on, Bo, I'm dying of thirst back here," Billy joked, slumping into his seat. He was no innocent choirboy. Hanging out with Max involved crimes, many with brutal violence, yet the Capellis were something else. They scared him.

Bo swung the car onto Grand Avenue at Pacific Beach and cruised toward the coast. He saw a bay in the center parking station and glided in. Arnie got out to figure out whether the location was suitable for them while the others waited. It wasn't long before he was sticking his head through the window beside Max.

"Boys, there's two bars on this strip. One we wouldn't get into because you guys don't have ID and they wouldn't serve us anyway, too upmarket. The other? Well, it's got a small crowd, and it's our kind of place. A few rednecks having a good time. Who said they wouldn't like us here in the ritzy part of town, Billy?"

"Let's go," said Billy, agitated by Arnie's constant snipping.

The gang drifted over to the West Coast Lagoon, a single fronted bar offering pool, pinball, and cocktails. They settled into a booth by the front door overlooking the street, ordering beers with tequila shooters. Max and Bo went off to the washrooms, and Billy moseyed over to the old jukebox to check out the music. He wanted to stay away from Arnie for as long as he could.

He flicked through the encased pages and the metal containers clanked as he searched for something that would brighten his spirits. Jimmy Morrison was Billy's hero, so he dropped two bits into the slot and brought up the Doors. They weren't in Los Angeles, but *L.A. Woman* seemed like an apt tune for their night of carousing. Who knows, maybe Max was right, and they would get lucky.

As the distinctive lyrics sounded out, he turned and leaned on the jukebox to survey the bar. A few booths lined the walls, limiting space for any conversations with strangers. At the rear, near the washrooms, was a games room. He could hear the distant pings of a pinball machine being rattled. Men lined the neon lit wooden bar with more coming in. He suspected the place was hotting up. A girl with a tattoo on her arm, swinging in time with the music, passing him a smirking glance. Things were picking up for Billy as he wandered back to the booth.

"Great choice, B-B-Billy," said Joe.

"If you're a fag, eh, Billy?" chided Arnie, smiling, hoping for a sting.

"Christ! Give it a rest, Arnie, will ya? You've been on my case since we left. Let's just have a quiet drink and stay out of each other's faces for a few hours."

"Fine with me."

Max suggested a game of pool, so they gathered their drinks and sauntered out back.

CHAPTER
3

"Sandi, you're kidding me. It's almost dark and we've worked darn hard all day. My feet are killing me, and we've done enough," an exasperated Barbara exclaimed. "Come on, let's go eat, I'm starved."

"You run ahead; I'll only be a few minutes."

"Sandi, I don't like the look of that place."

"No. Go ahead, order me a soda. I'll be back before they return with the order."

"All right, but make it snappy, I need something to eat."

Sandi scooped up her collection bag and made her way to the West Coast Lagoon.

The look in Alice Johnston's eyes said it all. The miracle she and husband Bernie prayed for over many years was lying in her arms snuggling and sniffing for milk. The bond between mom and daughter immediate and eight hours after the birth, the love between them obvious.

"You look so peaceful." A nurse was checking her chart, admiring the bonding.

"Life is so complete," Alice responded not taking her eyes from her baby. "The oneness I feel is as if we stay attached. I couldn't be happier."

11

Miracles don't happen often, and many suspect none exist, yet little Sandra Emily Johnston was evidence. She was a miracle.

"Whatever she wants she will have," Bernie promised, peeking at his girl in the loving arms of Alice. "I'll be there whenever she needs me."

Alice glanced up and smiled, her baby snuggling into her breast. "Bernie, you will be the perfect father, don't you worry." Alice had taken her eyes off her for too long and returned her gaze.

From a very young age, Sandi displayed various random acts of kindness, molding her character into her adult years. A stray cat or dog or injured bird would have a haven at the Johnston's house. As her menagerie grew, so did Sandi's reputation for helping others.

She worshipped the sun, playing any sport allowing her to be outside. Her olive skin darkened into a rich tan in summer, contrasting against her luxuriant hair, giving her a beach look, the envy of classmates. She did have the normal blemishes and concerns about body shape and worried whether boys would ever date her.

It wasn't long before friends were pestering her to make a career of modeling. She was not at interested in standing before the cameras of commercialism. She remained shy and ignorant to the wiles of the world, wanting to concentrate on her humanitarian interests. They pestered her and on her eighteenth birthday presented a photographic portrait voucher as a gift. Reluctantly, she booked a sitting.

"You make my work so easy," André told her during the shoot. "You are a natural." He worked around her, the motorized shutter flicking. "You melt into the camera, and you lighten up the entire studio."

When Sandi collected her portfolio, André asked permission to show several prints at an exhibition and send them to a few agents. At first suspicious, Sandi agreed, on condition he did not allow any publication of the photographs without her approval. She visited the exhibition's opening cocktail party and ventured through the milling guests; compliment followed compliment.

She weakened at the idea of becoming a model.

On Andre's suggestion, she auditioned with the Marks Agency. The principals so impressed they commissioned several assignments. Within weeks of joining, they had her striding catwalks and completing important photographic sessions. The firm soon had her as the public face promoting the San Diego Chargers and baseball with the Padres.

The veneered, self-interested fashion glitterati could never come to grips with a view of life not accompanied with champagne and caviar and disillusionment arrived. The men dating her were shallow, their groping, clammy hands did not bring her joy. She developed a dislike for the parties, the hangers-on, the abuse of drugs and alcohol, and the miscreants at the end of the night. Sandi missed her family and friends.

No one understood why Sandi rejected a lucrative career to pursue other secret interests. "Where I am going no one will care who I am or where I have been."

To Sandi, life required greater meaning than the whirring of a camera and fake smiles.

It did not surprise her friends when she joined the nursing staff at Mission Bay Hospital.

She never regretted giving away the heavy make-up and cynical falseness of the fashion industry for a nursing career as a clinical nurse specializing in microsurgery, the most tragic and intricate category of remedial medicine.

"Not for the squirmy" was how Dr. Gilchrist described it in an early lecture. A fact reinforced by the 75% dropout rate from classes.

Nursing introduced her to an intern, Tom Moroni, a dreamer, attracting Sandi to his ideas about improving the living standards of Americans, especially the homeless.

"How can we live in the greatest nation in the world, one with so many riches, and yet many of our citizens remain destitute on the streets?" he asked over lunch at the cafeteria.

"If anyone could come up with a solution, Tom, it would be you," a smitten Sandi replied.

They married on Valentine's Day, leaving soon after on an extended honeymoon to Africa. The hopeless poverty overtook the awe of nature's greatest animals. The biggest impact, Alexandria, on the outer limits of Johannesburg. A shantytown decamping 300,000 settlers in any slapped-together housing structure within an area no greater than a football field. The poverty overwhelmed them, and they resolved to return and work for the community.

On their return to California, they sought worthy causes. Their ultimate plan to go back as medical missionaries once Tom completed his training. Sandi volunteered for charities that sent funds to Africa. It was her way of helping until she could do more. She committed to their cause and believed her effort would help in a small way, relieving the appalling human tragedy that was Africa.

Sandi would set off with her friend Barbara most Saturdays, collecting money for her causes. Barbara had been her devoted friend since Sandi placed a reassuring arm around her shoulders on their first day of grade school; they had been inseparable friends ever since.

Barbara picked up Sandi from her home in La Jolla. The friends intending to spend the afternoon and early evening collecting. Later, having a quiet dinner as reward at Barbara's favorite nightspot in Pacific Beach called the Brewery.

The scorching sun had disappeared when Barbara pulled into the center parking station on Grand Avenue. They gathered their gear in preparation to walk over to the restaurant. Sandi noticed a bar opposite, and assuming she was close to a collection target, suggested Barbara save a table.

Sandi bounced into the West Coast Lagoon with the same bubbly confidence she always radiated. She silenced many patrons as they took in the lady before them. As an act of courtesy, she continued to the bar to ask permission to collect donations.

The bartender said she would allow collection for such a worthy cause and suggested she remember the drinkers out back in the games room. The crowded bar proved generous. She squeezed past a girl with a colorful tattoo on her arm and sidled up to a jovial group of men standing around others sitting in a booth.

"Can you help the African children?" Sandi asked a sweating fat man relaxing in the booth.

"Sure thing, little lady," his accent Texan. "Just let me make change at the bar."

"Thank you, sir. You are very kind. Shall I wait?"

"No, you skip back into the games room and when you head out just mosey on by and I'll drop money into your bag."

"Thank you, sir. I'll be back in a few moments." Sandi flashed the big guy a generous smile and squeezed past him, heading for the games room, collecting donations on her way.

She reached the dimly lit room to discover five men playing pool.

CHAPTER

4

The gang played pool for an hour with Arnie dispatching all comers, feeling cocky and ready for conflict. Adrenalin and alcohol a weird mix for excitable people often making them dangerous. Arnie more confident with his authority over the others.

The room was thick with putrid cigarette and marijuana smoke. Neon beer signs added to the gaudy atmosphere. Pin ball machines flickered, beckoning players at the far end of the room. The three centered pool tables beneath low hanging long shaded light fittings illuminating those who stood close.

"Come on, you guys who wants another game?"

"Arnie, you've d-d-done us, man, l-l-let's g-g-get out of here," said Joe.

"You guys are as weak as a hillbilly in shit."

"That maybe Arnie," Max said, chuckling. "But at least we have dicks like elephants. Your little pecker couldn't get its blood pumping in an oven."

The others laughed.

Arnie scowled. "You've got a big mouth, Max. Just big enough for your fag friend over there I bet."

"Geezus, Capelli, give it a break will you," Billy said.

"Why?" Arnie mocked. "What are you going to do fag?"

Billy sat up from lounging on a wooden bench, bolting to Arnie ready and willing to bust his face.

"Oh yeah? Come on. Let's see what you're made of you friggin' fag." Arnie tossed the pool cue onto the table, his brothers shifting in behind him.

Billy tensed his body, clenched his fists, and lunged. Max stepped in between them a bowie knife drawn and pointing toward Arnie's throat. Billy collapsed over Max's shoulders, trying to get at Arnie.

"You know pal," said Max, menacing his knife in front of his face. "When you insult my friend, you insult me. When you threaten my friend, you threaten me. And when you want to fight my friend, you fight me. So, you can either back off and give Billy slack, or Joey will call 911." Arnie hesitated. Max smiled. "Well, Arnie? Shall we be pals or do we come visit you in the hospital?"

Arnie's toughness was dangling him close to serious injury.

"J-J-Jesus! Look at that," Joe whispered, whistling low through his teeth.

Sandi bounced into the games room. Happy the big guy was going to give her a sizeable donation, and with five pool players likely to help her cause, she expected a rewarding few moments. Her eyes tried to adjust to the gloomy light, and an acrid smell flayed at her nostrils. As she approached, the hairs on her neck moved, triggering a sudden feeling of danger. *She was in a public place what could happen to her?*

The mood changed.

Max turned away to sheath his knife under his shirt and leaned against the pool table with his elbows resting on the green blaze. Arnie sat back against the table to ogle Sandi, and Billy resumed his seat in the dark.

"Can you spare a little money for the poor children of Africa?"

"Say what?" Arnie said, confused with facing a knife one moment and now a fine-looking woman.

"Can you spare change?"

"What for?"

"The poor children of Africa."

"Africans?" sneered Arnie. "You've got to be kidding me, lady."

Sandi quivered.

Bo moved closer to the table. Joe skirted behind, blocking any escape. Sandi felt uncomfortable, extending a warm smile.

"Just a few pennies to help the sick and injured."

"Piss off, honey. I give nothing for no Africans."

"Maybe we could give her something though, Arnie," said Max, conspiracy in his tone.

Sandi backed away, bumping into Joe.

"Yeah, Arnie," Joe said. "M-M-Maybe this is what you need. W-W-What do you th-th-think B-B-Billy?" Joe was almost at her ear. She tiptoed forward away from the voice as panic came to her.

"She's not our kind. Let her go," said Billy from the darkness.

Sandi's throat tightened as she tried to think of words to say. Her breathing quickened, as if her heart was about to burst.

"The fag thinks we should not donate boys." Arnie rubbed the stubble on his chin, peering at Sandi with a sinister sneer. "I think we should at least give her something to thank us for."

"Maybe I'll just collect more out front. Thank you for your consideration." Sandi struggled with the dryness of her mouth as she edged past Joe. She wanted to run, but her body wasn't reacting. Joe blocked her path. "Excuse me, please."

"Where're ya goin' honey?" Arnie stroked her arm, and she cringed from its ugliness. "I want to give you something."

"Ah look," Sandi said, breathing hard. "I don't want any trouble... I just want to leave. Let's leave it at that... I won't say anything, honest."

"No, I don't think we can do that." Arnie lunged, grabbing her by the hair at the back of her head, pulling tight. He grabbed her arm and swung her brutally onto the table. She hit the brass ridging of the pocket hard, knocking the wind from her. Bo grabbed her wrists and pulled tight from opposite, stretching her even further across the green blaze.

Arnie pressed a hand hard on her hips, making it impossible for her to move.

"Let me go... what do you think you're doing?" she gasped. When she lifted her head, all she could see was the rotting yellow teeth of an ugly man smiling, holding her wrists.

"Don't worry pretty lady, you can go soon," joked Bo, blowing a pouting kiss.

Arnie positioned himself behind her, grinding. He kicked her legs wider and rubbed his hands over her hips, kneading her buttocks.

"Come on, Arnie, this is stupid. Let her go... she ain't worth the trouble." Billy came from the darkness and tried to pull him away.

"Max, if you don't get him away from me, I'll friggin' kill him."

"Disappear, Billy, you're in the way," said Max. "Watch if you want but don't get in the way. Come on, Arnie hurry will ya, I want a go."

"Steady Max, this is what folks call foreplay."

With his left hand bracing Sandi down, Arnie slipped his right hand down to her knee and slid it up the inside of her thigh. She squirmed and kicked in opposition as best she could.

"Oh honey, I like it when you do that," moaned Arnie, and ground his hips harder. He flipped up her skirt, revealing the satin sheen of her white pants, and he groped his hand over her buttocks and between her legs. "Ooooh Lordy, you feel soooo good."

"Come on, Arnie. Hur-Hur-Hurry, someone m-m-might come."

Max had already unbuckled his belt loosened his buttons, his hand down his shorts squeezing himself into action. "If you can't get it up, let me have a go... I'm ready."

"Max, stop this," Billy urged. "This is wrong. The wrong place, wrong time, wrong girl."

"Shut up, Billy, will ya!" Max said. "I promised you pussy, didn't I? And here it is. All laid out, ready to go." His eyes were wild with excitement. "For Christ's sake, Arnie, will you get on with it!"

Arnie struggled to get his jeans open, but with only one hand to work the buckle and buttons he just fumbled, pulling, and shoving. Sandi fought hard to break free, bucking, kicking, and squealing, but each movement only increased her pain.

"Yes!" Arnie had his jeans down, positioning himself behind her. "Now bitch, just a little something for your cause."

"Hey little lady, what's keeping you?" a voice boomed from the entrance to the room.

Arnie turned away, tugging up his jeans. Bo released his tight grip. Sandi sprung up, swooped up her bag, and ran out. Retribution the furthest thing from her mind.

"Say boys, what's happening here?" The Texan was unsure what happened, but darn sure he wanted to find out.

"None of your friggin' business, fat boy." Max stood in front of him, re-buckling his belt.

"Who are you cussin' son?"

Arnie moved back into the shadows with Bo and Joe. Billy joined Max and placed a reassuring hand on his shoulder. He shrugged him off.

"You... ya fat tub of lard."

"Son, if you want to take this smart mouth of yours to the next step, then I am happy to oblige."

Max drew his knife, waving it in front of the Texan's face. "Yeah, well, maybe I'll just rip your friggin' heart out, you piece of horseshit."

"Son, that will be pretty hard to do with a hole in your head, now, won't it?" So slick was the Texan in drawing a 38 from his belt, cocking it and thumping it into Max's forehead he didn't have time to blink. When he did, he focused in on the cool greasy metal resting on his brow. The distinctive odor of burned gunpowder and the shiny bronze tips of slugs in the gray cylinder at the end of his nose, with hairy, stumpy fingers relaxed holding the gun had Max rethinking. "I would be very careful about that toothpick if I were you."

Billy pulled him away.

"Now boys, you can either finish your drinks and leave with your masculinity intact, or we can take this one step further. What's it to be?"

Joe stepped forward. "Well-well s-s-sir, if you put it in those t-t-terms we ma-may j-j-just wan-wander on."

"My view exactly." The Texan re-gripped his gun.

"W-W-We'll j-just finish our b-b-beer and b-b-bid you farewell." Joe was working hard. "We-We su-su-sincerely apolog-gise for any c-c-cussin' we may have g-g-given you s-s-sir."

"That's mighty fine of you, son." His eyes never left Max. "I hope your friend here learns the same respect. Finish your drinks and move on."

The fat guy lowered his gun and withdrew. Max trembling wanting to take it further, but not now. All thoughts of the woman gone.

Sandi stumbled from the room, clawed her way through the crowded bar, staggering out onto the street, gasping for air, bewildered, and confused. She felt sick and violated with the touch of clammy mauling hands still with her. She dry retched before staggering onto the roadway, falling against a car in the center parking station.

She composed herself, gasping in air. Fearing the men would follow she glanced back to the bar, scurrying her way to the Brewery and the comfort of her friend.

She found Barbara tucked away against a window. Sandi collapsed into a chair, shaking; wiping tears from her cheeks, she gulped her soda, trying to calm herself.

"Oh my god, what's wrong Sandi? Are you alright? What's happened?"

Sandi checked over her shoulder as the restaurant door opened. Barbara feared her friend might have seen something dreadful. She was pale, jumpy, and desperate.

Through bouts of worried tears and frightened sobs, Sandi related her story. She told of the large man then going into the games room to collect more donations only to be confronted by the thugs. She dabbed and wiped her face with a paper serviette. Her lips trembled and she bit them trying to hold back another wave of tears. When she attempted to talk about feeling the groping hands violating her, a shiver rushed through. She described how the large man interrupted.

Barbara moaned as she listened. "You must go to the police and report it, Sandi. You must."

"I don't know," Sandi said.

"Sandi, you must, you must report it."

"No."

"Why?"

"It'll mean trouble. Tom would worry. And even if they caught them, what would happen? Nothing."

"Sandi, they might do it again."

"Look, Barbara, was I attacked? Answer... yes. Do I have bruising, was I hurt? Answer... no. Was I raped? No. So nothing will happen, and I'd have to see them again. I just want to forget it," Sandi said, then recognized her friend's distress. "Come on Babs, let's have another drink. Let's just forget it."

"I think you're making a huge mistake."

"No, it's for the best. Let's forget it and have dinner," Sandi said.

"The police could be here in less than five minutes, if we call them now," Barbara suggested. "They would at least spend one night behind bars. Come on, Sandi, you must. Who knows what these guys will do next?"

"Barbara, they attacked me, not you." It hurt her friend. "It's my life, so let's just forget it."

As the fat man left the room, the gang mingled around each other, charged by the events.

"Boy, I almost had her," moaned a frustrated Arnie, tugging at the front of his jeans. "Just a little more time and I would have had it."

"Yeah," Bo grinned, "she was squirming like a stuck pig."

"Man, the blood's still pumping through my pecker," said Max, squeezing himself, dancing about swaying his hips. The others laughed.

"She was darn lucky alright," said Billy.

"What do you mean by that?" asked Arnie.

"If you ever got it up, she would have forgotten the experience in say…" Billy paused, glancing at the ceiling, "fifteen seconds."

"She was mine if you didn't get in the way you friggin' bastard," Arnie said, coming to the boil. "Christ, if you hadn't opened your friggin' mouth one of us would have had her. You even said she was too friggin' good for us."

"She was," Billy said. "Come on Capelli you know that." Billy stood firm. "Look, we do illegals who don't go to the police. If you had done her here... we would be in friggin' jail for the next ten years. You guys are just pussy crazy to even think you would have gotten away with it."

"He's r-r-right you know," said Joe. "S-S-She would have g-g-gone to the po-po-police."

"Crap," said Arnie. "You're a damn fag Humphries. I would have been happy to do the time. It would have been damn worth it."

"Ah, blow me, Capelli."

"A bit like coitus interruptus, eh, Arnie?" suggested Max, smiling.

The others tried to stay serious but cracked. Their laughter becoming more hysterical when Bo pointed out Max's bulging jeans.

"C-C-Come on g-g-guys let's drink up and h-hit the r-r-road."

"Yeah, the big guy might come back," said Bo. "He frightens me a bit."

"Yeah, we d-d-don't want him wa-wa-waving his c-c-cannon at us again."

"Stuff the fat pig," said Max. "I swear, I was ready to cut him."

"Not with a hole in your head," said Billy, sparking more laughter and banter.

Max didn't engage, pondering vengeance.

"Where to now?" asked Bo, draining his drink.

"Who cares," said Arnie. "Just so long as there's beer."

"Let's get beers and check out the beaches up north," said Max, tossing his empty bottle into the trash can by the door. He stepped back into the crowded bar and sidled past the Texan. "I look forward to seeing you again, fat boy."

"Don't bet on it you little shit."

The boys congregated on the sidewalk to discuss their next move. Billy voted for home. The others wanted local action. They decided on beer from the liquor store on the corner opposite, drink it at the beach and then head home in search of Billy's illegals. While the others clambered into the car, they sent Bo to the 7-Eleven, next door to the Brewery.

"Oh, my gosh there's one of them." Sandi ducked down.

"Where? Where?" Barbara didn't know where to look.

"The big guy in the parking lot, with the checked shirt."

"Oh, I see him." Barbara stared out the window. "Oh, my god."

"What?"

"Sandi, he's huge. Are you sure you don't want to go to the police?"

"No. What's he doing?"

"You can sit up he's gone into the store."

"Can you see any others?"

"No."

Sandi sat up, scanning the parking lot for any sign of the others.

"Sandi, call the police, please."

"Oh, for heaven's sake," she said. "Leave it will you?"

A black and white police car appeared in the parking lot stopping outside the entrance to the store.

"Look Sandi, this is our chance."

As two officers got out of the car, another police unit pulled into the lot, then another. The officers gathered outside the store in an animated discussion that seemed to humor them.

"Sandi, you've got to drop these guys into it, and you have to do it now. They must be punished. If they aren't, then they'll just keep doing it."

No response.

"Shoot Sandi. I could be their next victim for damn sake!"

Tears welled in Sandi's eyes. Her face pained in a grimace. She knew it was the right thing to do. She squeezed and rolled her serviette as she searched through the window.

"Barbara... I... I... I can't."

Bo stepped out of the store, stumbling into the laughing police officers. He appeared agitated, perplexed by them, almost dropping his brown bag of goods. The officers appeared to want to help him with his load. He brushed them away and scurried off out of the parking lot.

Out of sight from Sandi and her friend, Bo bundled the beer into the back seat onto Billy's lap, jumped into the driver's seat, ignited the engine, and gunned the car out into traffic. Sandi was glad the big guy had gone, and with him her nightmare.

CHAPTER
5

The cold beer numbed Billy's hands, sending a chill through him. He sighed and hoped things improved, wishing for it all to end.

"Damn it, we should have had that bitch," Arnie said, thumping the seat. No one responded. Billy dropped his head back. "Someone will take it tonight. I've got a load to dump."

"Yeah, well, don't come near me," said Max, squirming.

"I thought Billy was the fag?" queried Bo.

The others laughed, including Billy. Bo often said funny things.

"T-t-the fat g-g-guy would have st-st-stopped us, him and his g-g-gun," said Joe. "Christ, you wer-wer-were l-l-lucky buddy."

"Yeah, I should have slashed his guts open," said Max.

"She had a fine soft touch," said Arnie. "Satin panties, so smooth. I would have kept them if I got the friggin' things off her."

"Aw give it a break will ya Arnie. I'm getting hard," groaned Max. The others cackled.

"Turn here, Bo," Billy said. "That sign says beach park." The car cruised into Palomar, heading for the coast. "This'll do. Come on, I need to get this stuff off me, it's damn cold."

Bo turned into a parking lot, stopping away from the streetlamp, glowing as the evening sky darkened. They stumbled from the car, sprawling about after rummaging through the paper bag, grabbing, then opening a beer.

Billy dropped to the sandy grass, leaned back, and pulled a plastic pouch out of his back pocket. He unraveled it, helping himself to the marijuana, rolling a reefer. He lit it and passed it on to Max, who drew back hard. Billy rolled another. He embraced the mind-spinning buzz dope offered. He shifted his thoughts into a blissful world, listening to waves crash on the nearby beach.

Arnie, stretching out on a park bench bemoaned the lost opportunities for sex. "Man, she was a honey." He laughed.

"We'll get you laid tonight. If not, I'd hate to be your wife," Max said.

"I'd hate to be his wife anytime," chimed in Billy, lying back with a hand behind his head, blowing out another buzz of dope.

"Who asked your opinion?" sneered Arnie. "Anyway, she'll take one tonight no matter what happens. That's why I married her, on tap whenever I want." He sniffed.

The boys bragged and joked their way through the beer. They discussed their chances of grabbing a few girls for a little action. If they left it too late, they would waste the night. Joe stretched out on the car hood, studying the stars; Bo slumped against a tree almost asleep, Billy and Max laying together on the grass and Arnie spread out on the bench.

"Hey guys!" Arnie shouted, stirring the others. "What are we doing here, let's go?"

"W-W-Where?" asked Joe.

"Back home and get a little pussy," Arnie said, sitting up, his brain spinning.

"We'll need money," said Billy clambering to his feet pleased to be moving, brushing sand from his jeans. "We'll need it if we want more bud."

"I want to see a man with a handgun," said Max.

The others paused, gawking at him.

"What for?" asked Bo, yawning, getting to his feet.

"The fat guy had one, and if he can have one... then, I want one."

"Right..." said Billy. "You need a pistol because a fat boy had one? Are you crazy? Why?"

"I'm getting sick of having to use my beautiful Bowie all the time. I mean... there's nothing more exciting than scaring the shit out of a dude when I flash my blade. But a big shiny piece... man, that'll turn the babes wild." The others laughed, moving back to the car.

"Speaking of girls," said Billy, changing the tone. "Where do we go for the action you promised us?"

"You stupid dope," said Arnie, clipping Billy across his head. "We had one, don't you remember? You helped her get away."

"Listen here, you friggin' moron. It wasn't the time, the place, or the God damn girl." The constant berating stung Billy. "She wasn't for us. We know that. If you keep up this garbage man, I'll jam it down your throat."

"You had better watch your mouth you dumb punk. Or I'll..."

"You'll what?"

"I'll kick the friggin' shit out of ya."

Billy, tough, with a junkyard dog mentality when fighting for his honor, was flying high with bravado from the effects of the dope and alcohol. He faced up to Arnie, glaring him straight in the eye. "I think you're nothing but a bag of shit Capelli. And as for your friggin' manhood, stop letting your fingers do the stroking."

"You stupid fag," Arnie guffawed, tiptoeing back and straightening. He sneered, beckoning Billy closer with a limp wave of his hand. The others stepped away. The need to let off steam was obvious, and it seemed the right time to let them get on with it. Max ever mindful of stepping in to help his pal if needed.

"Capelli, you're a dickhead," Billy said. "You're so dumb you spend half your life in jail. You hang around us because you got no friends. And you only get laid if you rape someone, even your precious old lady." A mad opponent makes stupid mistakes, and Billy hoped Arnie seethed enough to make a costly move.

Arnie's hands clenched, waiting for the perfect moment to lunge. "Humphries, you've been asking for this."

"Stop talking ya dud and get your lard ass into action." Billy waved him on with outstretched arms and blew him a kiss. "Come to poppa."

Arnie lunged.

Billy cracked him in the cheek with a short, hard right. The thwack of the connecting fist bringing a satisfied smirk. Arnie dropped to his right knee. Jerking back, he swung his right arm. Billy ducked and ripped another right hard into Arnie's abdomen. Billy danced away, watching for another attack, fists at the ready. Arnie gazed up through knotted brow, gasping for air and sprung again, counting on wrestling

Billy to the ground. He missed. Billy kicked him in the ribs as he stepped aside and pile drove a hard straight right into the side of his face, gashing Arnie's eye.

Arnie's eye ached as he panted for relief. He lay awkwardly on a piece of wood big enough to grip as a weapon. He struggled to his feet, his back to Billy, hiding his new weapon and swinging around with the branch extended from his left arm. It distracted Billy enough for Arnie to kick him in the knee. Billy collapsed.

Arnie followed with a forceful blow to the side of the head, knocking him to the ground. He advanced and swung his boot into Billy's face. Billy rolled away and tried to get to his feet. Arnie, with blood dribbling from his nose and leaking from a gash over his eye, walked toward his prey, thumping him back to the ground. He twisted the dazed Billy over and straddled his chest. He picked up Billy's head with a handful of hair and punched him hard in the face. Billy groaned and coughed a rush of blood from his mouth.

"Now fag, how do you fancy these fingers?" Arnie readied himself to punch.

Without warning, Arnie's head snapped back, and a knife blade pressed hard against his throat. "What's it going to be, Arnie? An obvious, yahoo victory for you?" Max demanded. "Or damage to this throat of yours? Your choice."

"Max, what are you doing?" a surprised and desperate Arnie gasped, his hair pulled back.

"You've had your fun; it's time to get laid. Or do I lay you out here?"

"Yeah, sure, Maxie. Whatever you say. Let's go get pussy."

Max released his grip and stepped away, allowing Arnie to get up from a dazed and sore Billy.

Billy struggled to his feet, spitting blood, touching his nose. Max had a closer peek at him. "The nose doesn't look great, but I don't think its broken. You got good hits in there, but the old wood in the face trick will get you every time."

Billy snorted, then groaned. "Do I still look good?"

"We may just have to get you a blind date tonight, brother." He led him to the car to recover, ushering him into the front, nodding to Arnie to sit in the rear.

"Let's go find pussy," shouted Bo, responding to Max's invitation to get moving.

"Yeah, let's," groaned Arnie, hurting as he struggled to the car, wiping blood from his face.

"I still want that gun," said Max, stepping back from Billy and sliding into the back with Arnie.

"But we ain't got no money," said Bo, cranking up the engine.

"Okay, this is the plan," said Max, as Joe jumped into the front with Billy. "We kill two birds with one stone."

"H-h-how?" asked Joe.

"Who has a gun?" No one responded. "And who has the cash we need?" Still no response, as the others looked perplexed. "And who do I want to hurt?"

"The f-f-fat guy?" asked Joe.

"You got it in one, Joey."

"But how?" asked Arnie, perking an interest.

"We go back to the bar... wait outside until fatso comes out and then... zip, zing. He loses weight. I have a gun and we have the cash."

"What makes you think he'll still have money if he's still at the bar?" asked Arnie, wiping blood from his face with a cuff.

"Fat guys always have cash, man. They got nothing to spend it on."

"What if he ain't there?" asked Bo.

"He'll be there. We follow him until the greasy pig is by himself, then we roll him. I stick him, and then spit in his fat friggin' face."

"Yeah, sounds good, let's go do it," said Arnie.

Bo roared off back toward the West Coast Lagoon. Billy content to let the others figure he was out to it. His ribs ached and his eye throbbed.

They had only been traveling for a few minutes when Bo braked hard, stirring them into mild surprise. "Christ, is that who I think it is?"

The others didn't know what the hell Bo was talking about or where to look.

"Over there... on the sidewalk." Bo pointed to someone walking alone.

"Oh no, it couldn't be. We couldn't be that lucky," grinned Arnie.

"Oh yes, it is." Max shouted. "We've won the lottery."

"Quick t-t-turn around," said Joe.

"What's going on?" groaned Billy, lifting his head from the seat. "Aren't we going home?"

Arnie slapped the back of Billy's head. "Shut up. You stuffed the last one, now don't stuff this one."

Bo chuckled as he swung the Dodge to the other side of the road to cruise up behind a lone woman walking.

CHAPTER
6

Sandi and Barbara watched the big guy disappear out of the parking lot, then checked the front door. Sandi continued to search the parking area. Barbara peered at her, dropping her head, and shook it. They sat in silence for a few moments, Sandi wringing her hands.

"Babs you're a great support, but I'm okay. Truly, nothing happened to me. I mean, it could have, but it didn't. I'm okay, really."

"I know, and I'm sorry for troubling you."

"No way you could upset me. Look, it would be better if I just forgot the whole thing."

"Sandi, I know how you must feel. I'm sorry for being like this... I just thought we should shove it up those guys... you know?"

"Yes, I know Sandi. I just want to forget it. There's no justice through the courts. You know that. I just don't want to see them again."

"Okay, let's forget it. Do you want a soda?"

"No, forget that, let's have a gin and tonic. I think I need a stiff one."
Barbara laughed.

They ordered drinks and chatted before ordering a meal. They joked and laughed their way through memories tension lessening as they relaxed.

They counted the booty after dinner. "Barb, we have done very well," said Sandi, eyeing the large piles of money before them. "Today we set a record."

"What did we do?" Barbara asked.

"Oh, this is great." Sandi studied the total on her addition paper, toying with her friend. "The charity is going to love us. Listen to this."

Barbara couldn't wait any longer and tried to snatch the paper, almost tearing the entire sheet, but only disappointed with the torn piece having no information.

"Steady there Babs, be patient girlfriend," Sandi said.

"Come on Sandi, you're killing me."

"One thousand, three hundred and thirty-two dollars, forty-five cents."

Barbara squealed, disturbing other patrons who glanced over to the table.

"You're kidding, that's unbelievable," Barbara whispered as Sandi tried to quieten her with a finger to her lips.

"It must have been all those donations from those little businesses back at Mission Beach that set us running," said Sandi. "This is a great day, sister."

"Yes, it is." Barbara then remembered. "Except for those dirt bags."

"Oh Babs, life in South Africa is just so desperate. I hope this money offers hope for a few wretched children."

"Don't worry, Sandi, it will. I'm sure our work is doing good." Barbara said. "I have news for you. I'm going to Africa."

"What?" Sandi squealed, turning more heads. "When, tell me when?"

"Oh, I thought around Thanksgiving, for two weeks."

"Oh, you'll love it. Oh, I wish I could come."

"Why don't you?"

"Tom wouldn't let me. We have our sights set on going back as missionaries. We focus on that. He wouldn't let me go before then. But I would love to go. Maybe I'll ask him... who knows? Oh, this is magnificent news."

The two friends spent another hour talking about Africa. They planned and dreamed of what they could do. Two young women excited about their lives, pleased with their charity efforts, and nothing worried them.

"I suppose I had better ring Tom and ask him to come get me," Sandi said, yawning.

"Don't be silly. I'll drop you home."

"No, it's too far out of your way. I'll phone Tom." Sandi said, reaching for her bag.

"Sandi, he's been working all day. Knowing him, he's on early shift tomorrow. He's most likely asleep. Leave him to it. I'll drive you home."

Barbara was right. Tom had been working double shifts for two weeks and came home exhausted. Sandi hadn't seen him for any great length of time for about a month, but she understood the needs of an intern. She knew her husband would get out of bed to fetch her. Although he would be grumpy.

"You're right. Let him sleep. You're a great friend, Babs."

"You taught me."

They paid the tab and left with Sandi pushing the donations in her bag, intending to bank the cash first thing on Monday. They headed the car north to La Jolla and almost at once tiredness crept up on Sandi. She tried to stifle another yawn and regretted having the last liqueur coffee. As they approached Sandi's turn off, she asked Barbara to slow. "Let me off here. I'll walk the rest of the way. I think I need fresh air after all those drinks."

"Don't be silly. It'll only take a few more seconds and you will be at your front door and bed."

"Yes, I know, Babs, but you've got a long way to go. I need air. I'm spinning a bit."

"Are you sure? Ten seconds no more."

"No, just here will be fine."

Barbara cruised to a stop. Sandi leaned over and kissed her friend on the cheek.

"You are the greatest friend I've ever had. I love you so much."

"Aw shucks. People will talk," Babs joked.

"Let them. I don't care. Call me tomorrow?" Sandi dragged herself from the car. "Thanks for today, you've been terrific."

"Always a pleasure Sandi, I'll call you."

"Bye."

Sandi watched Barbara drive off, took in a deep clearing breath, and began the 50-yard walk to her home on Beaumont. The cool air revitalized her. She smiled to herself as she dawdled home. Neither of the girls saw the Dodge turn across from the opposite side of the street.

CHAPTER
7

"I don't believe it. It can't be?" said Billy, trying to focus through a throbbing squint.

"It is," Arnie said, leering out the window. "And won't it surprise her to see us?"

"No d-d-doubt she'll be more impressive th-th-this this time, eh, guys?" Joe said.

"Let's take her," said Max, focusing the others out of boyish excitement into the depth of evil.

Billy uneasy about the sudden alternate plan said, "Max, what about the fat guy?"

"Yeah, we'll finish him, but we'll do her first." Max focused on the woman. "Come on Bo, move in closer."

Sandi could hear the car but took little notice. Nothing seemed out of place. She began thinking about the keys to her front door and wondered whether she should start searching through her bag.

The gang in the car hung twenty yards behind, waiting for the road to clear. Their breathing now heavy and fast, anticipation building. Billy apprehensive. Bo waited for Max's word.

"I'll get her, but I may need help, Arnie," said Max.

"Man, I can't wait to get my hands on her." Arnie sat on the edge of the back seat, craning a look through the front window. They all knew what they were about to do.

Only Billy had doubts.

"Go."

Bo drew up alongside. Max jumped out and rushed her. The woman turned to the noise of someone fast approaching. When Max hit her on the left side of her face, she reeled backward, dazed, staggered, then fell. She groaned as she hit the pavement. Her face ached, and she tasted blood over her tongue. Still dazed she stared up to see two cloudy figures standing above her.

"Man, she is beautiful. I hope you didn't hurt her too bad. I want her fightin' later," said Arnie, picking her up at the shoulder. "Come on, help me get her into the car."

"What's going on?" she groaned.

"Honey, you is goin' to a party," said Max, taking hold of a leg.

"Leave me alone." She kicked out, collecting Max between the legs, buckling him. She screamed and struggled as if life depended on it. A light appeared from a nearby house, threatening the boys.

"Shut up, bitch." Max slapped her across the face, splitting her lip. She continued to kick, buck, and scream until Max, unable to control her, kicked her in the stomach. Now gasping for air, the thugs dragged her to the car.

Arnie grappled her around the neck, restricting her breathing even further. Max pulled her by one leg, the other leg still flaying collected him again, this time in the back of the head. Her struggling was making it hard to get her to the Dodge. Her desperate cries alerting residents.

"Christ, get her in. Goddamn it," cried Joe from the car.

"Help us will ya," Arnie said.

She fought hard. She bucked and kicked, flaying her arms, scratching nails across Arnie's chest, tearing his shirt at the buttons. He squeezed the headlock tighter, weakening her struggle. Max dragged her legs with him into the car and, although gagging, she hung onto the door, bucking, and grunting. Joe jumped from the car to help Arnie, prying fingers from her desperate grip of the door.

"Let her go. Leave her. Someone's coming," said a panicked Billy from the front seat.

Bo scanned the street and saw someone emerge from a property, walking toward the car to investigate the commotion. He leaned over the rear seat, raised his fist, and brought it down hard on her lower abdomen, weakening her. Arnie pushed the limp body into the car diving in after her. Joe picked up her bag and jumped back into the front seat.

Bo gunned the car and squealed away from the curb, leaving in their wake an intrigued citizen wondering what had happened. Max gazed back, giving him a flick of the wrist wave.

Someone rang the police, but there was little to report, only a vintage model Dodge with no visible registration tags, speeding north. The officer recorded the call on the duty log.

"Yahoo!" Bo thumped the steering wheel as the gang sped off with their prize. "We took her, we took her."

"Yeah... b-b-but is she alive?" asked Joe.

"Oo yeah, she's alive alright," said Arnie, running his hands up her disarranged skirt and over her pants. Max sat on her, bouncing up and down shouting and laughing. Joe searched the bag. Bo giggled, and Arnie moaned as he pawed the body beside him. Billy sat still, his head resting back.

The woman lay confused in pain on the rear seat exhausted and numb. She felt someone sitting on her, unaware of Arnie's pawing.

"Tonight's your lucky night lady," said Arnie. "You're goin' to have five boys give you a good time. You'll love it."

Max dropped to the floor of the car and kneeled facing her. He put his lips close to her ear and muttered. "You do what you're told, and no one will hurt you, understand? But cause us pain and we will hurt you real bad, understand?" He then kissed her.

She spat in his face.

"Man? I think she loves you," said a grinning Arnie.

Max responded by throwing a left fist into her face, already looking bruised. "Bitch."

"Yeah, but she sure feels real good," said Arnie, still mauling under her skirt.

"I'm first then," said Max.

"No way," argued Arnie. "She's mine."

"You stuffed it last time. There's no way you're goin' first. So, get out of the friggin' way."

"Jesus, Max. You're a mongrel. Stop mucking about. I need it real bad."

Sandi drifted off into a dreaming. She wandered in far-off lands, not aware of the scheming going on around her. She ached, and her face throbbed. Tom smiling, leaving her amongst the flowers, sun bright and warm days. "Tom?"

"You can just wait your turn you friggin' bastard. I'll take as long as it takes." Max began by unbuttoning her blouse, relishing the moment, only to have a button prove too difficult to detach, and in frustration he ripped it from her. "Where's my knife?"

Billy passed it back from where Max had left it on the dash. Max took it from the sheath and flicked his way through her clothes, leaving her in her underwear. "Christ, you are drop dead gorgeous," Max breathed, as he leered down on her listless body. He caressed his hands across her, cupping, then squeezing her breasts, licking her stomach.

"Don't cut up the pants, I want them," said Arnie, battling to tug them off.

Max was enjoying the moment as he sliced through the bra straps, then flicked his blade between the cups and they fell away. Arnie sucked in his breath and reached around Max to paw at a breast. Max slapped his hand away.

"Leave me alone, please don't hurt me," Sandi mumbled as she gazed at the boy pawing her. She convulsed as Max forced his hand between her thighs.

"Oh, brother, look at this," Joe exclaimed from the front seat.

"What the hell are you on about?" a distracted Max said, turning to look at what Joe had.

"The b-b-bitch is rich." Joe found the cache of donations and held up a wad of notes. "The-The-There must be a f-f-few h-h-hundred in here."

"Oh, lovely lady, you are my friggin' best friend," said Arnie, leering at her nakedness, trailing his fingers over her chest.

"Get gas, Bo," said Max, returning his attention to the whimpering woman, his eyes ablaze. "Lady, you are turning out to be one hell of a prize."

"Don't hurt me, please don't hurt me."

"Just do as you are told sweetheart, and no-one will hurt you," said Max, as he unbuckled and pushed his jeans away.

"Stop for booze as well little brother and we'll have a proper party with our guest," said Arnie with his hand down the front of his jeans, squeezing and rubbing as he watched Max pull and shove the woman into position.

"Sounds like a great idea," said Billy, unsure where the night was heading.

"Man, you're so beautiful," said Max, as he positioned himself.

"Don't fall in love with her, man," said Arnie, stuffing her pants into his pocket. "Just screw her, for God's sake, we all want to have a go."

Max dropped his mouth to moisten her, and she bucked at the violation. Once done, he drove forward. As she tried to reject him, he arched himself above her and shoved the tip of his Bowie into her nose and told her not to move.

Terror forbade her to do anything other than surrender. Her face ached, and she tasted blood. Her lower limbs were numb, and she shivered with cold and shock. The cool chill of the knife's blade pushed into her nose, petrifying her. Sandi could not feel the boy, but she remembered every dribbling detail. She would remember all of them in detail. When this night was over, she would seek justice.

"Christ, you aren't the man I thought you were," laughed Arnie, as Max grunted in less than a minute. "Give me a go." He pushed Max away, who collapsed against the door on the car floor.

"How was she?" asked an excited Bo, trying to see what was going on through the rear vision mirror.

"Don't worry boys, you'll all get to know real soon," smiled Max, satisfied with his moment.

Wasting no time, Arnie replaced Max. He picked her knees up and pushed them back toward her head, assailing her with more savagery. She groaned with pain.

"Please don't hurt me," she whimpered. "I'll do whatever you want... please don't hurt me."

"Shut up bitch," snapped Arnie, and he slapped her hard, twisting her nose.

His weight made it difficult for her to breathe, and she walked amongst the flowers once again, oblivious to the man on top of her. Arnie acted like a wild boar as he thrashed, slapping her head, biting into her breasts, and punching her thighs.

"Good timing, Arnie," said Bo, swinging the car into a gas station as Arnie grunted, then collapsed.

Bo guided the Dodge to the far side of the apron, away from the cashier and suspecting eyes. Joe hopped out ready to pump gas, while Billy walked over to the cashier's wired pen and paid fifty dollars.

Max stretched out from the back seat, adjusting his clothes. "Man, that was great." He walked around the car to Bo's window, alert for trouble. There was no one around.

"Where do you think we should go to give you and the others your little treat, Bo? And I'm not talking Wendy's."

"What about the beach we just come from?" asked Bo, hanging out the window.

"Nah, too open. I saw a sign back a-ways, saying a park was up ahead. We should move there. Should be plenty of nice, secluded spots for a party."

"Right, Max, sounds good to me."

Arnie stumbled from the car almost falling over, pulling up his jeans. "Man, what a woman." He staggered to join the others. "Man, she felt so good. I almost didn't make it... I want more. So where shall we go? And if we are going to party... we better get more booze."

"There's a liquor store yonder," said Bo, nodding toward the bright lights across the street.

"Pass me the bag Bo, I'll go get us a bottle of Daniels." He snatched a handful of bills before tossing it back. "You guys want anything?"

"Yeah, get me gin," called Joe, pumping the gas.

"I'll have a few Buds," said Billy, strolling back as Arnie strode toward the store.

The gang laughed and chattered, recalling the struggle to get the woman into the car. They didn't notice her stir.

Sandi could only open an eye as the other throbbed and swelling preventing it opening. Checking about, she came to recognize the inside of a car. She could hear the chatter of men. She tried lifting her head, but her shoulders ached, her head too heavy. Raising a hand to her face, she wiped away wetness, thinking it was tears, not realizing it was blood. The ache was intolerable, and she moaned as she strained to straighten, panting from the effort. Dazed, she tried to collect her thoughts as she rested her head higher on the sticking vinyl seat. A soft shaft of air ruffled a wisp of hair across her face. It moved again as Sandi pushed her eye up to see the door left ajar. An open door. *Where the hell was she?*

She lifted herself higher, bringing an elbow under to support her craning for a view. Staying back within the shadows of the seat, she tried to see where she was and if she could escape. She noticed a big guy in the front seat of the car hanging out of the window talking and laughing with a group of others. She couldn't figure how many there were. The men were on the other side of the car, leaning against it, paying no attention to her.

She strained to look behind her and through the open door. It was at a gas station, recognizing it. *She buys her gas here.* She was near home. She could see the cashier twenty yards away. Freedom and safety lay just twenty yards away. She collapsed back onto the seat, exhausted by the effort.

Surely the men would move to get back into the car soon?

Sandi decided her only chance to get away from these horrible men and the safety of home was to burst out of the car and run screaming toward the cashier. Her only chance to get away. But she had no clothes. Damn it.

Her moral dilemma soon overridden by a compelling sense for freedom. Her prudery would not hold her back. Naked escape or continued assault. There was no question in her mind what she must do.

Sandi gripped the end of the seat, fingers coiling around the tubular edging, dragging herself into position. It ached with even the slightest movement, but she forced herself ready. A leg draped over the edge, and she levered her foot against the hump in the middle. She inched further forward, her face now against the door. A cool draught of air fresh against her face excited her, refreshing her.

She planned to push the door open and burst out onto the pavement. Once out of the car, she would leap up and run toward the cashier's post, screaming all the way. The men were on the other side of the car. By the time they knew what she was doing, she would be there. If they valued their freedom, they would escape before the cashier put in a call to the police.

Push and burst. This was her plan. Push and burst. She waited for the right moment. Push and burst. She waited, frightened, apprehensive about her plan. What could go wrong? Push and burst. This was it. No time to wait. Push and burst.

Now!

She thrust herself into action. Her foot slipped off the hump, losing momentum. She leaned on the door as the internal light lit up. As she scrambled from the car, she felt the coldness of the concrete apron. The air was frosty, and she was free.

A large hand swung from the front of the car, gripping a clump of her hair dragging her back inside, almost tearing her scalp. He pulled her back across the seat and she bounced back.

"Where are you going, honey? I haven't had my turn yet." Bo was now in the back seat and the others were scrambling around the car.

"Help!" Sandi screamed with all her might. "Let me go... let me go."

The cashier raised his gaze from his reading, hearing a distant plea, but saw nothing. He returned to the lewd photographs before him.

Sandi kicked screamed and bucked against the man in front's powerful hold. He thumped her in the abdomen. Simple logic response was to stop the air, to stop the screaming. She stopped her thrashing, gasping for air, clutching her stomach.

Concerned about the fracas, the boys piled back into the car with Joe joining Max in the rear seat. He sat on her and bounced up and down. "You stupid b-b-bitch. K-k-keep ya m-m-mouth sh-shut and no-one will h-h-hurt you."

"Leave her, Joey," said Billy. "She's had enough. She won't be worth squat if you keep roughing her up like that."

"Yeah, Billy's right," said Max, with an admiring caress of her thigh. "We have more party to go yet." He pulled her head to his lap, undid his buttons, and pushed her face onto him. He gripped her hard around the neck, demanding she open her mouth. She obeyed, and he bounced her head like a balloon.

Bo gunned the car into action when Arnie made it back and headed north. Arnie tossed the drinks around, pissed to see Max with a smile on his face. "Christ, you're an animal, Max," he laughed, watching Max's tense, screwed-up face bouncing the woman's head up and down.

Max finished and brushed her away. Joe poured a splash of gin over her breast, licking it and biting hard, as she laid back, gagging for air.

"Go left," said Arnie, now up-front guzzling on a quart of Jack Daniels. "Any pathway will do."

After a drive north, past the country club, without warning, the Dodge swung off the road onto a small overgrown dirt trail that headed into woods. Low-hanging branches brushed the car as they bounced their way along the rough trail. The headlamp could not show beyond the undergrowth, and no one could see an open area.

"This'll do," an impatient Arnie said, when they traveled far enough. Bo rolled the car to a halt and turned off the lights. The woods dark and silent. A blue tinge of moonlight allowed them to adjust to their surrounds.

Max was first out, dragging the woman with him. She had regained consciousness and struggled against his will. He slapped her head and threw her face into the cold metal of the trunk. The Capellis bundled from the Dodge, leaving Billy swilling beer. Max kicked off his jeans, tossing them onto the roof.

"Well boys, I've given it to her in two holes. I may as well give it to her in the third, when it's offered like this," chuckled Max, leering at the naked body. He came up behind her, spat into his hand, and rubbed himself ready. With the woman beyond any spirit of rejection, he attacked her.

The woman screamed hard and loud.

"Geezus she's as tight as a monkey."

She screamed from the piercing pain, heightening Max's enthusiasm.

She screamed for help. She screamed to release pain. She screamed to forget. Max threw himself against her, roaring approval as she squealed. He rode her, bucking against him, until he fell away satisfied.

"Who's next?" Max asked as he staggered back. "Come on, Billy?"

"Stuff Billy," said Bo, as he brushed past and pulled the woman off the car. "I'm next... I can't wait any longer." He kicked his jeans off, forced her to her knees, and tried to push his way into her mouth. He held her ears and pushed her head back and forward. "Open your mouth, bitch." Bo slapped her ears.

The woman now semi-conscious, enduring pain far greater than the degradation. She'd given up caring, just wanting the pain to end.

Joe dropped to his knees, loosened of his jeans, and attacked her from behind, as Bo was at her head. This sight was too much for Arnie and Max. They collapsed laughing, swigging on their bottles, watching the brothers satisfy themselves. When Joe finished, Bo pushed the woman onto her back and lay on her.

Billy was on his second Bud, wasted, and didn't want to bother himself with the party. He sat staring out into the darkened woods, trying to block out the grunts and excitement of the others and the desperate, pathetic pleas of the woman.

Bo rolled off to be replaced by Arnie gawking at her.

The woman raised her head to see who it was, her eyes swollen.

Arnie took a huge last gulp of the Daniels, finishing the bottle, tossing it high into the woods. "It's me again, bitch." He kicked her hard in the ribs and she recoiled in pain and moaned a desperate, breathless groan. "You should have come across at the bar, otherwise, none of this would have happened."

Arnie dropped to his knees, pushed up her ankles to either side of his shoulders, leaned forward and attacked on her. He scratched and beat her until he grunted, smashing her head into the ground. After a few moments of recovery, he got up from her and kicked her as he stepped away. "That's done me. Now your turn, Billy."

"No thanks," said Billy as he sat in the car's doorway, drawing back on a reefer, and blowing his smoke into the cool night air.

"One in, all in," said Max, pulling on his jeans. He stepped to the door and tried to drag Billy from the car.

"No man," drawled Billy, rebuffing Max's efforts to drag him from the car. "I'm wasted, and even if I could get it up, which I can't, I wouldn't know what the hell I was doing."

"Man, you're friggin' hopeless," said Max. "Okay, well then, does anyone else want another go?"

"Yeah, I d-d-do," said Joe. "B-b-but I-I don't w-w-want Billy w-w-watching me like he is. If he doesn't w-w-want a g-g-go, I don't think he sh-sh-should w-w-watch. L-l-let's take her further down the t-t-trail."

"Yeah, good idea brother, let's do it," said Arnie.

Bo grabbed an ankle and lugged her further into the woods; she was like a corpse with her arms flayed out behind her head.

"This'll do m-m-me," said Joe, eager to have his turn after they dragged her twenty yards. He mounted her as she lay unresponsive. "Geezus, she feels g-g-reat." The others laughed as they watched Joe, and then Bo replaced him.

"Anyone else want it," asked Arnie as Bo finished. The others didn't respond, all happy. "No? That's great because I have been dying to do this. I've been saving it for her." He then peed over her, triggering the others to join him, chuckling over the ultimate humiliation.

Sandi stirred and inched herself she knew not where. "Tom? Where are you, Tom?" Delusion had overcome her as she crawled to a dry place; she wanted to let Tom know she was safe. "Shall we go home now?" She freed an eye open and saw the brilliance of a starry night; everything sparkled. She was wet and wondered why she had been lying out in the rain. "Tom? Are you there, honey?"

"What are w-w-we going to d-d-do with her?" asked Joe, keen to get moving. "W-w-we c-c-could leave her here. I d-d-don't fancy driving her b-b-back to La Jolla."

"She's seen us, and she knows our names," said Max.

"She won't remember," said Bo, stomping on her. "Will you, honey?"

The woman didn't respond.

"Max, you always said you wanted your pound of flesh," said Arnie. "Here it is man, go for it."

"Hey w-w-wait a minute," objected Joe.

"Look, she knows us from the bar. The fat guy will confirm it," snapped Arnie. "She'll do us in, then we're stuffed."

"She won't r-r-remember us. Don't be stupid."

"Man, if she talks, we do fifteen years," said Arnie.

"Just g-g-get on w-w-with it," Joe said, heading back to the car to get dressed.

"Leave it to me," said Max, with a glinting smile, drawing his knife from its sheath now on his belt.

The brothers left.

Arnie turned to see Max straddle the woman's back, grip her hair, and yank her head back. He turned away and hurried back to the car to join the others.

The woman gasped for air as her head snapped back. She raised her hand to her face. "No more... please no more."

Back at the car, Billy asked, "What's up? Where's Max?"

"He's just finishing up," said Bo, gunning the car into action and turning on the headlamp. The others stumbled back into the car, laughing.

Billy wondered why Max was taking so long. The boasting and laughing of the Capellis didn't help. Max staggered from the underbrush into the light, covered in blood.

"Oh my God, Max. What have you done?"

"Don't worry boys, the little lady won't be telling anyone what an unforgettable night she had."

CHAPTER
8

Nearing midnight, the gang swung on to the freeway heading south to Otay Mesa. The boys remained silent. Billy wishing he stayed at home. Joe speculating about a girl. Bo planning to sell the car first thing in the morning. Only Arnie and Max thinking about the woman, both for different reasons.

"Hey, we could go back and move her," Max said, smirking after Arnie complained about leaving the woman in the open.

"No way," said Bo, picking up speed.

"Did you cover her?" asked Arnie.

"Just a few leaves and shit like that."

"You're a raving lunatic man," Billy said. "You're friggin' crazy."

"I know, man, but it felt so good. Just so easy, ya know? Like slicing through butter. But the bitch was a bleeder," Max said, wiping blood from his hands onto his jeans.

"W-w-was she out to it?" Joe asked.

"Who cares," said Max. "The bitch deserved it... right?"

"Yeah, who cares?" Billy sighed as he gazed at the passing lights.

"What do we d-d-do with the c-c-cash?" asked Joe.

"Let's spend it," chuckled Bo.

"Nah, we donate it to someone worthy," Arnie said, slapping Bo across the back of the head. "Of course, we spend it dopey."

"Yeah, split it up," said Max. "How much is there?"

"I r-r-reckon about a g-g-grand, that'll g-g-give us two h-h-hund-d-d-dred each," said Joe.

"Let's split it up when we get home," said Arnie.

"Hey, I can buy that piece now," said Max, remembering his idea. "I think I'll get it tonight. Who wants to come and check it out?"

"Yeah, I w-w-will," said Joe.

"Count me out and I don't want any money either," said Billy.

"What?" Max said. "What's wrong with you, buddy? You've been acting strange all night, you okay?"

"Look, I just don't want to have any of her cash. It's blood money. She'll bring us trouble; I want no part of it."

"Since when have you worried about a bitch?" Max asked.

"I just don't want it this time. Okay?"

"You're a dick Humphries," said Arnie. "You proved you're a friggin' fag, and now you don't want any cash. You smoke too much weed."

"Up yours, Arnie," Billy said, starring at the road ahead.

"You've been on my friggin' nerves all night, you bastard," snapped Arnie. "And if it wasn't for your pal here, I would have finished you at the beach."

"Well, maybe it's you, you know? You went shitless over a bitch in a bar." Billy had enough of Arnie. "I said she wasn't one of ours. Did you listen? No way! You macho piece of shit. You couldn't give a damn about anything or anyone."

"Shut up, punk." Arnie said.

"We get thrown out of the bar because you and Max thought you were good fellas or something. Christ knows what was going through your friggin' brain."

"Leave it, Billy," urged Max.

"No, stuff you, Max. You're just as bad," snapped Billy. "You both went crazy when we picked up the bitch. You almost friggin' killed her getting her into the car. And then you both thought you were God's gift to women or something, as you friggin' screwed her like wild animals. You smacked her around so much she looked like a piece of raw meat."

"Come on, Billy, that's enough," said Max.

"I bet it was you suggesting sticking her; wasn't it?" Max didn't respond. "I guessed so. You're a friggin' crazed animal sometimes. And this dickhead Capelli says I get on his nerves. Christ. I don't trust you, Arnie, nor do I ever want to see you again. You're a total prick."

No one spoke for a few moments.

"Does this mean we're getting divorced?" asked Max.

After a brief pause, gales of laughter collapsed the tension, as the gang could not control themselves, but not Billy. He knew his life would change, and there was nothing he could do about it. The dark shapes of the city flashed past, and he wished he could go back in time.

Max was keen to shower when they arrived at Joe's house. Billy left for home, leaving the others mingling out back. Joe tossed a few beers about the others. Arnie suggested they should get rid of any evidence.

"Let's b-b-burn them," offered Joe, tossing all of Sandi's things in a pile on the back path.

"Nice one Joe," said Bo. "I'll get gas from the shed."

Once they splashed gas over the clothes, Arnie dropped a lit match, flaring the bundle. The brothers stood and watched, entranced, as the remnants of Sandi went up in acrid smoke, turning to ash. Bo went through Sandi's bag one last time, tossing the remains into the fire. Cosmetics, family photographs, key wallet, and assorted papers. He took the money and passed the bag to Joe who tossed it on the burning heap. They stood staring at the flames, ending their link to the woman.

Max, with a beer in hand stumbled from the house in Joe's borrowed clothes, having washed his own in the shower.

"Where's Billy?" Max asked, joining the others peering into the blaze.

"G-g-gone home," said Joe.

"Fool," said Max.

"Where's your knife, Max?" Arnie asked.

"Inside. I had to scrub it damn hard to get off the friggin' blood." They continued to watch the sparks in silence. "Well, I'm going to see a guy with a gun. You coming Joey?"

"Yeah," said Joe, draining his beer.

"We should get rid of the car," Max said.

"Good idea," Arnie said, watching the last of the flames.

"I'll sell it tomorrow," Bo said.

"I reckon we should burn it as well," Max said.

"Good idea," Arnie said, smiling at Bo and winking.

Bo nodded. "I'll get it done."

"Man, what a night. I feel great," said Arnie with a big smile. "Think I'll go home and wake the old lady."

CHAPTER
9

Detective Nicolas Garcia raised his head from his desk, struggling to focus on his surroundings. It throbbed; his mouth uncomfortably dry. His body racked with fatigue. He gazed around the squad room with bleary eyes, trying to recognize anything familiar. Nothing he knew so dropped back on his crossed arms.

The detective was suffering from too much alcohol and too many cigarettes. He already finished a bottle of Perrier and two mugs of thick black coffee, yet still could not function. His tongue wriggled in his mouth, trying to activate saliva to give the dryness its marching orders, but to no avail. He promised himself never to touch the demon drink again... well, not until the next time.

Garcia pondered whether a large dose of salty fries and a greasy burger would help, willing to try anything to get his body going. He suffered, counting down the minutes to when he could leave and buy revitalizing food without too much angst from his colleagues. The crumpled clothes still attached to him from the previous day reeked of a late-night bar.

He celebrated the second anniversary of his acrimonious split from a marriage, whose participants more concerned about individual careers than sharing their hearts. Blame and accusations led to a ruthless court case to separate them. How strange two lovers could finish a marriage with nothing other than hate.

The divorce devastated Garcia. He lost all his possessions, his dignity, and all remaining respect for marriage. Now more cynical about the motives of women, considering having a relationship would be the closest point to the devil one could ever expect to come.

No one could blame him for his snide attitude toward life. Yet, no pity ever handed over by his friends when he hit the bottle. It was destroying him. He could always find celebratory reasons for an alcohol bender and they were becoming more frequent for the talented detective.

The squad room had no ventilation. Ceiling fans squeaked in their toil to cool the air for those struggling under them. The Northern Coastal criminal investigation squad was a small team working on a variety of investigative cases. In this affluent part of San Diego, larceny was the highest caseload. Rumor of transferring the squad downtown to incorporate within the major crime teams remained rife and unsettled the team. Garcia considered law enforcement suffered when centralized and resisted the idea. His squad maintained a fine arrest rate reputation and admired within the San Diego Police Department for their work ethic. Yet the transfer plans remain discussed, to the continuing chagrin of Garcia.

The squad formed during the mayoral term of Gerard Wilton coming to office promising more from the City on crime and public safety. He devised a strategy to decentralize law enforcement out to the neighborhoods. He promoted a volunteer police unit and launched a program reaching two thousand officers during his first term as mayor.

Wilton's initiatives reformed San Diego law enforcement, ushering in a new era of neighborhood policing. Energized citizens became active in aiding law enforcers, and the scheme developed into the envy of other Californian cities racked with crime. The success of the program would support Wilton's campaign for the United States Senate. His administration of being tough on law-and-order issues would be the imprimatur for his entire political career. His advocacy for the death penalty was popular and remained within his policy platform.

Garcia was one of the more effective detectives and would have given up his four commendation awards for relief from this, his worst hangover. "Aw shoot," he cried from deep within his crossed arm headrest. "My mouth feels like the bottom of a bird cage."

"Stop your moaning, Garcia," said Richard Sylvester, his bemused partner. "You get no sympathy from me."

Intelligence and influence come to mind when first meeting Sylvester. The fact his intellect was superior, but he had little influence didn't seem to stop him from thinking he did. His partner begrudged his positive attitude toward all things. Especially when facing imminent trouble. But Garcia would work with no other.

"Aw shoot Dick. Do you have to shout so much? Keep it down, just a little, will you?"

"I'm not shouting, man, it's just the echo banging in your head... and don't call me Dick, you know I hate it."

"Ooh, someone slipped me a mickey. Either that, or I sucked on a bad beer."

Garcia leaned back in his chair, lifting his feet onto his cluttered desk. He tugged a crumpled pack of Marlboros from his jacket, drawing out his first of the day. He straightened it, flicked his lighter into action and drew back hard, sucking air deep into his lungs. A tickle developed into a cough preventing the smoke going deeper. He held what he could in his lungs for as long as he could, stifling a cough. Then exhaled before the hacking took over.

"Ah, that's better. You know, the first drag of the day always gets my head spinning."

"Partner, you need to get a life."

Garcia paid no attention to the barb. He continued to enjoy the cigarette, sucking more smoke into his lungs prompting another hack. Squad leader Lieutenant Reuben emerged from his office grumbling.

"Are you the only team on duty?"

"McPherson and Martinez are looking into a vagrant found beaten last night at Mission Beach. Seems simple enough. A bit of overindulgence, followed by an assault," said Sylvester, glancing at the duty roster sheet.

"A bit like your friend Garcia, by the looks of him."

"Sir, he thinks he's born again with that disgusting piece of garbage in his mouth. He'll be with us soon."

"And the others?"

"Monaghan and Lawrence are in court downtown until this afternoon. What's up?"

"I've got a body. First reports show a Jane Doe, found this morning at Soledad Park. Check it out for me. From what I have been told, we may call for the experts from downtown." Reuben's comments sparked Garcia's attention. The hangover becoming a thing of the past. "According to the uniforms at the scene, we may need the big city boys to resolve this case. Whatever that means."

"Over my dead body," said Garcia, kicking himself up from the chair. "No one comes onto my turf."

"Steady Nico. Are you okay?" Reuben seemed disappointed with the rumpled appearance of his most senior officer. He demanded certain standards from his team. "You know you're not supposed to smoke that crap in here?"

"Sir, I'm fine."

"That's my boy," said Sylvester with a huge grin. "Nothing like a pecker challenge to cure the shakes."

"Here's the detail. Let me know what the situation is as soon as you can."

"Leave it to us, sir," said Sylvester, taking the sheet.

"Yeah boss, the dynamic duo will have this wrapped up in no time at all," said Garcia, breezing out of the room.

"Try to control your pal will you Richard. He looks terrible."

"Sir, you know he lives for his work. He won't let you down. It's all he's got left."

"Yeah... well... he needs to lift his game if he wants to stay on this squad," said Reuben, returning to his office. He maintained respect but needed more return of effort from him. Too much carousing could lead to termination of services, and no one wanted that to happen.

The drive to the park was slow. Traffic hampered by roadwork and a minor vehicle accident. The heat of the day hitting the mid-eighties seemed blistering and affecting Garcia as tried to get the air-conditioner working.

"Christ, if I don't get water into me soon partner... I'll just drop and die."

Sylvester shrugged as he waited for cars to move.

"So Rich, my boy, you had better pull over at the next available store, otherwise you're going to have two corpses to worry about."

"Look, Nic, I know you're suffering. But man, you need to move on. It's affecting your work."

"Give me a break partner. I'm not in the mood for a lecture. I drink to forget. I'm told drinking kills the brain cells, so if I drink enough, I'll kill sufficient brain cells to help me forget."

"Trouble is partner, it may kill you before you forget whatever you want to forget." Sylvester cruised to a stop outside a convenience store and turned to his friend. "Nico, I don't want you to become a faded memory to me."

"Yeah, we'll see," said Garcia, clambering from the car.

He returned a few minutes later laden with four bottles of water and a large bag of steaming, salty fries. He attacked them with the relish of a man desperate to kill the mother of all hangovers. By the time they reached the park, he finished the fries and was on his second bottle. "I think I'm coming good." He belched. "Where are we heading? Have you directions?"

"There's black and whites up ahead, so I reckon, we must be close."

The detectives asked directions from the stationed uniformed officer and followed a trail into the undergrowth thick with coastal trees until they came across more uniformed officers at a crime scene ribbon setting a perimeter. They parked the car, collected their gear, positioned badges, and moved toward the tape.

"Where's the stiff?" Garcia asked as they approached a senior police officer from their station.

"It's another fifty yards further along."

"Who's here?"

"Nico, it's not a pretty sight. The forensic boys are here from downtown, so is the M.E.."

"What time did we have someone here?"

"We had officers here at eighty thirty and they cordoned off the site."

"Where are the boys now?"

"I've sent them back to the station house to prepare their report. I thought you might want it when you get back. I have a young guy getting temperature and weather readings."

"Male or female?"

"Female. And badly done over."

"Who reported it?"

"A university tutor. The M.E. has more details for you."

"Thanks Phil. Say... when are you pulling the pin?"

"In a month. I can't wait."

"Going fishing?" asked Sylvester.

"No, Richard, I can't stand it. I haven't got the patience. Just eating fish instead."

"Christ, what's the stink?" asked Garcia, screwing up his nose and wiping it with the back of his hand.

"That's our Jane. She's ripe."

"No kidding."

The detectives followed indicator flags to show where personnel could walk without contaminating the investigation area. They came to a small clearing with a ring of personnel investigating the surrounds. Officers in white protective gear were exploring for evidence.

Peering over the body were the medical examiner and his associate, taking forensic samples from various parts of the corpse. They already bagged hands and feet for closer inspection and scrapings at the city morgue. Now was the time to find evidence, and they took extensive notes to help with a later autopsy. Normal procedure did not allow detectives access to the crime site until they gathered all necessary forensic samples, so they waited. Bent over the body were Doctor Charles Malaxos and his assistant Sarah Whitman.

"What've you got Doc?" called Garcia.

"Oh, hello Nicolas. We have a woman around twenty-five."

"Oh, Christ," said Sylvester, seeing the blistered corpse for the first time. The naked body splayed face down with her head resting on an arm. Excessive blood loss obvious. Sylvester had investigated gruesome deaths. He fought hard against the sight and smell.

"They bashed her," said Malaxos, as he stood, shifting closer to the detectives. "There are heaps of contusions, so I would say she had a hard time of it before the kill. There seems to be resistance wounds to her hands."

"Cause?"

"I would say loss of blood from lacerations to her neck, but I'll know more when I autopsy."

"When was she done?"

"Hard to say. From the amount of rigor, insect activity and rectal temperature, I guess maybe two days. I'll have more later."

"Weapon?"

"You've got all the tough questions today, haven't you?" Malaxos thumbed his chin. "From the injuries, I would say an axe or a machete, perhaps a knife. Her head is almost severed. A blunt weapon, like a shovel maybe."

"Doc, if he had a shovel, he would have buried her."

"Oh yeah, I hadn't thought of that."

"That's why we're the detectives," joked Sylvester.

"Any abuse?" asked Garcia.

"Yeah, plenty," said Sarah, a shrewd forensic investigator who already worked with the detectives. "We have venereal discoloration and rectum damage, which may indicate sustained sexual attack."

"How many?" asked Garcia.

"At least two, maybe three. We'll know more once the toxicology results come in from the swabs. We also have foreign pubic hair samples and what looks to be skin under one or two fingernails, which could prove helpful," said Malaxos, snapping off his rubber gloves.

"Although there's no reason one maniac could not have done this," added Sarah.

"By disturbance of the long grass over there," Sylvester was pointing to a flattened patch of rye grass. "It could have been at least two."

"I think you're right partner," said Garcia, patting him on the shoulder. He turned to the police forensic photographer. "Can we get plenty of snaps on this one, Brian? I want color and black and white prints."

"Who found her?" asked Sylvester.

Sarah came toward them. "A lecturer from the university on his morning jog. He was doing exercises on the trail a ways and a familiar odor got him investigating."

"Familiar odor? What is he, a mortician?" asked Garcia.

"Sort of, he lectures in mortuary science. I'm in his class."

"Really?" Garcia smiled. "You good at handling stiffs, Sarah?"

"Only old, wrinkly, and dead ones, Nico." The pause timed with a smile. "A bit like you."

"Touché," laughed Sylvester.

"I'd like to get her back to the office as soon as possible, Nic," interrupted Malaxos.

"Do you want me to autopsy before you ID?"

"Wait twenty-four hours if you can. If we haven't had a formal by then, you had better go ahead."

"Is there any ID at all?" asked Sylvester.

"The only thing we have is a tarnished ring on her wedding finger. It may mean she is married," said Sarah.

"If it's a wedding ring, then there may be a Missing Person's Report," said Garcia, thinking ahead. "A married woman missing for two, maybe three days, is bound to have a frantic husband... unless?"

"Unless what?" asked Sarah.

"Unless the husband is the bad guy," finished Sylvester.

"We'll get the uniforms onto that," said Garcia.

"I'll go brief Phil now," said Sylvester, moving away.

"Can I have the ring? You don't need it do you, Chuck?"

Malaxos passed the ring in a small evidence bag to Garcia.

"Looks different," said Garcia, examining it through the plastic. "What do you think, Sarah?"

"Looks Indian to me. If not, Mexican. A spiritual symbol."

"I expect you're right. Is that rust?"

"Not rust," said Malaxos. "Blood, we've done the scrapings."

"Let's hope it leads to her identity, poor girl," Garcia said, pocketing the bag.

Malaxos and Whitman worked for another hour over the body before giving the all clear for it to be removed. They bagged the corpse and coroner's orderlies carried it to a darkened wagon and transported downtown. Malaxos then paid careful attention to the soil from where the body laid, looking for evidence.

"Nic, do you think we have a maniac on our hands?" asked Sylvester as they climbed into their sedan.

"Partner, I don't know. Only bad dudes could have done this."

"I can't help but think of the agony on that poor girl's face. She must have done it tough."

"Don't worry, Rich, we'll get these guys. Fear not my friend, they will fry."

"Man, frying would be too good for these dudes."

"Let's just do our job partner. Let the justice system handle those responsible."

"The way we deal with justice, I haven't much faith Jane will ever get the retribution she deserves."

"Just remember Rich; this is another day and another case. Don't make it personal, otherwise, we may not do the job well. Get too close and you may miss something."

"Yeah, I suppose you're right, but..."

"No buts, partner. Just do your job."

On the return journey to the station house, Garcia's ordeal of a hangover fog lifted, resolving to stay sober until they solved the case. He needed his wits to be on top of this investigation. The longer the investigation, the colder the trail.

CHAPTER
10

"We've got a Jane Doe with no ID other than this ring," said Garcia, slumping into a chair in Reuben's office holding the specimen bag. "She's been there at least two days. Weapon is unknown, could be a machete. Her head almost severed. We'll know more when they complete the autopsy."

"Nothing else?" a pessimistic Reuben asked.

Garcia lit a cigarette. "We've got squat so far, but that doesn't mean we can't do it, boss."

"I want to send it downtown?"

"What are you trying to do, piss me off or what?"

"We have nothing. How can you build a case?"

"We don't need wise guys from downtown. In their fine suits and shiny sunglasses. Our team will solve this, won't we, Rich?"

"We've got nothing other than a ravaged body. I don't believe in miracles, and I reckon that's what we need," responded Sylvester, standing by the door.

Garcia couldn't accept what he heard almost choking on the smoke he had drawn too hard into his lungs. He didn't want the hotshots from downtown muscling in. He knew the team could solve this homicide.

"I agree, Rich," said Reuben. "I'll give you seventy-two hours. If we have nothing by then, I'll pass it to them."

"Seventy-two hours? You know they're media junkies downtown and if I'm any guess, this'll be a circus. I'll expect it'll take over three

RICHARD EVANS

days," said Garcia thankful for that much time. "At least allow me extra resources."

"Do what you have to do, but seventy-two is all you got. And stop smoking those damn things in the office."

The detectives returned to their desks to prepare a case plan.

"Thanks for your support in there, pal," Garcia said. "What is it with you?"

"Nic, unless we get a miracle, I suspect we need extra hands."

The squad's secretary and administrator, Bonnie Lefroy, sensing tension between the partners prepared coffee for Garcia, and for her favorite, his usual Chamomile tea. As they sat down, she placed steaming mugs in front of them, deflecting any anxiety. "This case might be a drain on you boys, so you had better fortify yourselves before getting the gray matter burning. Try this special elixir to get your energy pumping." Her southern drawl an attractive feature. "You both look haggard already."

"It's bad Bonnie, the worst I've seen." Sylvester said.

"Bonnie, honey, you're a princess," Garcia said, taking a large draft of coffee and lighting another Marlboro with the butt he then stubbed out. "If I didn't hate women so much, I'd ask you to be my sweetheart."

Bonnie knew Garcia was kidding, although she harbored a secret fantasy of a tryst. She prolonged the game a little further. "You couldn't stand the pace, Nicolas. You're a five-minute man if I'm any guess." Bonnie offered Richard a knowing wink, and he smiled, relaxing back into the reality of policing.

"Best damn five minutes I'll ever experience," Garcia laughed, dismissing the game, searching for a pen amongst his cluttered desk. "Rich, where do we start?"

"Partner, my intuition tells me this case is an abduction, rape and murder. Bad guys, rather than opportunists. With the injuries to the victim and the ground disturbance, I reckon three, maybe four perpetrators."

"You could be right. A quick ID of Jane would help," said Garcia.

"If they are bad guys, then I reckon they may have done something before. We better get someone searching files."

"Good idea." Garcia took a note. "We'll need a greater search of the area. And we had better get Jane's dental records out."

"The ring could mean a Missing Person's Report."

"Yeah, good thinking partner," said Garcia.

"We should autopsy now."

"Maybe, I'd rather wait until the morning to see if we can get an identification."

"I don't think we should wait longer than we need. The trail may have gone cold," said Sylvester.

"Forensics should have something from residue within a few hours. We can afford to wait. The dentals will help us, I'll arrange those now and get the search organized." Garcia said, picking up the telephone.

While Garcia prodded numbers, Sylvester took the opportunity to call home to explain circumstances to his wife, Rosalie.

"Honey, it's a bad one and we need to get early wins, so I doubt I'll be home on any predictable basis for the next few days." He could hear the anguish in his wife's voice as she tried to reassure him there was nothing to worry about.

Garcia followed the call from his telephone, wondering why anyone would bother getting married. In his mind, marriage was for the love struck. An arrangement built on such mush could only sink. He would not be walking down the aisle again.

"Rosalie honey, I know you don't like it, but it's my job." He didn't sound convincing. "Okay. We'll talk about it when I get home." He dropped his phone on the desk and blew a heavy sigh.

"Not happy?"

"No. She thinks I enjoy this work."

"Welcome to the world of irrational thinking. Women teach you to die wondering why you bothered to pursue them in the first place."

"Nic, I may be taking her side. This case is getting to me."

"Snap out of it, Richard. One bad crime scene does not end careers."

"Yeah, I know, but I miss my family."

"Get on with investigating, detective. That's what they pay you to do."

Garcia refocused on telephone calls. He knew his partner would overcome the melancholy and knuckle down to the tasks at hand. Sylvester noticed Phil Collins enter the squad room and motioned him over to his desk.

"What have you got?" Collins brought with him a young police officer Sylvester had seen at the station but not yet met.

"Detective Sylvester this young man is Officer Chris Hayward."

"Pleased to meet you, officer." Sylvester extended his hand.

"Officer Hayward has only been with us for a few days."

"Oh, that's great. Welcome to the team. I'm sure you will enjoy your stay with us."

"Thanks."

"Officer Hayward reckons he might help you in identifying Jane Doe," said Collins.

"Oh well then, you both had better sit and tell me what you've got."

Sylvester pulled a pad from his draw and a pen from a cup. He readied himself to take notes. He recalled his own first nervous days and wanted to support the new officer. Whilst Garcia argued into the hand piece about a search of the crime scene, Sylvester gawked at the young officer. He could see the kid was nervous. The darting eyes, hesitant breathing and wiping hands were all signs the officer felt out of depth within the detective room.

"Tell him, Chris," urged Collins.

"Well sir, on Saturday I was on my first night shift. They told me at the Academy to expect my fair share of nights. I've only been here a few days, and I wasn't expecting a night so soon. My girl wasn't too happy about it, I can tell you. She was planning to go to the movies on Saturday and I told her on Friday I had to work. Boy, did she blow her top. Called me for everything."

"Just cut to the chase, please Chris." Sylvester stifled a yawn.

"Oh yeah, sorry sir."

"Don't worry about it. Just get to where you figure you know our Jane Doe. I'm interested to know how you could, given we haven't got photos yet. I don't think we assigned you to the scene, were you?"

"No sir. They don't let me out until I have been at the station for a few weeks. They have assigned me patrol duty when I do, though. I aspire to be a detective like you. My daddy was a DI in Seattle. I thought I'd follow in his footsteps. He was a detective for nearly..."

"Look officer, I don't wish to be rude, but could we focus here."

"Oh sorry, sir." He tugged a small notebook from his shirt pocket. Sylvester wished he were on the telephone and Garcia was dealing with the rookie. "On Saturday evening I had a Mr. Tom Moroni report about a missing person at around eleven-thirty-five. Mr. Moroni was expecting his wife home around nine-thirty. She hadn't contacted him or even texted, which was unusual for her, as she always messaged when she was running late."

"Go on," said Sylvester, taking serious interest in the officer's story.

"Mr. Moroni lives in La Jolla, on Beaumont. He hadn't seen his wife all day. She was out collecting donations for a charity with one of her friends. Mr. Moroni phoned her friend who told him she dropped her off near her home around ten thirty. Mr. Moroni said she didn't arrive. So, he came to us. We have a report out on her but no response from other precincts and no reported sightings."

"Why do you assume it's our girl?"

"It's her alright," interjected Collins. "I'll bet a month's pay on it."

"The hair."

"What?"

"Her hair," said Hayward, referring to his notes. "Mrs. Moroni has hair which could only be described as luxuriant. Mr. Moroni said it was her most outstanding feature."

"I don't understand."

"When Officer Collins returned to the station, he described the terrible crime scene. We all felt a little squeamish. I mean, at the Academy they advised us to expect this type of case, but when he told us, it was just awful."

Sylvester was about to interrupt but Officer Hayward was a quick learner.

"Anyway, it was the hair that struck a memory cord with me. He said how beautiful the lady's hair was. I remember he said it was like an 'oasis of beauty amongst all the death and destruction.' It jolted my recollection of Saturday evening, and I pulled the Missing Person file. Well, I guess it's her." Hayward passed over the file.

Sylvester opened it, exposing a photograph of a young woman and a completed missing person sheet. "Sandra Moroni," he said, mulling over the information. "It could be her, but I'm not sure. Where did you get the photograph?"

"Mr. Moroni dropped it in on Sunday morning, after I recommended a photograph might help," said Hayward.

"It's her. Check out the jewelry list," suggested Collins.

Sylvester read the register. Gold neck chain, watch with leather band and a Navajo wedding ring.

"You think the ring is ours, Phil?"

"Yep. She's our girl for sure."

"Has there been any follow up on the Missing Person Report?"

"To tell you the truth, Richard. Lack of personnel has meant we have done nothing, other than put her on the network."

"Okay," said Sylvester, closing the file. "I guess this may have just saved hours of investigation, which I can tell you we need. Outstanding work Chris."

"Oh, it was nothing, sir."

"Chris, in the context of this case, it's everything. Leave it to us now, thanks again. Welcome to the team."

Sylvester knew this breakthrough may transform the entire investigation, pleased to have such an alert officer working with them. If Hayward had not been on duty to hear Collins' story, they would have lost precious hours. It was a lucky break. After saying goodbye to the officers, thanking them once again, Sylvester sat smirking, studying Garcia, waiting to announce the news.

"Done," Garcia said, dropping the hand piece back into place and lighting up another cigarette. "We'll have every square inch of the scene picked through today. Not bad, eh, partner?"

"Not bad. Where are you getting extra eyes from?" a smug Sylvester asked. It wasn't often he had something over Garcia, so enjoyed this moment.

"I've convinced them to consider the media hell once the news gets out, and to bring out the Academy recruits."

"Not bad. Well done."

"Not bad?" The laid-back attitude of his partner surprised Garcia. "What are you smoking, boy? That's the best news so far."

"For small minds, maybe it is, but for enormous intellects like me... I have something better."

"Come on, Richard, stop blowing my trumpet." Sylvester's smugness frustrated and annoyed him. "I've got a headache."

"Well pal, this news will blow your cares away, including your headache."

"No, not a Bud partner. Not today."

"No, not for a few days at least," Sylvester said, grinning like the cat that just swallowed Tweety bird.

"Oh, come on Richard. Stop mucking me about," a frustrated Garcia declared.

"I've got a name for Jane," gloated Sylvester, waving the missing person's file above his head. Garcia bounced to his feet and in two skips reached Sylvester's desk, trying to snatch the file.

"What is it?" Garcia excited with the news kissed Sylvester on the forehead. "Partner, you're gorgeous. Tell me. Oh, what would I do without you?"

"Distributing parking infringement notices."

He handed over the file to Garcia who wandered back to his desk devouring it. "It's her."

"We should travel downtown to the morgue and check it out."

"No. Trust me on this one, partner. We'll go straight to the husband."

CHAPTER
11

The detectives rolled up outside 6534 Beaumont twenty minutes after leaving the station. A two-story, pink Spanish villa in a leafy part of La Jolla. The afternoon still sizzling, although a sea breeze drifted through, rustling the trees.

Garcia pushed the doorbell and waited. They hoped Moroni was home, but neither looking forward to the meeting. Tom opened the door. After polite introductions, he ushered the detectives into the sitting room where an older couple sat on the sofa.

"Mr. Moroni," Garcia began. "We would like to talk to you about your missing wife. Alone, if possible."

"Oh, it's all right detective. These folks are Sandi's parents, Alice and Bernie Johnston. I'm sure what you tell me, you can tell them."

"Have you found Sandi? Is she alright?" Alice asked.

"We may have Mrs. Johnston," said Garcia, moving to shake their hands. "Detective Sylvester and I are here to find out."

"Where is she?" asked Alice, seeking a sign from the men. Bernie took her hand, fearing the worst. Tom sat next to her, putting a comforting arm around her shoulders.

Garcia never cared for these moments. He anguished over small talk, wanting to move on with his news. After the tension eased a little, he prepared for his revelation.

"Look, there is no easy way of telling you this," he said, hurting as he studied the expectant faces, his hands trembling. "We found a body this morning which we believe to be your wife Mr. Moroni, and your daughter Mr. and Mrs. Johnston."

They understood but seemed unsure of what to say or do.

"How? Where?" Tom asked.

"Is she alright?" Alice asked.

"No, pet, she's not," Bernie replied, patting her hand. She turned to Bernie, and the pain of the news engulfed her. She wailed, falling into his chest sobbing.

"Sir, it's yet to be confirmed the deceased is your wife, Sandra." Garcia emphasized the point. "We found her at Soledad Park."

Tom stood and shuffled to the window, staring out into nowhere in particular.

Bernie comforted Alice and seemed disbelieving of the news. "No, it can't be. She never goes to that part of town."

Garcia cleared his throat and continued. "We suspect the perpetrators abused the deceased."

Tom collapsed to his knees.

"Was she..." Bernie fought for the words. "Was she treated harshly?"

Garcia couldn't answer, the lump in his throat preventing him from speaking.

"Yes, sir," Sylvester said.

Tom wept.

"How do you know it's Sandi?" asked Alice, wiping tears from her face, wishing for a sign of doubt from the men.

"Ma'am we don't know for sure," said Garcia. "All we have is Mr. Moroni's description and a photograph. Both match the deceased, and we found this ring." Garcia drew the plastic bag from his pocket, holding it up for inspection. Tom, fighting for control, struggled to his feet to inspect the ring.

"I can't be sure. It looks like our ring."

After a prolonged pause, Garcia said to Tom, "Sir, if you think you can manage it, we would appreciate you accompanying us to the coroner's office for a formal identification. We can then confirm whether the deceased is your wife, and we'll know for sure."

"Sure. Now?"

"If you wouldn't mind, sir."

"I wish to attend," said Bernie.

"So do I," added Alice.

"Ma'am, I am happy for Mr. Johnston to join us, as it may help the investigation. But I recommend you don't come with us."

"I want to," insisted Alice.

"Ma'am, it is very important that if the deceased is your daughter, then your last memory of her should be the last time you saw her. Not as she might be at the moment."

Garcia was firm. Bernie acknowledged his wisdom. He hugged his wife. "I'll ring Kay. She can wait with you while Tom and I go with the detectives."

Alice wanted to go but resigned herself knowing she wouldn't. It took ten minutes for Kay, who lived nearby, to arrive. Garcia and Sylvester waited outside, allowing the family to console themselves for a few moments. Garcia lit up and dragged, seeking to bring as much relief as he could to his system.

"Christ, that was hard."

Sylvester couldn't say a thing.

The thirty-minute trip downtown was hushed. The detectives answered questions from the men as truthfully as they could. Openness very important to a grieving family trying to come to terms with a tragedy. When they arrived, Garcia ushered both men into a viewing area. Sylvester organized the identification.

Garcia paced the room, hoping an identification advanced his investigation. Yet, for the men's sake, he wished the deceased was not Sandi. The sterile gray room had a viewing window shrouded in a curtain on a wall opposite the door. No furniture to rest emotional bodies. The wait was not long. A crackling intercom alerted the viewers of the impending exposure. The men moved to the window and waited, Bernie wringing his hands and Tom snorting, clasping the back of his head. The sudden retraction of the curtain startled them. Tom's panting increased. He then whimpered, putting his hands on the glass to steady himself.

The woman lay before them under a green sheet. An opening for her head, hair brushed out behind her. Garcia appreciated the work the coroner did to prepare her so well. He made a mental note to thank Malaxos. The sheet hid the wounds on her neck. Bruising distinct, with most of her face swollen and blistered.

Garcia waited a short while and then asked, "Is it Sandi?"

Tom was first to respond. "I don't know... I don't know."

Garcia wrapped his arm around Tom's shoulders.

Bernie broke the silence. He hadn't moved since the curtain opened. He felt a gnawing tightness in the pit of his stomach. The color from his face drained, and he struggled to speak. As he rolled his tongue through his mouth, he tried to speak, but only squeaked a few sounds.

"It's her." His body heaved into a sob. "It's my baby."

CHAPTER
12

"I hate this family thing with ID's." Garcia dragged on another smoke, coughing as they drove from the Moroni house. "I've got to give these damn things away," he said, eyeing the cigarette.

"Yeah, they seem to be a nice family. It's a shame for them having to go through all of this," said Sylvester, needing relief from the sadness.

"Yeah, a terrible shame. Drag Tom in for questioning in about an hour." Garcia had come back to the investigation. "And you better ask Barbara what's her name, as well."

Sylvester respected Garcia's pragmatism but wondered about his partner's emotions when he could switch from caring police officer one moment to a ruthless detective the next. "When do you think we should bring a team together?"

"Let's report to Reuben and see who is available."

When the detectives returned to the station house, it was nearing seven o'clock. They made a few telephone calls before reporting to Lieutenant Reuben, standing at his desk, packing his case, preparing to go home.

"Nice to see people get it easy around here," said Garcia.

"Yeah well, I have a date with my wife, who says it's tonight or never again. So, tonight I had better invest in family time."

"I don't understand you guys," a sarcastic Garcia said, waving his arm to include Sylvester. "What hold have your women got over you. You both bust your butts to keep them happy. Why?"

"Considering your latest disaster, you're no expert," laughed Reuben. "At least I'm happy."

"Are you?" a cynical Sylvester quizzed. Garcia's frown replaced the need for any spoken word.

"What have you got?" Reuben asked, keen to get home.

"We identified Jane as Mrs. Sandra Moroni. A twenty-six-year-old nurse. Married for two years. Lives on Beaumont in La Jolla and spent Saturday collecting for a charity." Garcia read from notes. "She was last seen around ten thirty in the evening, although that time is yet to be confirmed. She appears not to be implicated in any sordid activity and looks to be of outstanding character. We suspect an opportunist crime."

Reuben continued packing, dropping a file into his case as Garcia slumped into a chair at the desk.

"I've instigated an autopsy with results scheduled tomorrow morning. The husband is in for questioning in about an hour. We'll bring in her friend who looks to be the last to see her. No suspects identified at this stage. We've ruled no-one out yet," he said.

Sylvester considered Tom Moroni was not responsible.

"Little crime scene evidence so far reported, but an inch-by-inch search started earlier," Garcia said.

He knew his job, and Reuben relaxed with what he was hearing. "I should not inform media at this stage."

Garcia nodded in agreement.

"We need to complete the autopsy first. I don't want to give too much information to the killers," Reuben said, clipping his case closed.

"Good idea," said Garcia. "I'll start a M.O. search of the files. I expect it might be a group sex thing, spur of the moment, bash and slash. They just went overboard. Anyway, I'll know more after I talk to the husband and clear him."

"How many involved?" Reuben asked.

"I'd say at least two. What do you think, Richard?"

"Maybe four, tops."

"How many hands do you need?" asked Reuben.

"I could do with another two teams. The more we cover in these seventy-two hours the closer we'll get to these maniacs."

"Right," said Reuben, dragging his briefcase from the desk and leaving. "You can have Monaghan and Lawrence. I'll try to have Martinez and McPherson assigned to you once I know how they progressed with the vagrant assault. I'll talk to Gayle from the car."

Garcia seemed impressed with the increased help returning to his desk to think through an investigation structure. Bonnie had a cup of coffee waiting, and he squeezed her shoulder in appreciation. He took a large draught of caffeine, lit a smoke, and coughed hard to free his congestion.

"You should give those up, Nicolas. My men need all the strength they can muster."

"Hmm, nice thought Bonnie, honey. But a cigarette is cheaper."

Bonnie smiled, said good night, and left for the day.

"We'll need to build a profile once we talk to Barbara Smethers," said Sylvester, returning to his desk.

"Do we have contact with her yet?"

"I've spoken to Phil Collins, and he is on his way to collect her. She should be here in about forty minutes."

"Excellent, what about Moroni?"

"He's due in twenty minutes. I rang him before we met with Reuben."

"That's great Rich. You have been busy."

"I want these thugs," said Sylvester, anger in his tone. "She is my sister's age and for what they did to her family, these bastards deserve to fry."

"Stay focused Richard," said Garcia. "I need your investigative skills, not your vigilante sentiments."

"I saw something today which will live with me for a long time. Nothing you say will alter my focus on this job."

"Good. Then let's complete the friggin' paperwork whilst we wait for the husband."

CHAPTER
13

Tom Moroni sat at the table of interview room one, his head resting on his crossed forearms. A black coffee in a foam cup remained untouched. A sense of sadness shrouded him. A man who had his future taken from him appeared lost. He raised his head when the detectives entered. He pushed himself back into the chair, taking a few deep breaths, preparing to confront his tragedy. It was clear he had been struggling with the news. His face and eyes red and puffed.

Garcia sat opposite him as Sylvester stood by the window behind Tom, preparing then switching on a recording device.

"This is a voluntary interview with Mr. Tom Moroni, of 6534 Beaumont Avenue, La Jolla. The interviewing officer is Detective Nicolas Garcia, badge number 8934. Also in attendance is Detective Richard Sylvester, for the record detective. Please identify yourself?"

"Detective Richard Sylvester, badge number 9297."

"It is eight-ten on the evening of Tuesday, August 24th. Mr. Moroni, for the record please state your full name and address."

The interview began, the formality bewildering Tom, "Thomas Joseph Moroni. 6534 Beaumont Avenue, La Jolla."

"You are married to Sandra Emily Moroni, also of the same address?"

"Yes."

"Mr. Moroni, did you identify a woman's body, earlier today, to be that of your wife, Sandra Emily Moroni?"

"Yes," Tom whispered.

"Mr. Moroni." Garcia paused. He knew what to ask and already regretted it. "Did you murder your wife?"

"What?"

"Did you murder your wife? Did you bash her? Render her unconscious, willfully murder her and dump her naked body in Soledad Park in La Jolla?"

"You must be joking."

"This is no joke, sir. I repeat. Did you murder Sandra Emily Moroni?"

The intolerable silence confused them. Two men staring at each other. One with a silent rage building, the other, tough and thick skinned about the need to clear the husband from the list of suspects.

Sylvester had not moved. He felt uncomfortable; his breathing quickened, waiting for the response he hoped would come and end the conflict. He understood the need to clear suspects but considered Moroni to be innocent. However, the question they needed to ask and record the answer.

Tom shifted in his seat as he thought about how to respond. His mouth and throat dry, and he was conscious of his nervous cough as he cleared his throat. Beads of sweat appeared on his forehead and he wiped his upper lip. His eyes darted to all parts of the room, trying to avert Garcia's penetrating gaze.

Then with as much control as he could muster through clenched teeth, 'you are a crap detective, Garcia. You're a rotten scab festering over the most wonderful things in this life."

The comment wounded.

"Do you realize the pain I'm going through? Do you?" Tom's voice almost shrilling with rage.

"Mr. Moroni, I..."

"Sandi is... was... the most beautiful thing in my world. She is my life. Her very presence just took my breath away. Her touch tingles my skin and shudders my senses. I am in awe of her. My love surpasses no other emotion." Tears trickled down his face. "She is everything to me." He choked out the words. "And you ask, did I murder her?"

He brushed his face.

"Are you mad? Hurt my darling? You must be insane to think I would ever place a hand of anger on her." Moroni dropped his head and tears dripped from his jaw and chin. The detectives waited, passing each other glances.

"Once, I wept when she injured herself in the garden. Can you believe that? I blubbered like a baby when she came running to me with blood all over her hand from a cut on her finger." He stifled a chuckle. "And you ask if I murdered her?" Moroni screwed his face, glaring at Garcia.

"She is my life detective. Her breath is my breath. Her blood; my blood. Her pain is my pain. Her tears are my tears. And you ask if I murdered her?" Tom paused.

Sylvester brushed his face.

"Are you mad? Are you so stupidly mad, that you... that you treat my love for my wife with so much contempt? No detective, I did not murder Sandi."

Garcia breathed tension from him. "That being the case Mr. Moroni, can you please outline you and your wife's movements, from waking on Saturday until you filed your missing person report."

The hostility between the men remained as the interview progressed. Sylvester shuffled from foot to foot, pleased with Moroni's responses. He had been in many interviews with his partner, but the next thirty minutes were the most tense.

Garcia was professional and unemotional with his questioning. He wanted to learn every bit of information that may help track the killers. What clothes Sandi was wearing? Color of her shoes? Did she have hairpins? What type of underwear? What bag? Did she carry make-up? What brand? What credit cards did she carry? Which bank? Did she have any cash? How much? Garcia wanted to know everything so they could build a profile.

Tom answered the incessant questions, and after thirty minutes felt eviscerated. Sylvester indicated to Garcia that it might be a good time to end the interview. Garcia took his advice.

"Interview ended at eight forty-five."

It relieved Tom to end the questioning, and Garcia tried to comfort him. "Mr. Moroni, I have been in this business for fifteen years. Let me do my job and I will find the maniac who killed your wife. I have to get to the truth, and I must eliminate you from the list of suspects. If I upset you, then I apologize. But always remember, I'm on Sandi's team. I will not rest until I have the person who killed her behind bars."

Moroni lifted his head to gaze at Garcia,

"Detective, Sandi's love for me embodied me. If what I have just been through is a sign as to your zealousness toward this case, then I am confident Sandi will get justice. I'm satisfied with the knowledge this investigation is in your expert hands."

CHAPTER
14

Barbara was a wreck. She'd lost her best friend, her role model, and mentor. She couldn't understand it, nor could she come to terms with what happened. "I told her to report it. The police were even there. But did she? No. She knew better. She knew better," she said, trying hard to control her mix of emotions. "Can I have a cigarette?"

Garcia offered his last, flicking on a flame, holding it out. She was shaking, fighting to control her hand against the flame. Garcia recognized the distress and pain in her face, feeling sorry for the friend who dropped Sandi off curbside rather than her doorstop. He suspected she would suffer with that memory for a long time.

"Miss Smethers, can I just confirm a few points from your statement?" asked Sylvester. Barbara nodded, wiping away a tear. "You say you dropped Sandi at ten-twenty, is that right?"

"Yes."

"You said she carried the donations, about how much in total?"

"I can't remember. It was more than a thousand."

"Can you be a little more exact? It's important."

She thought for a moment. "No, I can't remember. I know it was a lot of money and it was a record for us, but I can't remember," she said, eyes welling.

Sylvester understood he would not get much more from her. "Just one last question, Miss Smethers. Did you get a good look at the other guys Sandi said molested her?"

"I've tried to remember," she said, moaning. "I've tried. But I can't. I just don't remember. I can't remember. I told her... I told her to call the police. Why didn't she? Why did she do this to me?"

"Interview ended nine thirty-eight," said Garcia

He and Sylvester left the interview room, giving Barbara peace and arranging a lift home for her.

"I need a smoke," said Garcia, walking off toward the vending machine.

"Yeah, I could go with one too," agreed Sylvester who gave up the dreaded weed years before.

"Profile meeting at ten," Garcia called over his shoulder. "Tell the others."

He had already assigned preliminary tasks to the team and, although operating on brief notice, he hoped they might have come up with early information to help develop the case.

They set up a whiteboard in the squad room and an assortment of detectives assembled in front, waiting for Garcia. The early details of the investigation waiting to be shared, then transcribed onto the board. The team completed basic steps for any investigation and now assembled to share information.

Gayle Martinez, an experienced homicide detective, waited by the board, tossing a whiteboard marker up and down. Asked to lead the briefing, she had already spoken to each of the team, identifying intelligence already collected. She had investigated thirty homicides with twenty-seven convictions from twenty-nine arrests. The unresolved homicides still nagged at her. She promised herself she would never miss evidence again. Hard on herself to perform, it drove her to obsessive thoroughness in every case.

She stood by the whiteboard, waiting to record the profile, anxious about valuable time being wasted. "Come on, where is he?" She tapped her watch with the pen.

In front of her sat a respected gathering of colleagues. She was keen to show her skills and although senior to the others; she carried the self-doubts of many when faced with a group of peers. Her theory of detection meant action. Not widening the gap between the good guys and the bad guys from lack of activity.

"He'll be here soon enough Gayle, he's had a hard day," offered Sylvester from his desk, grappling with his daily report. He couldn't get Sandi out of his head. He wondered how he would feel if it were his wife.

Detective Chip Lawrence leaned back in his chair, his feet on the desk twirling a pen between his fingers. A forensic expert, he preferred to chase bad guys rather than poke about a laboratory. "Do you think he's gone to a bar or something?"

The others didn't respond, preferring to reflect on the innocent comment, hoping it wasn't true.

A life of a bored scientist did not excite Lawrence, choosing instead the Los Angeles Police Department. He preferred working the streets and the thrill of overcoming the bad guys.

When his young wife demanded he move to the safer work as a detective, the Department did not agree. The hard-headed politics of Government Departments would not allow a compromise, so he transferred to San Diego. A new city, a promotion to detective and the thirty-year-old was again relishing good guy, bad guy assignments.

Red Monaghan appeared to all as the stereotypical perfect dead-beat. There was no way the fifty-year-old, hardened by thirty years of dealing with low life, could be anything other than surly. He didn't feel the need to apologize. He had seen it all and not wanted any of it. He looked dreadful all the time. His crumpled clothes never changed from one day to the next. He was fat, sweaty, crumpled, smelly and a pain in the butt, but as Chip often said, "I want him next to me when I face danger, because there is no-one more tough or sharper."

The last of the team waiting for Garcia was Lou McPherson. A hard man from hard times. He took no crap, and his absolute loyalty was to the squad. He enjoyed a military career until a hearing defect retired him. Legend has him touring the Middle East. His precise military background remained unknown. Garcia suspected he might have served in counterintelligence. His short, cropped graying hair, fit taunt body and cat like movements bellied the fact he was nearing retirement.

Garcia crashed backwards through the door, hunched over, trying to save two foam cups from spilling coffee. "Oh Christ," he muttered, through lips dangling a cigarette, as hot coffee splashed across his hand.

"Did you bring me one?" asked Monaghan, always on the lookout for a freebie.

With Garcia struggling to his desk, everyone began gathering in front of the whiteboard. They flicked through notes, preparing themselves for the briefing.

"Right, Gayle, what have we got?" asked Garcia, putting his coffee down, stubbing out his cigarette, and wiping his hand on his jacket.

"Okay, thanks Nic," started Martinez, focused on the task ahead. She snapped a graphic color photograph of the corpse in the center at the top of the whiteboard. Next, she placed another photograph of Sandi supplied by Tom. "As our photographs depict, we have the violent murder of Mrs. Sandra Moroni, nee Johnston."

Martinez referred to notes as she placed dot points on the board. "First reported to Central at seven thirty this morning by a Mr. Brian Southby, a lecturer at the university. The first officers at the scene sealed the area at eight o'clock." Martinez placed further crime scene photographs on the whiteboard as she continued her briefing. The others looked on, taking notes and waiting for their contribution. "Preliminary evidence suggests she had been dead two days. Autopsy will give us more definition of time and cause of death. They killed her where we found her."

"Nic, we have Mrs. Moroni confirmed until ten-thirty on Saturday night. Do you want us to go through them now or wait?" Sylvester interrupted.

"No, let's do them now. Lead us through, Gayle," Garcia said, sipping his steaming coffee then dragging on his cigarette.

"At around noon, Sandi, and her friend Barbara Smethers, began door knocking for donations along Mission Boulevard, near York in Mission Beach. They approached around one hundred businesses in the six hours they door knocked, raising over a thousand dollars. We suspect closer to twelve hundred," Sylvester said as Martinez took notes on the board.

"A handy little stash," chipped in Monaghan.

"We are compiling a list of the donors. Uniforms will complete that for us tomorrow," added Sylvester. "We will then have a better idea of how much money they collected. We may have an idea whether the killers followed them during the day."

"Good." Garcia nodded.

Martinez added. "We have the women arriving at Pacific Beach at Grand Avenue six-twenty-five. We are trying to confirm the time with patrons from the bars in the area. We'll have to wait until the morning to get a better picture. They then separated. Sandi went to the West Coast Lagoon bar and Barbara went into the Brewery Restaurant and Bar opposite."

"Why didn't they go together?" asked McPherson.

"Barbara was exhausted and wanted a drink," Sylvester said. "Sandi wanted more donations. Barbara went off to save a table and order drinks. Fifteen minutes later, Sandi presents to her friend in an anxious state. Distressed, pale and shaken."

"Are we getting someone to talk to patrons at the West Coast Lagoon?" asked Garcia.

"Yeah. We're planning to hit the place tomorrow," responded Martinez. "We're hoping to secure CCTV."

Sylvester continued. "Sandi tells Barbara about the guys in the poolroom. She tells her, they would have hurt her if it weren't for a patron, who came upon the assault just in time."

"The autopsy should show how serious this confrontation was," Lawrence contributed.

"When is it being done?" asked Monaghan.

"We should have results tomorrow, any volunteers?" Sylvester asked.

"I don't mind," jumped in Lawrence.

"Yeah, right partner," Monaghan responded. "You can have that on your own."

"Thanks Chipper," said Garcia. "Could you stay close to it, we need to know times and cause as soon as we can."

"I'm on it boss," replied Lawrence, taking notes.

"Continue, Gayle, please," said Garcia.

"Around seven, Sandi spots one thug in the parking lot next door. He went into the 7-Eleven to buy liquor."

"Do we have an ID on this guy?" asked McPherson.

"Around twenty-five. Caucasian. Heavy set, around 170 pounds.

Stands around five ten. Brown hair, cropped. Red checked shirt. Blue jeans and work boots," reported Sylvester.

"What about the footage from the 7-Eleven security camera?" asked Monaghan.

"We've already asked, and seems it was down that evening," said Martinez.

"Damn. That would have helped," said Monaghan.

"Okay, let's call these dudes from the bar, group A," said Garcia. "I don't know whether there is a connection, but who knows? They may be our boys. Right Gayle, move on."

Gayle noted, then circled the group on the whiteboard and continued.

"The women have dinner. They drink a bit more than usual, but they are not drunk. Tipsy maybe, but still in control. They count their money and head for home around ten fifteen. Barbara driving. Sandi insists on walking the last few yards to her home, for fresh air. She was feeling light-headed and thought the walk would help. She gets out of the car on La Jolla Boulevard, one hundred and fifty yards from her front door."

"You're kidding?" sighed Monaghan.

"No. They took her just a few yards from turning off La Jolla," confirmed Martinez.

"Unbelievable." Monaghan shook his head.

"What was she wearing?" asked McPherson.

"Red shirt with a yellow emblem. A denim skirt. Unsure about socks, but a distinctive pair of track shoes. White with red laces," Martinez read from notes.

"We're checking how unique the shoes are, because she bought them overseas and the brand may not be available here," said Sylvester.

"Could be a significant break, that," said Monaghan. The others seemed to agree.

"She also wore white panties and a matching bra clipped at the front. Hardly any jewelry, a watch, and earrings, all missing."

"And a wedding ring, which we have," added Sylvester.

Martinez continued. "She had a large patch leather bag which carried an assortment of material. Make-up and other trinkets, including a leather wallet. It also held the calico donations sack."

"When did Barbara last see her friend?" asked Monaghan.

"She drove off and watched her head for home from the rear vision mirror."

"No one else about?" Monaghan asked.

"No one."

"Is that it?" asked a concerned Garcia. "Is that all we have at the moment?"

"No. We have more," McPherson said. "Don't fret. We're working hard."

"At ten thirty-eight, Central receives a call from a Mr. Malcolm Vernon, who lives on La Jolla Boulevard," Lawrence said.

"Yeah, I thought I'd just follow up the call sheet, just in case there was anything for us," said Monaghan.

"Mr. Vernon heard screaming and went to investigate. He thought he witnessed an abduction but wasn't sure. He reported it anyway. Recorded, but no action taken," Lawrence said.

"Chip and I had a chat with Mr. Vernon earlier," said Monaghan. "He was sure of what he saw."

Lawrence interrupted. "It seems Mr. Vernon was out front, putting trash into his car, when he heard shouting and screaming coming from the street. At first, he thought it was just kids having fun, but then the screams became desperate. So, he went to investigate. What he saw unnerved him."

"What did he see?" Sylvester asked.

"Two dudes, struggling with a woman, matching our girl's description," said Monaghan.

Garcia was excited. "Why didn't you tell me?"

"You always tell me to follow the book and we just got back," Lawrence said, smiling.

"What else have you got? Give us the news," said Martinez, keen to transcribe the detail onto the whiteboard.

"Mr. Vernon saw the abduction. A vehicle, matt finished, perhaps gray, Buick or Dodge. No tags," reported Lawrence. "What alarmed him was the violent nature of the struggle. The dudes were punching into the girl. Once she was in the car, one dude went back and picked up a bag from the sidewalk. He piled in and the car speed off before Vernon could run to it."

"How many guys in the vehicle?" asked Sylvester.

"He was unsure. He thinks he saw two, though he isn't sure. If there were two and one driver, then we could consider three," said Monaghan.

"Any description?" asked Martinez.

"Not much I'm afraid," said Lawrence. "Small dudes dressed in jeans and jacket-type clothing. It was dark. Long hair maybe on one. Both could be Caucasian. Young, around twenty."

"It's them," declared Garcia. "Christ, it's them. Any ties with group A?"

"None," said Monaghan. "We'll know for sure when we speak to staff and patrons from the bar tomorrow."

"This is great. What a breakthrough, fantastic. Oh boy, I could kiss you both," said Garcia. "Well, maybe not you Red. This is significant news. Have we anything else?"

"We have nothing else until we hit the crime scene," said Martinez. "We found Sandi naked, with brutal wounds. We found no clothing at the scene, or anything else. We will have the cause of death tomorrow once the autopsy is complete. We have found none of her possessions except her ring. They ripped the earrings from her. Chip?"

Lawrence moved to the whiteboard to continue adding information to the profile.

"According to the ME's initial report, it was the kill scene. Three different foot imprints found, but it's difficult to be sure. We found a fourth set near a car imprint. So, we could search for four dudes. A flimsy link to your Group A, I suppose, Nic. I wouldn't count on it, though. There is little physical evidence, although we have a variety of dumped bottles, some recent."

"We're testing for prints and DNA," said Sylvester.

"We also have a variety of odds and ends, cigarette butts and a little marijuana residue. The forensic boys are running further tests over the site tomorrow morning. Your uniform search turned up very little," concluded Lawrence.

"Well gentlemen," resumed Martinez. "Other than the abduction sighting, we ain't got much."

"Oh, I don't agree," McPherson said, arousing interest amongst the team. "We have plenty."

"I agree," said Garcia, a wry smile of acknowledgement to McPherson as he stood to address the team.

"We have Sandi assaulted by Group A at six thirty, in a public place full of witnesses. A reckless act by a group of silly, stupid boys. I am sure we'll secure descriptions tomorrow. We have Sandi's likely murderers abducting her at ten thirty-eight. Another reckless act. Witnessed. I have a hunch Group A is our prime suspects."

"How come?" asked Martinez.

"Motive and opportunity, plus their collective stupidity," Garcia said. "They had a go once and waited for a second chance. The witnesses at the bar will help us further. If we can match descriptions of group A to the abductors, then we will have them. We are well ahead of the pace at the moment. I think group A is our boys. Chip, I want you and Red to follow up the bar tomorrow after the autopsy. There's the guy who broke up the assault. He's got to be our best witness to who these bad guys might be."

"It's a long bow, Nic," Sylvester said. "To link group A with the abduction is too great a hunch, there's too much time gap."

"I agree with Rich," said Martinez.

"What do you think, Lou?" asked Garcia.

"I agree it's a big hunch. But it's possible. They might have been pissed at missing out and waited for an opportunity to complete unfinished business."

"We have four dudes at the bar. A driver and two others at the abduction. And three, maybe four at the crime site. It could be them," said Lawrence.

"So, they stalked her?" asked Sylvester.

"Yeah, I reckon so," said McPherson. "They waited, then they pounced."

"No," said Martinez. "It's too long a bow."

"Let's just eliminate them first, shall we?" asked Garcia, trying to keep the team together.

"If they're in the same group, why not take both women?" asked Martinez.

A long pause of thought followed, considering her point.

"They didn't stalk her," suggested Monaghan. "It was opportunistic and may not have been the guys from the bar at all."

"Why?" asked Garcia.

"No lights in the mirror."

"What's that partner?" asked Lawrence.

"No lights in the rear-view mirror."

"Explain," said Garcia.

"Smethers said her last sight of her friend was in the rear-view mirror, as she drove off. She didn't mention any lights, and she thought no one else was even around. Therefore, if the stalking theory is correct, there would have been lights. She would have been able to see the lights from another car."

"Not if she couldn't remember," said McPherson.

"If there was a glare in the mirror from headlights, she would not have been able to see Sandi at all."

"Good point," said Lawrence.

"It was opportunistic. A split-second decision made when the bad guys saw a lone woman walking. They were heading south and spun around behind her."

"Okay. Let's assume group A is still group B," said Garcia, taking back control.

"Where did they go for four hours?"

"The 7-Eleven is the answer," Monaghan said. "They must have been buying booze. Maybe they went to a party up this way."

"Not the class for a La Jolla party," said McPherson.

"I agree," said Garcia. "They most likely went to a private spot to have a drink. Maybe the beach."

"Why not the class, Lou?" asked Martinez.

"The car. The clothes. The bar in Pacific, and the fact they may have been heading south, if Red's theory is correct. My guess is they come from south side."

"But if group B is not A, then all this talk is just crap," said Sylvester.

"Rich, it's all we have now," reassured Garcia. "Trust me on this one, partner."

"Let's just eliminate A from our investigation first. Or at least get more evidence. We are operating on shaky ground here," said Sylvester.

"You're right," said Garcia. "It's all guesswork at the moment. So tomorrow we should be able to firm up detail. It seems we are heading in the right direction."

The others agreed.

"Okay. Gayle and Lou, see what you can do about the car. A matt paint job and no tags may suggest recent body work."

"Big ask Nic," sighed McPherson.

Garcia knew McPherson would take on the enormous task of tracking an unknown vehicle with gusto. He may get lucky with reports of stolen cars.

"Chip and Red. Stay with the bar and try to track the big guy from the 7-Eleven. Is there other CCTV footage from the street? If you can confirm IDs, then talk to Vernon again. Richard and I will scan the MO's and rap sheets for like gangs. We'll be visiting a few friends tomorrow no doubt."

The meeting broke up.

"Guys, I'm keen for an early resolution. I'll begin media tomorrow, so the kooks will be out in force. I want these guys. Make sure you cross every T and dot every i. We don't want any mistakes on this one. We'll meet again at six tomorrow evening. So, plenty of work to do and very little time. Good luck."

CHAPTER
15

Billy woke on Wednesday morning unconcerned about the big story of the day; breaking news on all broadcasts and featured in morning newspapers. He didn't bother himself too much about the day-to-day business of the world, worrying himself about just getting through each day. His life offered him little prospect, and he was just smart enough to realize a destructive life of crime would be his forever.

After returning from his gruesome adventure, Billy got wasted. He accepted the cocktail of drugs Max brought with him on Sunday morning. He loved crystal meth. It generated a destructive attitude for one or two days. A prolonged bout of sleep followed. He was now waking from almost twenty-four hours.

For two days, Billy caroused through a spree of drugs and violence with Max. No innocence, first arrested when twelve for auto larceny, followed by underage drinking, assault, possession of an unlawful weapon and selling marijuana. Before he had reached the tender age of sixteen, Billy spent most of his teenage years in juvenile jails.

He committed his first sexual assault before turning thirteen when Max introduced him to the pleasures of criminal sex. They grabbed a teenage girl from a Mexican family and raped her. He loved it and pursued the fun whenever he could. Max told him to only take Mexican girls. Many illegals feared the authorities and the genuine possibility of deportation if they reported offensives against them. So, they never did.

By the time Max arrived on Sunday, Billy was ready to raise hell.

Money was the key to freedom, and the boys sat in the kitchen musing over Max's suggestion of mugging movie patrons downtown.

"It's too risky, Max."

"Only if we rob the bastards out in the open."

"How else do you rob someone, ya jerk?"

"In a parking lot," Max said, a satisfied smirk on his face.

"Say what?"

"Look, we hit 'em when they are least expecting it. In a secured parking lot. We do about four and we get out of there like a rat up a drainpipe." Max said, sneering. "We'll pull a couple of hundred, maybe more."

"Yeah, well, how do we do that?" Billy responded.

"We use this little baby." Max produced a 38 revolver from under his loose-fitting shirt hung outside his jeans.

"Christ, Max." Billy jumped up, backing away from the table. "Put it away, my sisters are here."

"Man, if a small cannon like this scares you when it's unloaded, what do you think it will do to rich dudes in a parking lot." Max laughed, putting the gun back under his shirt.

"I don't like it."

"Hey man, I'm not asking you to marry it. I'm not even asking you to touch it. But it comes with us."

Billy owed Max. He brought him a good life, but he remained shaky.

As they traveled downtown in a hot-wired pickup, Billy felt no more remorse or concern for his intended victims at the parking lot than he had for the woman they left abandoned twenty-four hours earlier.

"Do you think they will find her?"

"I'm sure they will," Max responded, sitting with his feet up on the dash. "Don't worry buddy, they can't connect her to us. How could they?"

"We should have given her a wide berth," Billy said.

"You worry too much."

"Hey look; I don't care about her. I just think there may be trouble."

"They won't have nothin'. We burned everything," said Max.

There was a pause as both reflected on the previous night.

"What did it feel like?"

"Oh, she was good," said Max, smiling.

"No, not her. I mean killing her. What did it feel like?"

"It felt like nothin', just slicing butter."

"It was a mistake. You know that, don't you?"

"Yeah, maybe, bud. Life's like that, you know? Sometimes you make mistakes. But I've got to tell you, Billy, you missed out on one helluva woman."

"Yeah well, I hope she doesn't come back to haunt us."

"There's no such thing as ghosts man."

They cruised into a multi-storied parking lot near a cinema complex and settled on level four to wait. Around ten-thirty, the first couples appeared, making their way to cars ready for home in the suburbs.

Max more alert said. "If we don't do it now, we'll get caught at the exit. You ready?"

"You bet."

"Then let's do it."

Billy wired the truck into action and glided out onto a down ramp, with lights out, looking for likely victims. "Look at the blue car on the left," said Billy; as he squealed to a halt beside the car, startling the middle-aged couple about to open doors.

Max jumped from the truck and ran in front to confront the couple. He reached for the woman, thumped his gun against her head, and shouted at the man. "Give me your friggin' money or I'll kill the bitch!"

"Don't shoot. Don't shoot. Here... here," shouted the frightened man, as he threw his wallet on the trunk of the car.

Max cracked the woman across the back of the head with his gun and ran back to the truck. Billy gunned it and squealed to the next level. They could see no one.

They slammed their way down the ramps to the next level, confronting a group of three couples arm in arm, searching for their car. The truck squealed to a halt and Max jumped from the cabin and rushed to the biggest man, slugging him across the face, knocking him to the ground. One woman screamed, and Max backhanded her in the mouth. The others seemed paralyzed with shock at what just happened. They complied with Max's shouts for money. He scooped up their wallets and handbags and jumped back into the truck.

"This is great," shouted Billy as he squealed away from the group. "Have we got enough?"

"Yeah, let's get out of here."

No cars were waiting at the boom gates as the truck reached them.

"Go through them."

Billy flattened the gas pedal, and the truck gained speed, smashing through the barrier and bouncing out onto the street. With wheels spinning, burning rubber, the truck sped off in smoky escape.

Max foraged through the bags and wallets, tossing discards from the window, after extracting anything of value. "Christ, we're rich."

"How much? How much?"

"Must be four, maybe five hundred bucks."

"Jesus, we are rich."

"Didn't I tell you buddy?" Max said, tossing the last of the bags out of the speeding truck. "Now let's get booze, broads, and dope. It's time to party."

"Yeehaw!" shouted Billy as he spun a corner against a red.

The boys partied for two days, making plans to hit Tijuana to spend the rest of their stash, and lie low. Tequila, hooch, crystal meth, and fine Mexican girls titillated them for hours. Diminished intelligence did not allow them to fathom they were running out of time.

Billy struggled out of bed, scratching and yawning. It had been a good sleep, but his head was fuzzy, and eyelids were struggling to open. He visited the bathroom, then shuffled to the kitchen to quench his thirst. Gaining the strength to pull the ice-box open, he peered in, searching for a water container. Groping past stale leftovers, preferring not to tempt fate with his stomach still suffering from the residue of alcohol, he couldn't find any water. He saw a Bud stuck at the back, behind a dark cabbage, flicking the top off, gulping half its contents.

Another large gulp of beer and he was feeling he didn't have a headache. He flicked on the radio sauntering over to the table and sat, resting his head on his hands. It had been a hard couple of days, but he was thankful for the sleep when it came. He gazed out of the window.

He tried to recollect what had happened but found it difficult to put too much together. He remembered one young girl though and smiled.

He recalled the booze, drugs, and the haze of love. Well, fleeting love at least.

It had been a party to remember. The biggest rage he ever experienced. He raised his arms high above his head, giving his body a good stretch. He felt good.

An announcer interrupted the music. "*We now go to our news desk for an update on the tragedy at Soledad Park.*"

Billy's smile disappeared as his arms dropped and listened.

"*We can now confirm an earlier report of a young woman found murdered at Soledad Park in La Jolla. Police have identified her as Mrs. Sandra Moroni of La Jolla. Mrs. Moroni, a twenty-six-year-old nurse, found murdered on disused grounds in Soledad Park had been dead at least two days before a passing university professor discovered her. We cross to Wendy Sloan at investigation headquarters for an update.*"

"*Thanks Greg. Mrs. Moroni, a geriatric nurse, spent last Saturday collecting for the Save Africa's Children's Charity. She was last seen a few short steps from her home in La Jolla by a girlfriend at ten-thirty on Saturday night. She never made it home.*"

Sloan added more solemnity to her presentation.

"*They found her Tuesday morning and confirmation of her identity made. It appears there are limited leads so far in the investigation, but to give us a clearer picture, I have with me the leading investigator, Detective Nicolas Garcia.*"

Billy let out a huge sigh on hearing there were no leads. He listened, pawing at his face.

"*Detective Garcia is this the worst murder you have investigated?*"

"*Good morning, Wendy. Well, I've been a detective for many years and seen gruesome sights, and this ranks as one of the worst murders. In particular, the ferocity of the attack.*"

"*Have you any idea of the murder weapon at this stage?*"

"*They bludgeoned Mrs. Moroni to death. We'll know more when we have more specific forensic information.*"

"*Do you have any leads detective?*"

"*Oh yeah. We have plenty. We are likely to make an early arrest.*"

Billy's stomach churned with an empty fear.

"*Thank you, Detective Garcia. Well, that's all we have at this moment. More reports later. Back to you Greg. This is Wendy Sloan reporting.*"

Fear surged into Billy like a hot poker. Anxiousness clouded his uncontrollable thoughts. "Oh Christ, they're onto us. Oh shit, we're dead." Billy ran from room to room in a panic, grabbing a bag and shoving clothes into it. He didn't fancy meeting Detective Garcia. The chill in his voice made him fear of ever meeting him. Convincing him he had nothing to do with the murder would be an impossible task.

A sudden banging on the front door startled Billy, and he leaped in fright for security behind a sofa. He lay there, squeezed between it and the wall, expecting the door to burst open and a SWAT team to charge in. The anxiety of the wait excruciating for him. A droplet of sweat tickled from his hairline across his temple as he strained to hear any action. His breathing rasping in a desperate pant.

"Billy?"

The voice sounded familiar.

"Billy, it's me. Max."

"Max?"

"Billy, open the door. I've gotta talk to you."

"Max?"

"Billy, come on, open up, we've got trouble."

Billy came out from his hiding place and moved toward the window, peering through the curtains seeing Max waiting on the stoop, hands thrust against the door.

"Hey Max?" Billy smiled, pleased to see his friend. "Just a minute. I'll get the door."

"Billy where the hell have you been?" Max was almost shouting as he rushed through the open door.

"Max, we've gotta get out of here. The cops are onto us."

"No, they're not, dummy," said Max. "But we should head for Mexico."

"I'm with you, man. When?"

"Tomorrow. Let's get a few things together today and go tomorrow."

Max was always right about these things, and Billy remained confident a new life started tomorrow.

CHAPTER
16

The arc lamps snapped on and a hurtful glare bore into Garcia's eyes as he tried to see who was standing by to question him. As he waited for the throng to settle, he imagined the headlines and the sensationalized lead storylines.

Woman brutalized. Killer still at large. Or maybe. *City gripped by fear as killer walks among us.*

Accurate, but not even coming close to resembling the truth. The sensationalization of stories could never be justified, yet Garcia knew he needed to get a message out about the case so the perpetrators would worry about what the police knew. Nervous criminals make mistakes. They feel under pressure and begin making irrational decisions. This murder was big news. He just wished the media would do their job and report facts, rather than seek entertainment and good rating points by distorting police investigations.

Garcia stood ready to answer questions at the front steps of the precinct station house. He knew it was important and the impact his words would have on the community. His hands trembled, and he thought a cigarette might calm him. He tried to prompt himself to stay cool, yet grave about the severity of the case. He recognized he could talk to the killers; so, he must stay guarded to protect the investigation, yet project reassurance police were in control. Just enough information, said with conviction, could influence the killers to act silly.

"Detective Garcia, do you have any answers for this terrible crime?"

The first question came from the milling pack of radio, television, and newspaper reporters.

Garcia paused for a moment; his throat dry. The warmth and glare from the lights increasing his discomfort. "We have a victim, Sandra Moroni. A married woman from La Jolla. They kidnapped her from La Jolla Boulevard, Saturday night, around ten thirty. We found Mrs. Moroni murdered Tuesday morning, in Soledad Park in La Jolla. She was murdered and we have many lines of inquiry, so we expect early results."

As he finished, the reporters spoke at once, and the clamor made it impossible to hear any question. One television reporter persisted and got her question through the cacophony.

"How many people involved?"

"We are unsure of the exact number. The investigation team is considering at least three, maybe four perpetrators."

Again, the commotion instantaneous as Garcia stopped talking.

"Is there a likely weapon?"

"Unknown at this stage of the inquiry. We will know more once we complete the autopsy. At this stage we assume an axe or maybe a military machete."

"Do you suspect military personnel, and will you seek support from the Navy?"

"We will follow all leads and seek as much help as we can to solve this gruesome case."

"Do you have any witnesses and are they helping your inquiry?"

"Yes, and yes."

"What is the current status of the victim's family?"

"I advised them yesterday. The victim's parents are under supervisory nursing care. Her husband is helping the case."

"Detective, do you have anything at all?"

"Yeah, we have plenty. We expect early arrests." Garcia lied. He knew if the killers were listening, it might put doubt in their minds.

The questions kept coming and Garcia handled each one on its merit until he thought they had asked enough and signaled an end to the press conference. As the pack broke up, Wendy Sloan from the local radio station beckoned Garcia for a live interview. He agreed.

As he waited, he wondered how the team members were progressing.

He wished for positive news at their briefing tonight. If the team could get enough intelligence, early arrests are a possibility. The longer they waited for information, the colder the trail would become. Luck would play a part, and he hoped they were lucky.

"Detective Garcia." He realized he was on air. "Is this the worst murder you have investigated?"

"Good morning, Wendy. Well, I've been a detective for many years and seen gruesome sights, and this would rank as one of the worst murders. In particular, the ferocity of the attack."

"Have you any idea of the murder weapon at this stage?"

"They bludgeoned Mrs. Moroni to death. We'll know more when we have more specific forensic information."

"Do you have any leads detective?"

"Oh yeah. We have plenty. We are likely to make an early arrest."

The interview ended with Wendy signing off and Garcia giving pleasant goodbyes and a thank you. He pushed his way through the milling throng and returned to the squad room, optimistic of a quick breakthrough.

CHAPTER
17

"Remind me why we're here again, will you, Red?" It had been a long day, and as the car cruised to a stop at their third La Jolla park, Lawrence was losing faith in his partner's hunch. "I know you think these guys are from south side, but why are we north at yet another park?"

"Don't you trust me no more partner?"

"I do, but the autopsy was a little tough this morning. I'm not feeling well."

"Think what that poor young girl must have gone through on Saturday and perhaps you might liven up a bit."

"Unfair. Unfair," Lawrence said. "Just explain it to me again, will you, please?"

"Okay. Okay, the bad guys, group A, do you recall them? We know they hassled Sandi in the bar. Mr. Curtis gave us a damn excellent description."

"He would, wouldn't he? I mean you would too if you were about to blow a head off."

"Yeah, I would. And the knife was a good get," Monaghan said. "Anyway, they come out of the bar all pumped up, ready for action and wanting to kick on somewhere. The trouble is, they had nowhere to go. My bet is, they want to party, rather than go home. So, they go buy beer from the 7-Eleven," Monaghan said. "We know from the store records, two dozen bottles of Bud. Which means six each. Now, rather than drive all the way back south, they think they might have their party nearby. If they are group B, they must have headed north."

"Yeah right, I've got all that, but why these damn parks?"

"From the story Curtis gave us, it would appear they are south side boys. Their dress was not your standard north side dude, they all looked scruffy, so, who would they know north side?"

"No one, I guess."

"Correct Chipper. So, if you have no friends and no place to go, where do you go, if you want to have a boozy party?"

"The beach if it's warm, a park if not so warm."

"Right. So, we are looking in parks, my boy. We are looking for any possible residue that may have been a recent party."

"I still don't get it." Lawrence yawned. "Is this the magician trick you entertain the kids with, Red?"

"If my hunch is right, and the gang went north, then we might just find a beach park with residue. If we happen upon the pre-crime party scene, then maybe we find the used bottles we know they purchased. And if we find bottles, then maybe they have fingerprints and DNA. You see how it works son? And if we find prints and DNA, they may link us to the crime scene. And if they do, then... POW." He smashed a fist into his hand.

"We have the bastards."

"Yeah sure, Red. And if the president was reliable, there wouldn't be any riots." A doubting Lawrence nudged his partner. "You wish."

"Maybe, son, you'll see if I am right. In the meantime, Mr. doubting Thomas, what is all that crap over there, near the trees?" Monaghan said, squinting through the windshield and pointing toward scattered trash.

"Oh, now you're living in fantasyland," a still doubting Lawrence said, stopping the car and climbing out to investigate. He strode over to a patch of sandy grass, crunching twigs and other debris. As he approached the strewn trash, his doubt in his partner faded. Before him lay discarded Bud bottles.

"Are there any bottles?" Monaghan called from the car.

"Yeah, around twelve," called back Lawrence.

"So why didn't they put them in the trash-can yonder?" asked Monaghan as he approached.

"I suppose you're going to tell me they don't know what trash-cans are south side?"

"You said it, son."

"How many beers did the big guy buy?"

"Two dozen."

"We have twelve here and a couple of cigarette tails, which look like they might be the reefer variety." Lawrence was now on his knees inspecting an assortment of litter.

"You had better call the forensic guys to join us. We may be onto to something here."

"We?" shouted Monaghan as he headed back to the car. "We? Boy, you sure change your tune quick young lad."

"I never doubted you partner. We are partners, aren't we?" laughed Lawrence. "You had better let Garcia know as well." He prowled head down, circling the area.

It took Monaghan ten minutes to get instructions through and return to his partner, checking to show a pattern for the trash.

"We have to change our friggin' method of communication. It's like talking to a friggin' brick wall. What have you got Chip?"

"I can confirm five distinct footprints, which may be a problem. If I remember correctly, there were only four at the crime scene."

"They could have dropped one off, or maybe someone just walked by since then."

"Yeah, maybe, but we only have sightings of four in group A and only three for group B, the killers. I also have two dozen bottles which confirm a match with group A, and I suspect marijuana joints."

"This is perfect, Chip. I think we may have hit on something."

"I also have what might be clothing fibers which could show anything from a fight to blow by rubbish. I'll leave that to the experts to figure out."

"This might be our boys. I can feel it in my water. And this could be the place they partied."

"Yeah, but five is not four. And we only need four."

"Who got the extra beer, I wonder?" queried Monaghan.

"Say what? What are you talking about?"

"If there were five guys, one missed out on a beer. They all had

107

five and one had four. So maybe there were four after all and the other footprints might be someone who came by later."

"Maybe you're right. The forensic boys will say one way or the other."

"These are our boys, Chip. I know it. They had a party, headed for home, saw the girl and did the business."

"Yeah, bad luck for her I suppose. I mean, they must have seen her just after her friend drove off. One minute either way and Mrs. Moroni would have been alive today."

"Sometimes fate remains out of our hands."

"How do we link this group with the kill site?"

"If they only bought two dozen beers, when did they get the bottles we found at the crime site? Where would they get them?"

"They stopped for more I suppose. They bought high grade alcohol because they were now flush with money from the charity collection?"

"Now you're thinking, Chip. If they did all of that, a liquor store must be where?"

"Between the pickup and the kill scene," said Lawrence, warming to the discussion.

"Chip, you are beautiful," said Monaghan, as he kissed him on the cheek.

"Get off me, you sick bastard," said Lawrence, wiping the slobbery kiss from his face.

"We'll wait for the uniforms to seal off this site, and then we can check out liquor stores on the way to the park."

"We should get them to door knock the area."

"Yeah, nice one, partner."

CHAPTER
18

"That's it. One hundred and forty-seven likely autos," sighed Martinez, not looking forward to that many interviews, clicking the print tab on the computer.

"That's bad news for us, I suppose. How many stolen recently?" asked McPherson from his desk, happy to let his partner do the work on technology he had no wish to understand.

Martinez turned in her chair and stretched for the printed copy of the detail on the vehicles. "Just fifteen." She smiled.

"Hey my lucky day. We'll do those first, let's go."

The partners held a silent bond of communication. They respected each other for their policing qualities. Neither interested in each other's private life, and did not care to ask. They sat watching traffic motoring south, pondering the tasks ahead.

McPherson broke the silence. "How many body shops in the Otay Mesa district?"

"Four."

"If we get details of our car from the owner, we should be able to track it to one of those shops, I'd reckon."

"Why so?"

"I reckon our boys are as dumb as a mule. How stupid are they to have left the victim the way they did, tossing bottles all over the place? If they are that dumb, then there should be clues all over this area, unless the stolen car is part of a bigger scam."

"How do you mean?"

"They steal a car; their next move would be to go to their pal at the body shop for a quick paint job. If we can get an ID on the car, then the body shop guys would then be able to ID our boys."

"Seems reasonable. But, what if it's a scam, and no-one wants to talk to us?"

"Scamming stolen cars is one thing. Accessory to murder is another. I reckon we can nail these guys."

"You may be right, Lou."

Silence again for another long period. Comfortable in each other's company, they preferred it that way. Two police intellects wasting no time with casual chitchat.

Interviewing of the stolen Dodge owners proved difficult. Trying to get coherent descriptions from Mexican owners, without a firm command of English, proved hard. Memory for detail was not good and although each professed great loss, it was only the marine corporal who gave a reliable description. McPherson suspected the others were not keen for the return of their automobiles, wanting the insurance money instead.

Each meeting with a body shop proprietor became more of an inter-rogation, as frustration beset the detectives. They knew the task would be hard yet did not expect the resistance they encountered. It was the third shop they had a response they could use. Phil Hanson, a tough former marine, who played life right down the middle, operated Devil Dogs Body and Paint Shop. Never interested in skirting the law, Hanson always kept meticulous records of all his dealings.

"Yeah, I remember the Dodge. A guy came in one day and wanted to change the color to red."

"What color was it?" asked Martinez, a list of stolen car colors at the ready.

"It was a blue. A vibrant blue. He wanted red, and I told him it would take a few coats to get the base required for such a change, so it would take a few days." Martinez checked off the marine corporal's car.

"Got the tag number?" asked McPherson.

"Sure do, I even have the guy's address and license number if you want that."

"Yeah, that could be helpful," said McPherson with a broad smile.

"You never know whether they are real. I take them down just the same." Hanson took out his log and flicked back through the days to find the entry. "Yeah, here it is. It came in on Wednesday and we cut it back and coated it with a primer and then an undercoat. Gray. The guy wouldn't leave it over the weekend, and he was due back on Monday but never showed."

"Got a name?" Martinez wished.

"Yep. And the dude's address. Brett Capelli. License number MLT 562749. The address he gave was twenty-four Tico Place, Otay."

"Thank you, Mr. Hanson, you have been a great help," said McPherson, shaking his hand.

"Yes, Mr. Hanson, you have been most helpful." Martinez said, busy taking notes.

"Aw, don't mention it. If the dude is bad, then you need to get him. Just remember if there is a reward then you know where I am."

"Mr. Hanson, you will get anything that is available, I promise you," said Martinez, leaving the workshop.

"I told you, I told you," a smug McPherson said as Martinez got into the car. "These guys are so dumb. What a jerk to leave a name and address."

"Yeah, if they are correct."

"Shall we go see him? Or maybe we should wait."

"Rather than see him now, we should wait. If we go see him too early, it may frighten the others off and we may lose them. At the moment, they don't know we have this information, so let's wait. We should report back and see where the others are at with their day."

"I'm with you, Gayle. Although it's tempting to pay Capelli a visit right now."

"Yeah, wouldn't that be nice? But we've got nothing other than a stripped car, and that ain't worth squat to our main game. We should go do a profile check on him."

"What a break Gayle, these boys are dumb, and my guess is we shall have them soon."

CHAPTER
19

"Right, Gayle, away you go," exclaimed Garcia, cigarette stub dangling from his mouth as he took up a position in front of the whiteboard, almost full of information. The detectives shuffled to positions around the board, arranging notes ready to report.

It was just after six, and the day had been long and tiring. As Garcia waited, he mused whether they would complete arrests in time to meet Reuben's deadline. Sending the case downtown was not an option for him, and it prepared him to put in the extra effort to secure an arrest.

"Nic, we have a fair chunk of evidence from a lot of good police work today, especially Red and Chip, who had great luck. So, let's begin right at the beginning," said Martinez, taking a position in front of the assembling group.

"Nice place to begin," said Monaghan, laughing as he sat down.

"Sandi Moroni walked into the West Coast Lagoon at six-twenty-five, which we have confirmed with three staff. They remember her bouncy nature and seeking donations. They liked her manners."

"She met a Rudi Curtis, who promised to donate money on her return, after visiting the poolroom. Curtis can give an excellent description of the bad guys."

"She's in the poolroom for around five minutes before Curtis wonders what's holding her up. As we know, what was holding her up was the assault and attempted rape."

"We have a confirmed statement from Barbara Smethers, who

recounts the assault as described to her by Sandi," said Sylvester, holding papers aloft.

"Curtis, who could wait no longer for her, interrupted the assault. He worried about her and wondered what was keeping her," continued Martinez. "There is no CCTV, unfortunately.

"He says he heard strange cries coming from the room and went to investigate," added Monaghan.

"Thanks, Red," said Martinez. "He sees young men gathered around Mrs. Moroni. He approaches and confronted by a young punk, as yet unknown to us, but we are working on it. The punk pulls a Bowie knife and wants to have a go at him. Cool as you like, our loveable Rudi Curtis draws a 38 and warns off the boys."

"What happens to the girl?" asks Garcia.

"While this confrontation is happening, she collects her things and scampers from the bar," said Monaghan.

"How many men?" asked Garcia.

"Curtis is unsure. He thinks four," said Monaghan.

"You know, in hindsight, this scuffle may have been the trigger for what happened later," suggested McPherson.

"Doesn't excuse the bastards," said Sylvester.

"I wasn't suggesting that," a bemused McPherson said, taken by Sylvester's snappy response. "But, if they had their jollies in the bar, she might be alive today."

"Yeah, well maybe, but they didn't have to go on and do what they did," said Sylvester.

"Quite right, Richard. Gayle, please continue before these guys are at each other's throats," said Garcia, placing a reassuring hand on Sylvester's shoulder.

"Mrs. Moroni scampered out of the bar and found sanctuary with her friend at the Brewery Restaurant and Bar opposite. The bad guys then leave the bar. One sent for beer at the 7-Eleven, next door where Sandi is sitting with her friend."

"Barbara Smethers verified this," said Sylvester.

"And the employee at the 7-Eleven confirms the purchase of two dozen bottles of Budweiser," said Monaghan. "Regretfully, no security camera footage but given us a rough description which matches what Smethers told us."

"They then jump into a gray 1980 Dodge, owned by Corporal Tom Stenman. A marine living in Otay Mesa," a smiling McPherson said.

"Impressive," smirked Garcia, lighting up another cigarette.

"The gang drove north, looking for a spot to party," said Martinez, signaling to Monaghan to continue the briefing.

"The boys hit Hermosa park on Palomar, in La Jolla. They partied and finished the beer, which means, they were now pretty much under the influence."

"We found all twenty-four bottles lying about the park and other residue which, is at the lab now. They have advised there are good fingerprints on the bottles. We have them being reviewed for matching now," interrupted Lawrence.

"You mean we have fingerprints for these guys?" asked an amazed Garcia.

"You bet, and DNA samples, and more," said Lawrence.

"More? Well then continue..." said Garcia. "Please."

"The boys stayed and drank their beer and seemed to party hard. We can confirm four, but the surprise may be, that we could have five," continued Monaghan.

"Five?" asked Garcia.

"We can't confirm sightings, but we have five definite footprints at the park," responded Monaghan.

"We only have four at the crime scene. Don't we, Rich?" asked Garcia, baffled by the news.

"Yes, only four confirmed at Soledad. It doesn't mean we can't have five."

"Okay. So, we could be seeking five. That may change a few things," said Garcia.

"Not really, Nic," said Martinez. "Although we have no sightings, Lou considers these guys are as dumb as all hell and could still be together."

"They are beyond having a small amount of smarts. Even so, we can't take it for granted these guys are even in the country, let alone the city," Garcia said. "Five? They were a gang looking for damn trouble, weren't they?"

"Thanks, Red," said Martinez, connecting facts with lines on the board. "At around ten thirty both parties move and ultimately meet each other."

"Unfortunately for Sandi," offered Sylvester.

No one spoke for a moment until Martinez broke the silence.

"We have a confirmed sighting of the kidnapping. A Mr. Vernon could give a good identification of the car, confirming our information from Corporal Stenman. Mr. Vernon also has given good confirming identification of the driver who presented the car at a body shop on Wednesday last week."

"Do we know who?" asked Garcia.

"In a moment, Nic," said McPherson.

"Vernon could only confirm three bad guys," said Martinez.

"He can't help us with any more than three?" asked Garcia.

"No. He could confirm Red's theory of none, or little traffic. Although he can't confirm squealing tires. He can confirm a car turning around from heading south."

"That's a help," said Garcia.

"Yes. Which puts our park boys in the right place, heading in the right direction, with motive and opportunity," said McPherson.

"Yes, but we only have three at the abduction. If it is our park boys, then we need to have their car ID'd, before the abduction, hopefully at Pacific Beach. If we can, we should try to get another sighting further north. Did they stop for more booze? We found a fresh bourbon bottle at the crime scene. Maybe they stopped for more." Garcia was speculating.

"Boss, you sure are one hell of a theorist," laughed Monaghan. "It's lucky we think the same. We have another sighting of the car and the boys, but only four."

"You boys have been busy, haven't you?"

"What do you expect from this talented team of detectives?" asked Monaghan.

"Early arrests if we can get them," Garcia said and lit another cigarette.

"Nic, you may get your wish and be happy when we finish the briefing," Martinez said. "The gang traveled north and stopped for gas at a station on Torres Pine Road. An attendant confirmed this. We can't confirm how many in the car, and the attendant didn't see a girl. Across the road from the gas station, is a liquor store, and we verified a purchase of various quantities of alcohol. Including, you guessed it, Nic, a bottle of bourbon."

"What time was it?" asked Garcia.

"We have a copy of the cash register receipt for a car at ten fifty-three. Pretty much in the right time frame for our boys from the park," said Sylvester.

"Do we have a description of the alcohol buyer?"

"Yeah, we do," said a smiling Martinez. "Let's just come back to that information."

"Oh, I see, more secrets. Are you stringing me along?"

"That could be your interpretation. We like to think of it as a structured briefing, which we are all trained to provide," said McPherson.

"Well then, I can't wait," said Garcia, bemused by all the secrecy.

"Chip had the unfortunate duty to attend the postmortem, so I shall let him give the details," Martinez continued.

"Hmm, yeah, I'm afraid to say, it was grim," said Lawrence. "Not the prettiest forensic inspection I have been to, I can tell you."

"Have you got the report?" asked Sylvester.

"Yeah, here," replied Lawrence, passing the report and accompanying sketches and photographs to Sylvester. "It's all a bit messy. The best guess the M.E. can come up with is an estimated time of death between eleven thirty and midnight on Saturday."

"So, the bastards played with her for about an hour," interrupted McPherson.

"Yeah, seems so." Lawrence referred to his notes. "She fought for her life. Vigorously, it appears, confirmed by Vernon. We have skin scrapings from under her nails, suggesting one of our gang will have a decent scratch. The M.E. took foreign hair samples, which are confirmed as male. DNA testing is now proceeding," Lawrence said.

"This is fantastic news for us. It will help," Garcia said.

Lawrence continued reading the report. "Mrs. Moroni has multiple fractures to her ribs, her cheek, and a finger. She has bruising to her head, neck, arms, back, and most of her torso. She also has severe bruising to her breasts, buttocks and legs. She has several superficial scratches and gashes, mostly around her legs. A broken nose, punctured lung, a bruised kidney, and a ruptured chest cavity. Internal bleeding is extensive."

"They beat her real bad," said Sylvester.

The other team members expected the worst and got it from Lawrence.

"Now this is the gruesome part. The M.E. thinks the murder weapon was a large carving or hunting knife."

"Or a Bowie?" suggested Garcia, glancing at Sylvester.

"Or a Bowie. There are no hesitation marks which show a deliberate, cold-blooded murder. She has defensive resistance damage to her fingers and hands. They cut her from ear to ear, almost severing the head from the body. Two major fatal wounds, with four minor slashes."

"Jesus," said Sylvester, slumping his head into his hands.

"The M.E. got semen residue samples from her injured vagina and her anus. He could not extract any sample from her mouth because of the extensive lacerations." The others sat hushed. "Death almost instantaneous," Lawrence said, closing his file and handing it to Garcia. "And she was seven weeks pregnant."

Nothing could be heard, other than the sound of the ticking second hand on the squad room clock.

"Right. Thanks Chip," a sullen Garcia said. "Now, you said you may have a secret, Gayle. What is it?"

"We know for sure who one of the gang is."

"You're kidding. Who?"

"We have him confirmed at the body shop. Curtis has him at the bar. Vernon is unsure, but we might have him at the kidnap. We also have him at the liquor store, but the best news is, we have confirmed his fingerprints on a bottle at the crime scene."

"You're kidding, we have all of this?" The news surprised Garcia.

"He is a small-time criminal. He has a long record of petty offences, but he runs with his brothers one of which has jail time for violent assaults. We are seeking more information from the local boys down south. Boss this might be your early arrest."

"The more interesting news is that his brother is one, Arnie Capelli," Martinez said. "Capelli has a history of violence, extortion and served time at Donovan."

"I know him," said Garcia. "I've had the pleasure of doing business with that thug before."

"If we link one Capelli to the crime, then his brother is involved, I reckon," Monaghan said.

"Any evidence?" Garcia asked.

"Prints at the scene on a bottle," McPherson smiled. "A description from the liquor store where he purchased the bottle."

"Is that enough to bring him in?" Sylvester asked.

"I reckon it is," said Monaghan.

"Where is he?" asked Garcia.

"His dumb brother left an address at the body shop. I can confirm that address is current for Arnie Capelli," said McPherson.

"Well," said Garcia, springing to his feet. "Let's go get the son of a bitch."

"What do we do with the others?" asked Sylvester.

"Let's bring in big brother first. If I know Capelli, then he is up to his neck in this," Garcia said.

CHAPTER
20

Sylvester was aching. His head jammed against the cold window as he tried catching a snooze. His body craved rest; just a short numbing of the mind would help to relieve the intensity of the investigation. A smoke haze nestled above, clinging to the inside roof from the chain-smoking habit of his partner, and he squirmed, shifting in his seat away from it.

The detectives had been sitting for two hours in Tico Place, waiting for the light of a new day to strengthen. Since the briefing, the team opened intelligence channels to establish Arnie Capelli's whereabouts and gain an arrest warrant. It wasn't until two o'clock that confirmation of him settling in for the night, after carousing the neighborhood, searching for sport. They learned his wife to be away, and he remained alone. Now they hoped he was sleeping like a baby, though hardly innocent.

The plan was to take Arnie first, then search for his brothers. He was the most violent, and the squad didn't want him to escape their net if they arrested Brett.

Garcia remained optimistic about an incident free arrest, but the wily detective took nothing for granted. He requested SWAT support, although conceded it could be an overreaction. Confident an arrest would not cause many, if any problems, he sent the rest of the team to their beds, asking them to return to the squad room next morning.

"Do you think we have enough to charge him with murder one?

I mean, would it stick if he didn't knife Sandi?" Sleep now out of the question. Sylvester evaluated the consequences of the arrest ahead.

"I know Capelli's form. He's a two-bit thug. If it involves him, which seems likely from the weight of evidence we have against his brother and even him, he'll deal to beat any capital offence."

"We will get him though, won't we? I mean, he'll make major time, won't he?"

"We have his prints at the scene, that's enough for murder one. If he doesn't help us, then he'll get a shocking end to his life." Garcia smirked. "If he sings like a canary, then he'll do twenty years minimum."

"He better."

"Rich, you sound as if this case is getting to you. Don't let it pal. I don't want any mistakes, which come, when we get too emotional."

"Yeah. Okay."

They continued to sit and wait for more light, Garcia coughing through another cigarette. Sylvester shifting in his seat, irritated by the pollution.

"Look, do you mind if I open a window a little? Your smoke is driving me nuts."

"Go for it."

Sylvester cracked the window and a surge of chilled air cannoned in, drafting the smoke from the car. He laid back, amused by the swirling haze drawing and shafting out of the window. He pondered whether the shivering chill was worth it. Deciding it wasn't. Enough fresh air had replaced most of the stagnate stale fug he endured, so he closed it.

"Feel better, pal?"

After a few moments, Sylvester asked. "Where do you know this guy?"

"Oh, I collared him for running drugs and consorting. He ended up being a snitch. The punk has no respect for anything other than himself. And he'll do whatever it takes to survive. He is the typical guy never to trust and steer clear."

"We should go."

"Yeah. Let's do it." Garcia took the radio hand piece and advised the SWAT team entry within ten minutes. The light had brightened, although the sun was yet to rise.

Sylvester shivered as he got out of the car. "A bit chilly, Nic."

"Chilly or chilling?"

"Chilly," said Sylvester, reaching through the back door dragging out his police parka. Garcia went to the trunk. Flicked it open and unlocked a gun casket. He selected a pump-action shotgun from a rack of long arm weapons and slid it into operation. The sound of cartridges clicking into the stock magazine seemed loud, disturbing the early morning calm. The cautious detectives glanced up to see whether they attracted attention. The neighborhood remained deserted.

Sylvester struggled to strap on a bulletproof vest. "These things are a damn nuisance to put on," he said, fumbling with the ties.

"It'll save your life one day, partner," replied Garcia.

Sylvester tugged on his parka and checked his standard issue 38 revolver before arming himself with a shotgun. The chilling sound of the snapping and cocking a pump-action sharpened his focus. "Is he dangerous?"

"This scumbag could do anything. Volatile and unpredictable."

"Take care then, partner," Sylvester said as they trudged toward the house. He shivered as he scanned the sky, searching for any hint of warmth. Shrugging shoulders settled his nerves, and he looked for any suggestion of life at number twenty-four.

The house was downhill from the car. Early morning mist clung close to the road and amongst the trees. It would disappear with the day, but it added an eerie foreboding to the detectives as they strode to the house.

The men came to the front and met with armed officers. Garcia flicked a command to three SWAT members to move to the rear of the house. He wanted an easy capture and hoped there would be no need for a firefight.

Sylvester made a brief twitch as they entered the yard. His shallow breathing quickened with each step as they crept onto the stoop. He figured his adrenalin rush was the reason for the trembling. He braced himself in preparation. No matter how long they had trained him for this contact, he still feared using a weapon. The oily, cold metal of the shotgun heavy in his hands, adding to his nervousness. He never faced a rogue criminal in armed combat, and was twitching.

Garcia had experienced gun battles. He carried an indented scar on his abdomen from a battle, during a search and seizure operation, gone wrong six years earlier. Had he not been wearing a protective vest, the slug fired by an illegal immigrant may have ended his life. Death held no fears for him.

The detectives braced themselves for an entrance, as a SWAT member surged forward with a long, red lump of metal called the doorknocker. He positioned himself in front of the door, gripping the tool from handles at either end; he swung it past his hips into the lock. The door burst open, another effective entry.

Garcia lunged forward into the darkness of the house, shouting, shotgun butt tight into his shoulder, waving the barrel into the unknown. Sylvester took a deep breath and followed.

"Police!"

They danced through the front rooms. Finding no one and hurrying to the next.

"Police!"

Garcia kicked open the bedroom door. The bed slept in, but empty. He could see no one. He checked under the bed. Nothing. He searched about, thinking Capelli might be armed and hiding. A SWAT team entered through the back door and were making their way to the center.

"Police!"

Room by room they hunted; yet Capelli was not to be seen. The police groups met in the center of the home, tense and baffled by not being able to capture their quarry. Garcia uncocked his weapon, resting it on his shoulder, and ambled back to the front bedroom, hoping to see a sign that may lead to Capelli.

"Where is he?" shouted Garcia. "The friggin' dog must be here. We have intelligence to say he is. He hasn't left since we've been sitting outside for the last two friggin' hours."

"Check the ceiling and under the house," called Sylvester to the SWAT members. "He must be here. Our boys could not have gotten this wrong."

"Well, he ain't here now, partner," a frustrated Garcia said, banging his fist into the door.

A familiar sound came from behind a small door in the bedroom. Neither detective had checked. The flushing toilet was louder as Capelli emerged. In his own little world; eyes squeezed shut, dancing to music blaring in his ears from his iPod buds. Strangling musical sounds to sing in tune, his grunts, oohs and ah's helping his music appreciation. He didn't know he had company.

Sylvester drew his revolver from its holster. Cocked it, pointing it at Capelli, inches from his forehead, waiting for the moment of realization. If it wasn't for the gravity, the moment would have been funny.

Dressed in tee shirt and denim jeans, the bare foot Capelli inched closer, absorbed with music. Then he stopped and opened his eyes. The look of genuine confusion on his face brought a smile to Sylvester.

"You are busted, man."

"Shit."

"Didn't you just do that?" asked Garcia as he went behind him, snapping on handcuffs and proclaiming his Miranda rights.

"I've done nothing wrong. Ouch! What are you doing here? You're hurting me."

"As I said, you slug. You are busted. We have you sighted and your prints, and now we have you," said Sylvester, re-holstering his revolver.

"For what? You've got no right to do this."

Garcia rounded on him and stood nose to nose. "You, my friend, don't deserve squat for what you have done. So don't you be asking for any favors because you won't get any."

"Ah, Detective Garcia. Long time no see, thank God."

"Capelli, we have you. And this time you'll be lucky if they commute your sentence to life."

"What do you mean?"

"Are you so stupid, to not know why we are here?"

"You people are always blaming me and my family. You never leave us alone. This time? Let me guess, I kicked an old lady's dog or something. Hey, maybe I ain't paid a friggin' parking ticket? Why don't you guys ever knock?"

"Aw, shut up." Garcia pushed him in the face with enough force to make sure he fell backwards onto the bed.

Sylvester withdrew to inform the police officers and arrange a thorough search of the house, optimistic about finding the murder weapon or some of Sandi's possessions.

"Hey, look Garcia, what are trying to set me up with this time, you snake?"

Garcia began rummaging through the bedroom, searching for

evidence. "You, and your dumb brothers, met a nice young lady last Saturday, and you had a party with her."

"Only slut we met, was your mother, and she don't party."

"You roughed her up at a bar in Pacific Beach, then took her to a private place."

"No way, man. Did she name me? No way."

"She's not talking."

"Well, there you are, then. You've got nothing, pig," Capelli said, struggling to his feet. "I want to see my lawyer. This is harassment and you'll pay for this."

Garcia turned on him. "You friggin' low piece of scum. You rape an innocent woman. Brutalize her. You murder her, and you want privileges?"

"You're damn right I do."

"You're lucky I don't have my way with you now, you friggin' bastard."

"You ain't got the balls, pig."

Garcia raised his knee, plunging it into Capelli's soft groin, sinking him to the floor. "Neither will you, by the time I finish with you."

"What happened to him?" asked Sylvester, seeing Capelli on his knees dribbling into the carpet.

"Oh, he's searching for a contact lens he dropped."

"We should get him back to the station house and see what he has to say when confronted with the evidence," suggested Sylvester, helping a snarling Capelli to his feet.

"Slip these on him." Garcia tossed loafers to his partner.

"You'll pay for this, Garcia," gasped Capelli as he struggled past, leaning on Sylvester.

"Man, I haven't paid for pleasure like that for a long time. Just remember Arnie, my dearest, unless you give me what I want, I'll ring the friggin' things off with my bare hands."

Sylvester assisted Capelli into a squad car. "Take him to the station and process him for me, please Jim."

"You bet Rick." The squad car drew away with Capelli laying on the rear seat, still in pain.

"We need this place done over," said Garcia, searching his pockets for his sunglasses. "It sure has warmed."

"Listen Nic, I appreciate you and Capelli have a thing going, but roughing him up like that will not make our case."

"Yeah, I know pal," Garcia replied, putting on the glasses and tugging a cigarette from a crushed packet.

"You could face action over your methods. And after earlier warnings, they may suspend you."

"Yeah, I know." Garcia lit his smoke and took a deep drag.

"Come on, Nic. You're the one wanting quick arrests and conclusions. And when we get close, you whack the bad guys."

"Yeah, I know."

"Is that it? Yeah, I know?"

Garcia blew into his partner's face. "Yeah, but it felt so *gooood* partner. Real good. Practically as good as this smoke. Do you want one?"

"You kill me," laughed Sylvester, shaking his head. "And so would Rosalie if I ever took another cigarette."

"How is the little woman, anyway? You keeping her happy?"

"I would, if I could get to see her."

"I reckon the way this investigation is panning out you might get the weekend off. So, why don't you plan a few days away, maybe a week, and treat the little lady. We'll cover for you."

"No fooling?"

"Yeah, take off. Go to Mexico, or why don't you go to Vegas?"

"You're beautiful, man. We've been talking about doing something like that for a long time."

"Just do it, if we get this job done, and I suspect we will, just do it."

"We will."

"Hey Richard, now you're daydreaming, son." Garcia broke into his consciousness. "Get the forensic boys organized and let's head back and have a chat with Capelli."

"Sure, boss."

"You don't have to suck up to me, son. I've already said the weekend is yours."

They laughed.

CHAPTER
21

"Hail the conquering heroes," declared Martinez as the pair wandered into the squad room.

"Thanks, Gayle," smirked Garcia.

"With one suspect in the sin bin, I assume we're very close, Nic. Well done to both of you." She pecked both colleagues on the cheek as they moved past her toward Reuben's office.

"Has he dropped anyone else in?" asked McPherson.

"Not yet. I think he will though," said Garcia.

"What makes you so sure?"

"His manhood may depend on it." This comment baffled the team. Garcia often left them gob smacked with the obscure things he suggests. No one could figure this one out.

Only Sylvester remained unsettled by the remark.

After updating Reuben, the detectives accompanied him to the observation anteroom of interview room one. See, but not seen, through the one-way mirror.

Reuben took a long, hard look at Capelli. "There's no compassion in that boy, is there? Check out the hate seething from him. His body language just says guilt, doesn't it?"

"Boss, it shouts up yours, if you ask me," offered Garcia.

Capelli sat silent, sometimes fidgeting, oblivious to the three detectives observing him.

"Who's going to interview him?"

"Rich and I will."

"We need early results, so don't hang about. If you have nothing within an hour, then use Gayle. A touch of woman might send this guy over the top."

Martinez was a tough cop, she specialized in breaking down the macho wise guys who thought better. They knew better alright. Gayle seemed to use her charm to advantage to get information an investigation needed.

"I'm happy giving Gayle a go, but I reckon this guy will break before then and give up the others."

"Do you suspect his brothers?"

"To be honest, we do. We have evidence on one of them, and we are working on the other. We brought this thug in first because he would have skipped town if he sniffed he was in trouble. With a little help from brother Arnie we might just wrap it all together."

"No rough stuff, Nic."

"Who me?"

Sylvester winced.

"Remember we want the entire gang not just this guy. So don't go putting our case in jeopardy by breaching civil liberties."

"Aw come on, boss. I don't do that stuff. You know that."

"Yeah, sure. Get a result as quick as you can." Reuben left the detectives to it.

"Set up the tapes Rich, I might just talk to our little pal, Arnie."

Sylvester prepared the recording equipment to prepare for their interview. Garcia entered the room, closing the door behind him.

Capelli slumped in his chair, his arms resting on the table before him. Other than the other chair at the table, there was no furniture in the room, which was about the size of a large bedroom. He understood the routine. He held no fears about what was to come.

Arnie knew the charade of the good cop, bad cop routines. He also thought saying nothing helped more than squawking to the pigs. The longer he could go giving no information, the better it was for him. It has all to do with leverage and negotiating power. Right now he was powerless. In the meantime, he keeps quiet and plays the game of worried and frightened suspect, who knows nothing.

Capelli, by instinct began fumbling through his pockets for a cigarette. Not recalling he had cleaned them out when brought into the station house.

A crumpled packet of Marlboro slid across the table, followed by a book of matches. Capelli weighed up his options. Refuse and keep his silence and owe Garcia nothing. Or enjoy a much yearned for cigarette and restore his silence. The nicotine urge was thumping. He snatched at the cigarettes, withdrew a stick and lit up, sucking in deep, giving his lungs the craving he wanted.

"Was that good, Arnie?"

He didn't respond. He sat and enjoyed the relief. The standoff continued.

Garcia waited.

He stood leaning against the wall by the door, staring at Capelli. No matter how hard he tried to avoid it, he could not help thinking of what he had done to Sandi. The wailing father and the deep shock of her husband. Confused and angry, he wished he could vent on Capelli. Police regulations meant he could not.

So, he waited.

The constant flicking cigarette the only sign of Capelli's state of mind. He was getting nervous. He finished the smoke and lit up another. Hoping the nicotine would calm him.

Garcia pondered his own addiction, knowing it would be a little while yet before he could take a few puffs. Twenty minutes passed and not a word spoken between them. Not even a furtive glance from Capelli, as Garcia stared at him.

Capelli had not been in an interview like this. It was unsettling him, and he lit another cigarette. He weakened. "What the hell do you think you are playing at Garcia? You can't keep me here like this. Ask your damn questions or let me go."

Sylvester turned on the recorder from behind the mirror.

"Patience, my dear Arnie. Patience."

"You've got nothing on me about nothing. This is another setup. You pigs blame my family for everything."

"All in good time, Arnie. Just a little more patience."

"Who the hell is going to pay for my door. You can't bust into somebody's home. Who's going to pay?"

"Arnie, I said patience."

"Aw, this is bullshit. I want a lawyer and I call for one now. It's my constitutional right and I demand one now."

"Now Arnie, you're upsetting yourself." Garcia had not changed his soft tone in response to Capelli's bellowing. "You know we can get a lawyer for you. You will need one if you are guilty, as we think you are. Only, we haven't started the interview yet, have we? So don't stress yourself."

Capelli stood, pushing back his chair and kicking it aside. He turned on Garcia, frustrated and wanting an end to what was going on. He wanted an interview he could understand. "Either charge me, or I'm walking, you bastard."

Garcia kicked himself off the wall and lunged toward Capelli, taking him by surprise. He grabbed him hard in the genitals and squeezed.

Capelli gagged in pain as Garcia lifted him, increasing the pressure. He whispered into his ear. "I'm coming to get you. I'm going to send you off to death row, where you'll wait in the stinking dark, until they strap you into a chair and stick a needle in your arm and you squirm as they feed the drugs into you. Or maybe even better, they turn on the power. I'm going to watch your eyes pop out onto your cheeks, as you writhe in agony when the volts rocket through you. I'm going to suck in the smell of your burning flesh as you shiver and shake against the electrical current."

Capelli's head sagged to Garcia's shoulder, enduring the monkey grip.

"Or even better than that, I would love to hear the snapping of the rope as you drop through the crashing trap doors. Gagging for breath as you swing back and forward." Garcia fanned his fingers and squeezed harder. The contorted face of Capelli meant there was not much more left to endure. He was on the verge of passing out. "You don't deserve to live you, bastard. You give me what I want, or I'll take these little fur balls and feed them to my cat."

Capelli was just able to gasp. "Okay, I'll give you whatever you want."

Garcia gave him one final tweak and let go. He collapsed to his knees. Garcia resumed his position by the door, as if nothing had happened. To the knowledge of anyone outside of the room, nothing did.

Sylvester entered after a few moments, joining his partner. He moved to Capelli, helping him back into the chair. He didn't agree with his partner's methods, but Capelli was a thug.

Capelli regained his composure and passed a sneer to Garcia. "You bastard. You can't do that to me. I want a lawyer."

"Arnie," Sylvester said. "You have the right to a lawyer, but I would like a few details from you first, if you don't mind? In fact, I need your help."

"Say what?" The novel approach amused him. "You want my help?"

"Arnie, we have a young woman murdered."

"So what? What's that got to do with me?"

"It seems we have an empty bottle of alcohol at the crime scene, Jack Daniel's, which you purchased on Saturday evening, at a liquor store in La Jolla..."

"I wasn't in La Jolla on Saturday; my brothers can back that up, I was with them."

Garcia's eyes lit up. It involved the brothers, that's three.

"Arnie, I hear you man, but this bottle of Jack Daniel's, it's got your prints on it."

"So what? There are plenty of JD bottles at my place. All empty, with my prints."

"Yes, maybe, you may be right. The problem is this Arnie, the one we have was lying beside the murdered woman. And we think you might know how it got there. Arnie, my simple mind says, if your fingerprints are at a murder scene, then you are involved. Do you understand where I'm coming from?"

"Well, I don't know how it got there. You planted it; you guys do things like that."

"On Saturday, when you say you weren't north of the city, we have a confirmed sighting of you in a Pacific Beach bar. Strange that, wouldn't you say?"

"Never been there."

"It seems several eye-witnesses have you in this bar in Pacific Beach. Our victim was being assaulted by a gang of men at the same bar. And much to our surprise, our witnesses have picked you out as a member of this gang. This woman in the bar is the same woman you later murdered."

"You're wrong," Capelli said. He lit a cigarette and blew the smoke into Sylvester's face. "Can I have a coffee?"

"No, you can't have a coffee." Sylvester was losing his patience. "We need you to tell Detective Garcia and me what happened."

"Haven't you been listening? I don't know what you're talking about."

"Arnie, you aren't doing yourself any favors by acting like this. You are facing a murder one charge. Help us and we might help you."

"How?"

"We could speak to the D.A. and come up with some sort of deal."

"Like what?"

Sylvester passed a queried glance to Garcia, troubled by the abrupt change of heart. So rapid a change was rare, especially from a bad guy yet to concede anything. "What do you think, Nic?"

"I reckon we could do something, but the return has to be impressive. Not just outstanding, but impressive. So impressive that we would get convictions. Convictions so good, that we have an injection party, gas sniffing, skin burnings, or even neck crackings. Because unless we get that, then it will be your body getting strapped to the chair."

"Boy, that's a motivating factor." Capelli sounded sarcastic.

"What have you got for us, Arnie?" Sylvester probed.

"Why, nothing for you friggin' Moreno cocksucker."

It him cut deep, really deep. The equivalent term seldom used in English, but the increasing use of the Spanish to describe African Americans carried the same racist hatred. Sylvester thought it didn't worry him. This time it did.

Capelli leaned back in his chair, dangled the cigarette from his mouth and put his hands behind his head, pushing the chair back onto its back legs, chuffed at his little game and assumed he was ahead on points.

Sylvester could not bring himself to say anything. He tried to swallow to relieve his tension, but knew if he did, the uncomfortable action would give away his feelings.

Capelli passed a smug expression toward Garcia.

"I guess the only cracking you'll be hearing is your partner's knuckles as he thinks hard about whether to thump me. Look at him. The boy is seething. He wants to hit me so bad. Knowing this Moreno, as I reckon I do, he hasn't the friggin' stomach for it. Have you boy? Still a whipping boy, aren't ya, boy." Capelli smirked as he gazed at Sylvester. "Now you

Garcia, that's another matter. You're a crazy bastard. You think you can get away with hurting me like you have. Well, think again, pal. I'll be pressing charges against you as soon as I see my lawyer."

"Capelli no amount of macho crap will save you," said Garcia, prowling the room. "We have you. We know there was more than one, but you'll do. And you will pay big time."

Capelli knew there was a certain truth to what Garcia was saying, but it didn't wipe the smug smile off his face.

"Now Arnie. If it takes all day, let us get your story and perhaps your help." Sylvester began standard procedure. "Where were you at ten thirty on Saturday evening?"

And so, the arduous task of procedural questioning began. The detectives probing, prodding, and cajoling responses from Capelli. All to no avail. He was stone faced in his responses.

They tried reason. They tried threatening. They failed.

Capelli knew what he had to do. Say nothing. The longer he could string the police out, the more opportunity he had to make a deal. He was in serious trouble and although capital punishment in California wasn't popular, he couldn't risk the chance he may face death row. As he stumbled over his answers, he reminded himself that the pigs would deal. They wanted the entire gang and although they had his print; they wanted more. He was connection to the others. He could afford to wait. A good lawyer could argue away the damaging evidence against him. So, he waited.

After an hour of questioning, the detectives were no closer to any further information. They needed more evidence to trigger answers from him. Something. Anything which could implicate him further. Something more direct. Something more immediate. Yet they had nothing. They could not break him.

In frustration rather than defeat, Garcia rushed from the room, demanding Capelli dress in prison fatigues. He wanted forensic tests on his clothes. Sylvester had prepared the clothes waiting outside the room and tossed them to Capelli as he left.

"I want my lawyer," shouted Capelli as the door closed, leaving him to change. He chuckled to himself as he lit another cigarette and began undressing. He knew the frustrated pigs would begin dealing soon.

They had nothing other than the fingerprint. They would find nothing at home. He was well ahead. His chuckle turned into a laugh.

Garcia stood at the anti-room window, contemplating Capelli, as Sylvester arrived at the door.

"You okay?"

"Yeah," Sylvester said, shrugging. "Heard that crap before and no doubt, will hear it again."

"Don't let it get to you," Garcia said, touch his partner's arm. "Although, that's easy for me to say."

"What do we do now? This guy will not give us anything. Do we give him to Gayle? He wants his lawyer. Man, if only we found something at his house."

"What color were Sandi's panties?" Garcia asked.

The question surprised Sylvester. "White, I recall. Why?"

"It seems our Mr. Capelli likes the same color. If I was a betting man, I would bet he likes the same brand as well." He was pointing into the room.

Sylvester peered into the room.

Capelli was struggling to get the one-piece, orange fatigue over his hips and shoulders. Across his chest spread a four-finger scratch. He was wearing Sandi's white panties.

CHAPTER
22

Sylvester could not contain himself. The tension shrouding him too great. He stumbled back into the squad room, holding his convulsing stomach in a fit of laughter. The other team members confused, then bemused, then tittering as Sylvester's fit of laughter became contagious.

"What?" asked Bonnie, catching the bug and giggling along with him.

"It... it's... oh, I can't." Sylvester tried to stifle his laughter.

"Oh, come on Richard, what the hell is going on?" a frustrated Martinez asked.

Sylvester gulped water handed to him by Lawrence, trying to contain himself.

"It seems our Mr. Capelli... oh dear... it seems our Mr. Capelli enjoys getting into women's panties."

"Yeah, no doubt. Why is that funny?" a frustrated Martinez asked.

"He enjoys wearing them."

"A cross dresser?" mumbled Monaghan.

"Not exactly." Sylvester was now back in control, a tear trickling over his cheek.

"He's wearing Sandi's."

"You're kidding me," laughed Lawrence.

Monaghan scoffed, and McPherson allowed himself a brief smirk. Martinez had not quite got the joke. "So what?"

"He states he was with his brothers last Saturday. He also states the fingerprint on a bottle means nothing. I'm sure he thinks it will not pass the scrutiny of the court. If he is in possession of physical evidence, which he is wearing, then we have the bastard."

"And his brothers," McPherson added.

"Right Lou," said Sylvester.

"That gives us three. Who is the fourth? Has he said?" asked Lawrence.

"Capelli has given us nothing. He knows the drill, but with this little discovery, we might change his attitude and get him to give us a few names."

"Will he deal?" asked Martinez.

"Yeah, he might. I don't think we should do it. We have enough on him to go all the way with murder two. Maybe enough for murder one with DNA."

McPherson tossed his pen down on his papers and stood up, making a move to leave. "We should go get his brothers. Do you have their address, Gayle?"

"Yeah, partner I do. They're at seventeen Marsha Court in Otay."

"If they are likely to be implicated, I suppose we should go get them," said Lawrence, flicking on his jacket and moving to the exit.

"Hang on," said Monaghan. "We ain't got probable cause; we need it if we arrest them now. We need paperwork."

"We've got probable cause," argued McPherson. "Their brother implicates them. When forensic gives us their prints from the party bottles at the park, we link them to the assault at the bar. That should be enough to pick them up, at least to an interview status."

"I don't think we need any paperwork, but I'll do it just in case," said Sylvester. "You guys get going. Bring them back as soon as you can. You'll need to get intelligence on them. We've had a profile being developed by the uniforms that should be ready. Pick it up on the way out. I'll send the paperwork down to you." Sylvester began riffling through a draw for the forms.

"We may need back-up," suggested Monaghan.

"Leave it to me," said Sylvester, picking up the telephone hand piece punching numbers to connect with the duty officer. He sat at his desk, waiting for the connection.

"If these guys are like their brother Arnie, you might get into trouble."

"Who knows? They may still be in their jammies," scoffed McPherson.

"Or better yet, sound asleep in lacy attire," joked Monaghan.

"Yeah. We should watch out for their swinging handbags. Who knows what might be in them?" laughed Lawrence.

"Come on, guys, let's stay focused," interrupted Martinez, troubled by the jokes. She didn't like ribald, sexist humor and hoped her colleagues would not allay the danger of their mission through their silliness. As the detectives left the squad room. Martinez turned to Sylvester. "Don't forget the paperwork, Richard."

Sylvester still talking into the handset to the duty officer flicked her away with his hand and nodded. The room fell quiet. Bonnie walked to the coffeepot and refilled her cup. She caught Sylvester with an inquiring eye, showing whether he wanted a cup. He understood the gesture and nodded. He finished his call and thanked Bonnie for her welcomed cup of coffee. Drawing on the steaming cup, he prepared documents for the warrant to cover the likely arrest of the Capelli brothers.

Although the squad had enough probable cause to bring the brothers in for questioning, warrants cover any detail, which may not be part of their investigation.

"Partner, I need you." Garcia poked his head through the doorway.

"Yeah, hang on, I just need five minutes to complete this application."

"Come back to it. I need to have another short crack at Capelli, now."

"But I need..."

"No buts. Let's do it now." He disappeared.

Sylvester knew Capelli would almost be ready to make a statement, now that they had further evidence to put to him, so he resolved to come back to his paperwork. He also knew Garcia was in a mood needing his compliance.

"Thank you, Bonnie, honey. The coffee was beautiful." He drained the cup. "Just like you."

"Why thank you, Richard. Anytime my dear."

CHAPTER
23

Lawrence drew his car to a halt across from number five in a deserted Marsha Court.

"What's the intelligence on these guys, do you know, Chip?" asked Monaghan.

"We know they're here. They are enjoying an extended party. These guys seem in party mode all the time; you'd think they would pull their heads in after last Saturday. The message seems to be that they are oblivious to our suspicions. Hey look at that."

Across the street, two women left the house, walking toward the mall two blocks away. "We either have the Capellis playing twiddley thumbs on their lonesome," said Monaghan. "Or the coop lay empty."

"What do we do?"

"Check with our fearless leader. She might have a good idea."

Lawrence picked up the microphone. "Unit twenty to unit thirteen. Unit twenty to unit thirteen over." No amount of static could seduce Martinez's voice to crackle from the radio. "Unit twenty to unit thirteen. Are you there, Gayle?" No response over the static. "Gayle are you there?" an exasperated Lawrence said.

"She ain't there, Chip. She's over there," said Monaghan, pointing to number seventeen.

"What the hell is she doing?" Lawrence stared through the windshield. "She goes over the top sometimes."

Martinez marched up the path, carrying a folder under an arm, looking very much like an official on business. She paused at the stoop and passed a squinted furtive glance to the detectives who were at a loss to understand what their colleague was doing. She moved with confidence to the door, thumping hard, letting the entire neighborhood know she was on the prowl. McPherson was nowhere to be seen.

"Good afternoon, sir," said Martinez. Bo seemed baffled by a woman knocking with an official-looking clipboard in her hand.

"What can I do for you?"

"Good afternoon, sir, I'm from the City Health Department and we are testing sewage capacity. I would like to ask you a few questions. If you wouldn't mind?"

"Sewage?"

"Yes sir. We have an increasing capacity in this area, and we are unsure of the total population. We are asking residents the number of people living in each house. We want to figure out the capacity flows."

"Capacity flow?"

"Yes, sir. The capacity flow is the amount of sewage moving through the system. If the capacity becomes overloaded, then we get blockage. Blockage means back flow, and this could mean health problems."

"I see." He didn't.

"We would like to know how many people live in the house, sir." Martinez poised her pen over the clipboard, waiting for a response

"People who live here?"

"Yes sir. On a permanent and part-time basis."

"Permanent?"

"Yes, sir. How many people live here?" Martinez wondered whether she should have bothered.

"There's me, Mom. There's me. There's Joey, my brother. And that's it. There are a couple of girls staying over. They're me brother's girls and that's about it."

"I see. And how many now, sir?"

"Right now?"

"Yes sir, right now."

"Just me, me brother, and me. My mom's out of town with Arnie's wife for a few days. Um, I suppose the girls have gone shopping."

"There's only you and your brother here at the moment?"

"Yeah."

Martinez feigned a back scratch and raised two clear fingers, showing the occupants.

"Man is she crazy or what?" Lawrence bemoaned.

"Chip she may be. At the moment, she is signaling there are two bandidos at home. Call in the cavalry and let's go party," Monaghan said, struggling from the car.

Lawrence called for backup and jogged after his partner, checking his pistol as he went.

Martinez said her goodbyes at number seventeen encountering her colleagues in the house's driveway next door. "The brothers are by themselves, and they seem out to it. By the sounds of the television blaring, they are in the front room."

"What do you want to do?" an apprehensive Lawrence asked. "And where is Lou?"

"He's out back. Let's do it now." Martinez drew her pistol, releasing the safety.

"Hang on. I've called for backup, and we haven't got the paperwork yet. We should wait," pleaded Lawrence.

"Stuff the backup. Let's do it now."

"I'm with you, Gayle," said Monaghan, storming past, running up the path with the others behind, pistols at the ready. The detectives paused on the stoop, ears straining for any sudden noises of detection.

"You knock Red. And I'll announce. Okay?" whispered Lawrence.

"Yeah okay." Monaghan approached the door. With a giant hefty kick, he busted it open, rushing inside screaming. "Police."

Lawrence and Martinez remained outside, stunned at what just happened. They rushed in after him. "Police. Everyone on the floor." As the others rushed into other rooms, Lawrence danced into the lounge and found Joey half asleep on the floor.

"Stay down. Turn on your face. Hands stretched out to the sides. Do it." He thrust a foot on Joey's back and pointed his gun at the back of his captive's head. "Right hand behind you, son." Lawrence withdrew his handcuffs from his belt and snapped onto the right wrist of Joey. "Now your left."

Joe responded in a haze of confusion, bewildered at what was going on. He could hear shouting from other rooms, but he did not know where Bo or the girls were. One minute he was watching cartoons, pretty much out of it. Next, in his own animated scene.

Lawrence snapped the cuffs shut; tension relieved. He holstered his gun as Monaghan came to join him. "There's no sign of the other one, Chipper."

"He couldn't have disappeared. It was only minutes ago he was at the front door."

A crashing noise had them joining Martinez scurrying through the kitchen to outside. The wailing of police sirens now filled the air as they ran to further noise, toward the back of the yard.

"Move and I'll cream you," the familiar voice of McPherson shouted from behind the shed.

"Don't shoot. Don't shoot," a frightened Bo pleaded, hands over his face.

"Just give me a reason scum bag and you're a dead man."

The detectives rounded the corner of the shed to find an ashen-faced Bo trembling on his knees before McPherson, his Magnum cocked and shoved into the forehead of his quarry. The sight troubled Martinez, who moved to reassure her partner the situation was under control. She placed a calming hand on his shoulder; the other covered his gripping hands.

"It's okay, Lou, we have him now."

McPherson lowered his hands as a petrified Bo wet himself.

CHAPTER
24

The haze of cigarette smoke swirled around the interview room, wavering within the shaft of light above Bo's head. He was tired and wondered when his lawyer would arrive. He requested one more than an hour ago and he knew the police must allow such a request.

Lawrence and Monaghan questioned him without result.

Monaghan sucked on a cigarette, lighting another as he stubbed out a completed stick. He sat in front of his suspect, blowing smoke into the non-smoker's face, which became more and more uncomfortable with each suffocating minute.

Bo's asthma was choking him. He couldn't breathe and a wheeze begun, adding to his discomfort. He was hot and suffered flushes and needed fresh air. The detectives sat watching him and each time they asked a question; he responded in the Capelli code, say nothing.

"Come on, Brett." Lawrence almost pleaded with him. "We know you're involved. You can tell us what happened."

"I'm not telling you nothing until my lawyer gets here."

"You are in serious trouble, you know that," Lawrence said. "Your brothers are talking to other detectives at the moment. Why can't you?"

"I'm not telling nothing, until my lawyer gets here."

"When we charge you, you can have your lawyer," sighed Lawrence. "Why not answer our questions?"

"We have your brother's statement. We have physical evidence. We have witnesses who place you at all the crucial sites in this investigation."

Monaghan blew smoke into his face. "You can't sit there and refuse to speak to us."

"You were part of it, Brett. All we want to know is, who used the knife?" asked Lawrence. "That's all. Who was the knife man?"

"Brett, we know," Monaghan said. "We know you stole a car and re-sprayed it. We know you assaulted the woman in Pacific Beach. We know you went to a park and had a party. We know you kidnapped her. We know you raped her. What we don't know is, who killed her? Was it you?"

Bo shifted in his chair as Monaghan accused him.

"Alright," said Monaghan. "I didn't want to tell you this. I know how close you think you are to your family, but your brother has given you up."

"Bullshit!"

"He has, Brett, I swear," said Lawrence, hoping his confirmation might get him thinking about his position. "He said you started it. He said it was your idea."

"Joey would never say that."

"It wasn't Joey," said Monaghan.

Bo flicked his eyes over at the detectives, wondering whether there was any truth to their accusation. No matter how much he loved his brother, he was never sure whether Arnie had the same devotion. "Arnie wouldn't either." The Capelli code of silence seemed to work.

"Arnie said you did all the talking," said Monaghan. "He said you bought the beer at the 7-Eleven."

"He even said you did all the driving. He said it was your idea to go to Pacific Beach." Lawrence guessed, hoping it might loosen his tongue.

It did nothing other than dry Bo's mouth. He swallowed hard and wrung his clammy hands, hoping they were wrong. Faint perspiration beads appeared on his upper lip.

"I have nothing to say."

"Oh yes. Your brother was a real squawker," said Monaghan, noticing subtle changes in his demeanor. "Arnie said, not only was it your idea to take the woman, but it was also your idea to rape her."

"No, it wasn't."

"And it was you who killed her. Even though your brothers said no."

"No." Bo snapped, slapping the table.

"Your brother has signed a statement saying you were the murderer. He is doing a deal with the D.A., dropping you into the breach and he has fired you straight at the D.A.. What this will mean Brett, after the courts are done with you, you'll do twenty-plus years. Arnie will do one."

"No. It wasn't me."

"Brett it was you." Monaghan used the opening. "You murdered Sandi Moroni." He opened a file for the first time, tossing graphic color photographs of the bloodied corpse.

"No." Bo recoiled at the sight of the glossy prints. Images he hadn't seen.

"You raped her and then you killed her." Monaghan demanded.

"It wasn't me." said Bo, staring at the photographs shaking his head in denial.

"Yes, it was. It was you who raped her. It was you who butchered her, and your brother Arnie agrees with us. You friggin' punk." Monaghan stretched out of his chair and stood scowling above the cowering Bo. "Detective Lawrence, please prepare arrest papers and tell the boss we have our man. We can get his lawyer now and begin the formal interview." Lawrence began making his way to the door as Bo fidgeted in his chair.

"No wait. I tell you it wasn't me."

"We've got our man. Brett, you're it. They will gas you, boy. Or better yet, get the shock treatment from the chair, or a jab. Do you like needles, Brett? And even if it wasn't you, it doesn't matter, you'll do."

Bo just wanted it all to end. He was sweating, wheezing, holding his hands to his ears to block out Monaghan's accusations. He was out of control, rocking back and forward in his chair. "Stop it. Stop it. It wasn't me," he shouted.

"If it wasn't you, then who?" asked a soothing Lawrence.

"It was Max. Max did it."

"Who's he? asked Monaghan, looking surprised at Lawrence. "Another brother?"

"Max Roberts," sobbed Bo.

"Were you there?"

"Yes."

"Who else?"

"Arnie. Joey. Max. And Billy."

Five. Five bad guys. The detectives glanced at each other with a mixture of surprise, excitement, and shock. Five bad guys. Not three. Not four. Five. What a breakthrough.

The footprints at the park were right. There were five.

"Who's this, Billy?" asked Lawrence.

"A pal of Max. Billy Humphries, they're always hanging out together."

"Where are they now?"

"I dunno."

"Come on Brett," attacked Monaghan. "You're spinning us a line to save your own skin."

"I'm not. The last time I saw them was a couple of days ago at the mall. They were as high as kites and driving a stolen truck. They had been in the city robbing people in a car park, or something like that."

"And you say this Max guy sliced up the girl?"

"Yeah. We all did her over, and Max killed her. I had nothing to do with it. And neither did my brothers. And that's the truth."

"Interview interrupted at four fifteen." Monaghan led Lawrence from the room.

"Chip, we've got these guys," Monaghan said, punching the air. "We got the knife man and a fifth. We've got the bastards."

"Partner, you never cease to amaze me with your damn skills. How the hell did that happen? One minute he's wanting a lawyer and then the next... he's spilling it all to us?"

"Just lucky, I guess. Let's go tell the others and brighten their day. We've got the bastards Chip; we have got them."

When they walked into the squad room, they assembled around the whiteboard, drinking coffee and sharing information. "What have you got guys?" asked Lawrence, waiting for the right moment for him to announce their news.

"Arnie's about to turn our way," Sylvester said, more with hope than any conclusive facts.

"We've got nothing from Joey," a sullen McPherson said, disappointed in his failure to secure a confession. "We have three brothers who we know did it, and still, we have nothing."

"Yeah well, who do you think the others are?" asked Martinez. "If there was a fifth bad guy. Do we have any further evidence from the fingerprints at the park?"

"Inconclusive," said Sylvester. "We'll know more in an hour. We should have DNA tomorrow or the next day."

"We only have a day left before we have to bring those jarheads in from downtown. It's a pity, we're so damn close," said McPherson.

"Over my dead body," a tired Garcia said, resting his head on his hand.

"I have good news and bad news for you," a chuffed Monaghan said, plonking himself down at his desk and throwing his feet on top.

"Tell us the bad first, will you, Red?" sighed Garcia.

"Brett didn't do it."

"That's bad? What's good?"

"There's five bad guys. The two missing gang members are, a one Max Roberts and a Billy Humphries."

Silence.

No one moved. They just looked at each other and then more attentively at a beaming Monaghan and Lawrence. Garcia dropped his hand from his face and drew himself up from his desk.

"Roberts is the sole knife man," chimed in Lawrence.

"You mean five and not four?" asked Garcia. "We sure got that wrong."

"The big guy just told you this?" asked McPherson.

"Yeah. Don't ask me how. God knows we were with the dunce long enough," sighed Monaghan.

"This is fantastic," said Martinez, dancing a little jig.

"All right!" shouted Sylvester, throwing his arms into the air.

"Good news maybe guys, but we have more to do. We can't afford to celebrate just yet," said Garcia, bringing the happy team back into focus. "We don't know where these other two are. We need a murder weapon, the knife. We need signed statements from the Capellis. And I want it done tonight. Now we have this breakthrough we must press forward."

The team shared Garcia's urgency for a result and looked to him for direction.

"Gayle, follow-up the where-bouts of this Roberts and Humphries. Red, you and Chip... look, well done, guys. Can you now get a signed statement from him? Do it in front of a lawyer. Lou grab someone, perhaps the boss, and pressure Joey with this additional information. Get him talking. Who knows, he may give us more. Whatever you do, get it down on paper and have him sign it; make sure you do it in front of a lawyer. Richard? You and I will have another go at Arnie. And Bonnie, honey? Can you call the D.A. and get their people down here. We might just need them tonight."

"Right, Nicolas," said Bonnie, pleased to be included.

"Guys, I see a light at the end of the tunnel. But we have more to do. Let's put our heads down and get a result. I want the other two in here tonight."

Garcia's sternness faded from the joy the others may have harbored. They owed it to Sandi's family to stay focused on the tasks ahead.

CHAPTER
25

"**M**ax, I reckon the pigs must know by now," a skittish Billy said. "Nah. They'd have us by now. Joey won't drop us in." Max checked the road behind, searching for any sign of police, as they motored toward sanctuary over the Mexican border.

"Are you sure they arrested the others?"

"I'm not sure about Arnie. No one has seen him since last night, but the cops are swarming all over his place."

"Doesn't mean they have him though, does it?"

"You might be right, Billy boy. I would bet my balls on him not being busted. If he is, and we aren't, then that means they don't know about us yet. Knowing the Cappelli's as I do, we should get out of here whilst we can."

"Do you think we'll get over the border?"

"Man, you've got to learn to trust me." Max slapped Billy's knee. "We'll be sweet. In less than thirty minutes, we'll be in Mexico and safe."

They motored through the side streets, away from highway traffic, edging toward the border. Billy's idea was to stay off the highway in case the cops were searching. Get as close as possible to the border before taking the major road through the checkpoint. They still had the truck from their adventures last Sunday and hoped to sell it in Mexico.

Border authorities were more interested in people coming into the United States than leaving. The boys confident they would get through the checkpoint with no hassle. They had been through without even being stopped and remained convinced they could pass through without stopping this time.

As they crossed over each street, they scanned the roadway for any sign of police activity. "Man, I could kill you for getting me involved in all of this." Billy said. "I said she was trouble when we saw her in the bar. I bet I'm wanted for murder right now."

"Hey man, you ain't in trouble. You did nothing and I'll tell the pigs that. You have nothing to worry about. It's me they'll want to execute pal, not you. You'll be okay. Take a left here."

Billy turned the truck into a tree-lined avenue. It was almost night, and they hoped to time their approach to the border as it turned dark.

"Max, how long do you think we'll have to stay in Mexico?"

"Buddy, I don't think we'll ever come back."

Billy sighed. He didn't like his crummy life. It was a no joy, no hope existence, though it would be better than a life living in a downcast third world country. Since hearing the news of the police hunt on radio, he spent his time in the roof cavity of his mother's house, hoping to escape any house invasion from the police.

He blamed the Capellis. They were to blame for the mess. They were the ones who provoked Max. They dragged him along to the bar in Pacific. They wanted the woman. They were the ones who raped her. They hurt her and urged Max to kill her. Yes, the Capellis were to blame for the trouble.

If Mexico was the way out, then so be it. He just wished he could reclaim his life by going back in time for just one week. If only he didn't go with the Capellis. If only he didn't have that drink, if only.

"Oh shit," Max mumbled.

"What man?"

"Cops."

"Where?" Billy searched in the rear-view mirror, fear gripping him. He saw a flashing red light atop an unmarked car. Flashing headlights meant he should pull over. It was not yet dark. The sky flashed with orange streaks, and the pulsating red light illuminated the neighborhood.

"You'd better pull over before they call for backup," Max said.

Billy stopped the car. His breathing rapid, eyes wide.

CHAPTER
26

"**N**ic, if I don't get this paperwork done, we'll get agony from the D.A.'s office."

"Rich, you can do it when we get back. We've got a vehicle sighted."

"Where?"

"South in Otay Mesa. A blue truck, fitting Brett's description and matching the report of the vehicle used in bag snatches last Sunday. It's our boys, I bet."

"This paperwork needs to get done."

"Listen partner, the others are on their way. If you want to be part of this arrest, then we have to get going now. So, what do you want to do? Paperwork, or bag a couple of killers?"

"You know, paperwork is an integral part of the investigation. We have procedure to follow. I don't want to jeopardize the case."

"Okay, you stay, and I'll go get these guys." Garcia left.

Sylvester sat at his desk, trying to work on his computer, but his mind was elsewhere. It didn't take long for him to pick up his jacket and scamper after his partner.

As they motored toward the border, Sylvester ran through several outstanding issues.

"We need to go see Moroni when we get back."

"Check." Garcia took notes.

"We should keep him informed. Perhaps we should visit Sandi's parents as well."

"Agreed."

"Barbara Smethers needs to run an eye over Brett in a line-up."

"Check."

"That guy Vernon, who saw the snatch, needs to come in and update his statement. A line-up with the Capellis would be a good idea."

"Check."

"The boys from the West Coast Lagoon as well, in particular Rudi Curtis, need to ID the Capellis.

"Check."

"We've got these guys, haven't we?"

"Check." Garcia snapped his notebook shut. "Partner, it has all fallen into place fast. Yeah, we've got enough to jab them." A slight pause of reflection. "I reckon your weekend away is a safe bet. Boy, what a day."

"You can't even consider how I feel about wrapping this case up. Not just for the weekend away. I want these guys behind bars. I can tell you the long nights have been worth it. But Nic, honestly, I'm concerned about the paperwork."

"Don't worry partner. We have probable cause since we picked up Arnie. It'll be all right. Do it when we get back."

"Yeah, I will. I just want to cover all bases. Who knows, we might get a loopy judge and miss out. I need to be certain."

"We get the knife man, and he'll be happy to tell us everything. Especially, when we tell him the Capellis have already given statements implicating him."

"Arnie hasn't."

"Yeah, I know, but he will, Rich, once we have Roberts."

"I can't believe our luck in this case. Just twenty-four hours ago we had nothing.

Now we have them all."

"Just remember, these guys are dumb. I mean, who wears the victim's panties to bed just days after you murder her? These guys are so dumb. Prints left at the crime scene, how stupid."

"Yeah, but we have been lucky."

"Amen to that, brother. Hey, look at that."

Sometimes bad guys just fall into your lap with no good police work. Luck plays a large part. Tonight, luck continued. Crossing the street at the intersection was a blue truck matching the description.

"Richard, my boy, you are the luckiest dude I know. Do the tags match?"

"They sure do. What do we do?"

"Get into the street behind them for starters." Sylvester cruised into the tree-lined avenue and followed the truck ahead. "Two occupants, maybe our boys. I think we should call for backup."

"Partner, if we wait for help, we may lose them. Light is fading fast, and we may spook them if we keep following them whilst waiting for the cavalry. Buzz them over now, before it gets too dark."

"Okay. Let's do it." Sylvester slung a magnetized police light onto the roof of the car through his window, switched it on and began flashing his headlights until the truck pulled over. It stopped and Sylvester cruised the car to a halt behind it.

Garcia barked instructions into the radio hand piece as Sylvester climbed out of the car, drawing his pistol anticipating sudden movements from the truck.

"Wait a minute, Rich," said Garcia, trying to complete backup instructions.

Sylvester focused on the truck and didn't register his partner's plea to wait. His eyes fixed on the driver as he moved to the front of his car his pistol at the ready. "You in the car. This is the police. I have a weapon drawn and at the ready. Get out of the truck one at a time, starting with the driver. Keep your hands where I can see them at all times."

Billy could not hear the police officer calling out instructions. He was shaking with fear. Max reached into the glove compartment and grabbed his gun, cocking it. "What are you doing, man? Do you want to get us killed?"

"Shut up will ya," said Max, as he opened his door and slipped out.

Garcia finished his call for back up and pushed open his door, grabbing a shotgun from its rack by the door. As he climbed out, he took his eyes off the truck and did not see the passenger getting out.

Sylvester repeated his command to the driver and cocked his pistol. He wanted the driver to make it easy on everyone by getting out. But the driver hadn't moved. He edged to the rear of the truck. the passenger was not in his line of sight.

Garcia looked up as he was getting out of the car, pumping a cartridge into the breach of the shotgun. He swung around to support his partner and glimpsed the passenger out of the truck, advancing on Sylvester with the gun at the ready.

"Passenger out."

As Sylvester swung his pistol to the right, the passenger squeezed off two shots. The windshield cracked and the splatter of blood had a fatal impulse for Garcia, discharging his shotgun at the passenger.

The zing of another round flashed past his ear, too close for him to consider proper police procedure. He pumped another round into the breach and fired again.

It was all over in less than five seconds.

The passenger lay in the gutter lifeless with a hole as big as a fist in his chest.

Sylvester squirmed on the hood of the car.

Garcia rushed to the driver's door, pumping another round into the breach.

"Get out of the vehicle you friggin' moron," he screamed. The driver shaking climbed out onto the road sobbing, his hands behind his head.

"Kneel you little shit, or I'll blow your friggin' head right off."

The driver followed the shouted instructions. His arm thrust backwards, and the other arm then brought into place behind his back. Handcuffing done, Garcia thumped him to the head with the butt of the shotgun, knocking him onto the roadway.

"Stay down."

Garcia skipped back toward Sylvester, jumping up onto the bonnet next to him, cradling his partner's head.

"Oh shit, Richard," Garcia said. Fragments of bone, tissue, and blood covered Sylvester's head and face. "You'll be okay partner. Help will be here soon."

Sylvester convulsed. Garcia squeezed him tighter. His partner's bulging eyes wide, listless. He shook as he gurgled and coughed blood.

Then all movement stopped, and a lifeless Sylvester slumped in the cradling arms of a rocking Garcia.

CHAPTER
27

The work had piled up. Papers strewn, in no logical order, over a desk bursting with several in-boxes stacked around the desk and office. At these moments, Anna Booth regretted ever thinking law was a career for her. She wanted justice for others and assumed the law would help her meet her dream. The legal process frustrated her with a complex court practice in the greatest democracy in the world.

A free democracy without justice. What a paradox, but this is the system that evolved in the United States of America, land of the free. Common sense left the court system long ago, and justice is rarely found.

Anna, a wide-eyed idealist, wanted to represent the underprivileged in their quest for justice. Her ideals were not enough to pay her bills. Escrow paid her bills.

She wanted to be a litigator yet lacked the courage to give up reliable income for the uncertainty and risk of representing what the community called losers and deplorables. Nagging doubt plagued her. She believed that whilst she continued transferring real estate, she would be a loser.

Anna twirled the pen between her fingers as she rested her head on her other hand. Before her lay a transfer. A happy couple buying into their first home. Their hopes and dreams for the future, creating a family and contributing to the community now reliant on Anna. And she couldn't give a damn.

Her mind skipped from the file to the wasted opportunities at the party of the most eligible bachelor in town last Sunday. Why did she have so many cocktails, adding to her legend of being a fall down drunk?

She thought about food and pondered what cancer it would promote if she had another TV dinner. Maybe chicken and vegetables tonight. For the third night running. Thankfully, she likes chicken.

Another heavy sigh came, and she doubted whether life would ever improve. Life had given her many opportunities, but she missed them all when they came knocking.

She longed for excitement. Stimulation to get her living again. Blondes are supposed to have more fun, yet she had zero fun for a long time. She had the highs and many lows of being on the rough end of disappointing relationships. Her irrational choice of men her weakness. She always seemed to be attracted to the go-getters, who often got going whenever she raised talk of a future together. She tired of being the handbag for an ambitious man.

Her colleagues considered Anna to be a brilliant prospect as a litigator yet did not see her potential in a courtroom. Her private life always seemed to impede career advancement. She was a sucker for the smarmy offer of uncomplicated love and often embraced it, even if she knew it was just for a night. The mind-numbing work of escrow was not only her livelihood. It was her security.

The thirty something years lay before her, and she was not looking forward to them. The romantic fairy-tale of happiness and love were nothing more than a pleasant dream on a Sunday morning. Her quest for the happy ending kept her in a life she regretted.

"My life sucks," she sighed.

Anna tossed her pen against the files. Frustration at not meeting her idealist college goals haunted her. A sudden startle from the buzzing telephone beside her broke her morose drift.

"Hello, Anna Booth," she murmured absent minded, not caring who was online.

"Booth? It's Kramer from the Public Defender's Office. Got a sec?"

"Oh, hello Kramer." Anna recognized an old acquaintance from her college years. Kramer was a tutor she admired and although he remained disappointed with her life choices, they remained in contact. "What's up?"

"We are looking for a defender and I mentioned your name."

"Is this one of your sick jokes? You know I hate being set up."

"No, it's for real."

"You smoking that strange weed again, Kramer, because you know I'm an escrow girl." She didn't know how to respond. Her colleague could not be serious. He has to know she has done little court time in the past six years. And since college, the fingers of her two hands could count her cases before a judge. "You must be desperate to even suggest such a thing."

"Anna, I am."

"What's happened?"

"I've contacted everyone on my list, and I've come up with a big fat zero. I'm now faced with taking a student or not being able to get my guy a fair trial. You are my last call."

"Why can't you do it?"

"I'm in court on a fraud and conspiracy case that will run for another four weeks, at least. I don't have the time. If you want a chance, then this might be it."

"Kramer, you know?" She fudged. "I'm very busy and I haven't been in front of a judge for an awful long time."

"Yeah, I know all of that. But hon, I'm desperate and frankly, if you can assign real estate, then you can speak for my guy."

"Who is it?"

"William Hubert Humphries."

"Never heard of him."

"Where have you been, girl? Billy and his buddies picked up a woman a week ago and did a number on her in La Jolla, leaving her dead. He is a sleaze bag and as guilty as all hell but deserves a good defense. You must know the case."

"Yeah, maybe I do, now you remind me." Anna lied. She knew the case and why Kramer could excite no one into taking it. Humphries will go down is the common cry amongst her friends at the vibrant Dobson's Bar downtown. A place she went to meet her lawyer friends and hear of challenges and conquests.

"Christ, escrow must bury you under a pile of dirt, girl. Don't you think it's time to dig yourself out of your career grave and have a crack at a little casework?"

"How much?"

"Judas Priest, Anna. You're on the bones of your ass, with no immediate prospects. You have no future and your chances of ever moving before a judge again are slim. And you ask me how much?" exclaimed Kramer. "Let's forget it. Thanks anyway."

"I'll do it," an overanxious Anna snapped.

"Good. My office, tomorrow at ten." Kramer ended the call.

Anna sat dumbfounded, dropping her phone to the desk. She sank her head into her hands and ran her fingers through her lank hair. "What the hell am I doing?"

A chance to change her life and here she is, remaining fearful of the uncertainty. She fretted. She laid back in her chair, raising her arms above her head, sucking in air, hoping to calm negative thoughts. She rose from her desk and stumbled to the window, sitting within the frame on the ledge. Her mind racing and confused.

Humphries was the youngest member of the notorious gang who violated and then butchered a young, married nurse. Kramer was right. He was as guilty as sin. There was no way they could not deliver a guilty verdict.

"What am I doing?" She gazed out of the window toward nothing in particular. "The guy will go to the chamber or whatever they do with murderers." Her mouth was dry, her tongue struggled to moisten it. As she did, a sly smile appeared and turned her mouth. "The publicity would be good for business."

CHAPTER
28

The cold crisp air of the dank, windowless interview room sent a shiver through Anna as she waited for Humphries. It had been a whirlwind few days, as she tried restructuring her affairs to allow enough time to put an adequate defense together.

Kramer briefed her about the need to emphasize justice and seeking a fair trial. She pondered a motion for dismissal, based upon the overwhelming media reporting of the case. They published every scant piece of information about Sandi Moroni and her family. The biased media reported the need for justice; they called for the death penalty and a fair trial in San Diego did not seem possible.

A motion was a long shot, but worth considering, given the overwhelming evidence showing the guilt of the gang members. Kramer was against the idea. The public wanted justice and revenge. He was of the view a quick trial would help Humphries and lead to a jail term, rather than the death penalty.

Anna tapped her red nails on the bare table. The chill of the metal chair adding to her discomfort. She struggled to control her shivering and made a mental note to wear warmer clothes next time. She pondered whether she shivered because she was cold or just nervous about meeting a murderer.

A clanking of metal echoed through the room, startling her. She wondered if inmates ever get used to the coldness of prison metal. Crisp to touch and a strange chilling of spirit feel to the echoing noise. Jail was not the warm and cozy place many thought it to be.

Jangling of a key inserted into the door and a buzzer sounded. She rose from the table, preparing to meet her client. The door swung open. A guard entered the room, followed by Humphries shuffling toward her. Another guard followed. Her client manacled at the ankles, with a light-weight chain extending to his wrists, which were handcuffed to a sturdy belt at his waist. He carried any excess chain to help his shuffling. The orange overalls two sizes too big for his waif like body. His face etched with confusion, darting eyes giving away fear and misery. The lead guard hustled him into a chair opposite Anna.

"No touching and no transfer of materials without approval." It was as if it was a standard piece of information delivered many times. "One of us will stay in the room, as required under the State's Correctional Code." He didn't even bother glancing Anna's way before leaving the room.

The room now weirdly calm. The fat guard's heavy, sweaty breathing the only sound to pierce the silence. Humphries squirmed in his chair, rattling chains. Anna resumed her seat, watching her client, wondering how long it would be before he peeked her a glance.

Before her sat a bedraggled, frightened, frail boy accused of murder. It was a pathetic sight. He looked like any other teenager. Not the creature of hate and loathing portrayed by the media. *What manner of boy was he?* Anna searched for clues from him to justify taking a life. *What could have been his reason to murder another human being? Where was the evidence of evil from this boy?* She opened her leather case to prepare for taking notes. Anna cleared her throat, ready to question the boy. A disappointing figure of a feared murderer.

"I didn't do it," Billy mumbled. His chin resting hard on his chest.

"I beg your pardon?" responded Anna.

"I didn't do nothin'," Billy said, louder this time.

"William, my name is Anna Booth. I am your court-appointed attorney. The police have charged you with the felony of first-degree murder of a Mrs. Sandra Moroni in Soledad Park, La Jolla." Anna read from prepared notes. "Evidence has placed you with the deceased, during an assault a few hours before her death." Anna paused for a moment to study the response.

"Evidence points to you being at the crime scene. Given you are not stupid, how in heaven's name can you sit in front of me, and deny any involvement in this horrendous crime? How can you do that when the District Attorney believes it implicates you in murder?"

Anna's aggression to her client unsettled her. She considered she should be more compassionate. *To hell with it. He is guilty.*

He lifted his head to look at her. His eyes watery. He could have been under stress, but his lips tightened with determination, and he said, "I was there. But I had nothin' to do with it."

"Why should I believe you, William?"

Billy sunk lower into his seat hunching his shoulders and bowing his head even further.

"Ma'am, I've done bad things. I've robbed. I've stolen and I've bashed. But I would never do what they say I've done. The lady wasn't one of us."

Anna shook her head. "Explain?"

"She was good. Not bad like us. And good needs protecting not destroying."

Anna sat back and laughed. "You must be joking. Are you a comedian, William?"

"No, ma'am."

The craziness of the scene was too much for Anna, and she regretted agreeing to handle the case. She was dumbfounded. She turned to the guard for reassurance. He shrugged, shuffled his feet and stared down to study the pristine tiled floor, leaving communicating with the nutter to the attorney. Billy sniffed and struggled to wipe his nose against his shoulder.

"Who did it then, if it wasn't you?"

"Max killed her. I didn't even touch her. The Capellis messed her up, and they did her over in the woods. I had nothing to do with it."

"You were there, were you not?"

Billy nodded.

"You didn't stop them?"

"Nah. Well, kind of, at the beginning, you know, in the bar. I was too out of it later."

"Then you are as guilty as the others."

They glared at each other; the guard's breathing now more noticeable.

"William, you are in deep shit. You understand me?" Anna stood and moved about the room, stopping to lean against a wall. She peered down at her client irritated at the task ahead. "If the jury finds you guilty. And I am pretty damn sure they will. They will sentence you to death. My job is not to get you out of here, my job is to make sure you live."

It began quietly, then after a few moments Billy's sniffling dominated the interview.

Anna ignored it and continued. "When they sentence you, they will send you to the gas chamber or maybe you'll get a lethal injection."

Billy was wiping his nose as best he could.

"If you agree to turn testimony for the prosecution, they may offer a plea."

"No way."

Anna paused for a moment. She needed to tell him of his rights. At the moment, she preferred she was back solving escrow problems. "You may get fifteen to twenty years, but at least you'll live. Which is more than I can say for your victim, you bastard." It just slipped out, and Anna turned away.

Surprised, Billy raised an objecting face. "Hey, you can't talk to me like that."

"Listen, you little jerk. You took part in the worst, most vicious crime this city has ever known. You are going to court with only one friend. And that's me."

Anna wanted to smack the kid around the head and vent her anger.

"I'm the only fool who would take this case, and already I'm regretting it. I thought, yep, I can do this. But I was wrong. You are a piece of shit. How dare you sit there and say you did nothing? Who the hell do you think you are kidding?"

Billy didn't respond.

"I make you this promise. If you do as I say, then I will fight hard to save your miserable, pathetic life, even though I consider you guilty. Screw me, and I will drop you like a hot potato, and you die without friends. Do we understand each other, William?"

The room echoed Anna's words.

After a long pause. "It's Billy."

"What?"

"My name is Billy and I'll do whatever you want."

Anna returned to the desk and snapped open her briefcase. She flung papers toward him. "Sign them."

"What are they?"

"Now Billy, didn't I just say to do as I ask?"

He struggled to his feet and Anna put a pen in his hands, held the papers down and pointed to a spot for his signature. Billy struggled to use the pen, eventually signing Anna's appointment papers, allowing her to act on his behalf.

"Thank you, Billy." Anna collected her things and snapped her briefcase shut. "Speak to no one unless I'm present. I will need to talk to you again in a few days. I'm expecting to go to preliminaries at the end of the week."

Anna left, leaving Billy to struggle back to his cell.

As he shuffled back, Billy could not help thinking his counsel was the only chance he had of getting out of this horrible place. She had the fire for justice that might just lead him to a short prison term. He understood he was part of the gang that murdered the woman, but he didn't take part and the law will know that. He considered a couple of years in jail as a just retribution.

When he returned to his cell, the guards unshackled him, and he withdrew into the gloom of his little alcove and the metal doors clanged behind him. There was nothing inviting about his cell. A cot with the bare requirements for sleeping. A seatless metal John and basin. There were no possessions. He did not have enough reading skills to have material to read. He didn't write or draw well, so he had no tools. Other than a bar of soap there was no other sign of habitation.

The noise of fellow inmates with little respect for others made it impossible for him to sleep. He had not been in jail long enough for him to become accustomed to his surroundings, to get used to the constant noise. He was not looking forward to joining the criminals in the main prison where he would face many tests. If he was going to be sentenced to a jail term, he hoped it would not be too long.

The thought sent a shiver of regret through him.

Anna kicked off her shoes as soon as she entered her apartment. Almost three hours after leaving Billy. It had been a long day, and her feet were aching from walking and standing. Escrow was a pain in the butt, yet the only thing that got sore was her butt.

She dropped her briefcase beside the sofa and wandered into the kitchenette, loosening her clothes. She picked a tumbler out of the sink, rinsing it under cold water. She stretched her arm into a cupboard above the icebox and took hold of an old friend, the almost empty bottle of Jameson's Irish Whisky. She filled her glass with ice and poured herself a stiff shot. The whisky had little time to trickle through the ice before she gulped it down and refilled the glass. The whisky felt good as it burned its way through her system.

She struggled to reach for the zipper of her clothing as she walked toward her bedroom. Stepping out of the frock, leaving it on the floor, she went into the bathroom, discarding underwear. A quick splash of refreshing water, and she was feeling a lot more comfortable after a long day. She slipped on a large sweatshirt and returned to the sofa, picking up her drink from the dresser on the way.

Nestling onto the comfortable sofa, pulling large cushions about her, she took another gulp of whisky and snapped open her briefcase to work on the lost cause. As she studied information sent to her from the District Attorney's Office, she accepted her task would be difficult.

Anna read the briefings, taking notes well into the night. She was not conscious of time, relishing the intellectual stimulation in preparing a case. Her ease of application to the work pleased her and she could feel confidence growing. In the past, she had the ability, but always shrunk at the thought of having to prove herself.

The sharp shrill of the telephone startled Anna awake, and she lunged for it to stop the noise. "Hello," she croaked, annoyed at the few hours of sleep now disturbed.

"Anna? It's Kramer. Got a sec?"

"Shit, Kramer, you pick the damn worst times to call," she groaned, seeking full consciousness. "What do you want? And it better be good."

"The D.A. wants a meeting. Do we negotiate?"

Anna sat up from her cuddled sleeping position, more attentive, keen to know more. Her mind switched to go mode. "What's he want to meet for?" she asked, running her fingers through her hair. "We've got full disclosure, haven't we?"

"Yeah, we have. He wants to deal so he can strengthen the case against the others, I suppose. Geez, I don't know. What do you think?"

"I doubt it," yawned Anna. "He must have something important to tell us. Knowing him, as I do, it could also be a tactic and a damn waste of time. When?"

"This morning at ten."

"I'll meet you there."

CHAPTER
29

Anna often wondered whether an office with a view across Mission Bay was worth the hassle of corporate dealings, the backslapping, the false friendships and the pure, unadulterated itch for power. Squashing anyone who got in your way to achieve your selfish mind set. Was the view worth it?

She stood before a floor to ceiling window, soaking in the scene. Yachts battled the breeze out on the beautiful blue waters, and Coronado Island looked idyllic. She gazed over the military installation, pondering the need for military espionage, when military secrets were so easily seen from downtown office towers. A navy fighter took off from the air base with a silent grace and she thought how peaceful a weapon of war could look without noise.

She stretched across the table and poured herself water from the crystal jug and settled into a chair. A file closed in front of her. She sighed, tired at the wait for her appointment with Jonathan Morriarty.

Kramer slumped opposite, the victim of a heavy night of abuse. At fifty, his thinning hair different from the thick thatch of wavy curls he wore long to his shoulders, almost twenty-five years earlier. A skilled attorney, his career swung from the highs of academic achievement and exhilarating courtroom successes to abysmal failures. There were more defeats these days than expected, such is the lot of a public defender. Defeats still hurt. Although defeats kept growing, he wore each as a scar across his chest.

Both lawyers were becoming impatient.

Kramer cleaned his fingernails with a paper clip, while Anna tapped the beat of a vague Latino number with her long nails. She rested her head in her hand and glanced at Kramer, raising an eyebrow of impatience. They didn't know what to expect. The DA invited them to the fount of greatness and wondered why they were wasting time.

"Christ, what is taking so long?"

"Try to stay calm," responded Kramer, aware of the failed relationship she had with Morriarty. He knew his young friend had exorcised herself of all feeling, yet he remained uneasy. The wait was not helping. He hoped Anna could stay calm and not jeopardize any further legal dealings. He didn't want to contend with antagonistic former lovers. The Humphries case was challenging enough.

Anna smiled, suggesting a wise insight into his thoughts. "It finished long ago, Kramer. I have no feelings at all. I just get annoyed; no correction… pissed off, when people keep others waiting past the scheduled time. Especially twenty minutes, like this pompous, lard ass, dude."

The conversation ended as the door swept open and the distinguished District Attorney, Jonathan Morriarty, and a female colleague entered. He rushed to Anna, snatching her hand, cupping it as she rose from her seat. The clasped hands lingering a little firmer and longer with more subtext than protocol would have expected. "Anna, how wonderful to see you again," beamed Jonathan. "It has been years, you look wonderful."

"Jonathan…" answered a nodding Anna. "It has been a while. You seem every bit the successful counselor you wanted to be."

"Thank you, Anna, and you are every bit of what I expected."

The subtle jibe scorched through her. She knew what he meant. No more an innocent compliment than a kick in the pants.

"Are you enjoying escrow?"

Morriarty preferred a political career and wallow in the public adulation, feeding his nature. A stellar political career lay ahead. First, the Governor's Office, then perhaps a shift to the White House. That is the plan. He once considered Anna the perfect partner for his political journey until he learned her ambitions went no further than the front gate and the crippling ties of family life. Suburbia was not in his plans. Anna didn't share his dream, so he discarded her.

"Jonathan... you haven't changed either," Anna gushed, with a wide smile, hiding gnashing clenched teeth. "Still a choice prick."

The mood changed.

Morriarty dropped her hand and greeted Kramer. He shook his hand and gave a knowing wink to let him know everything was under control. A sign to say all was well, relaxing tension.

Sweeping his hand in an exaggerated gesture, he beckoned his colleague to join them from waiting by the door. "This is my assistant, Jennifer Hennessy. She will prosecute the case against your client. Lawrence Jordan will support her."

"Ah, another student. Good man, young Lawrie," Kramer said.

"Yes, he is. Please take a seat. Would anyone care for a drink? Coffee perhaps?"

Both Kramer and Anna said no, gathering themselves as they sat waiting for the news Morriarty would deliver. He sat at the head of the table, resplendent in blue suit, crisp white shirt, and red tie. A man used to getting his own way, oozing confidence and arrogance. Anna considered him and wondered why she ever bothered. Such a gracious man on the outside, yet such a ruthless, ugly monster.

"What's the story, Jonathan?" asked Kramer. "Why are we here?"

"No more pleasantries?" Morriarty responded, chuckling.

It was all too much for Anna. "Jonathan. Cut the sanctimonious crap and tell us why you want us here. Already you're twenty minutes late. There are better things to do than sit here and listen to your friggin' shit. Either get on with it or I'm punching my ticket and I'm out of here."

"Escrow calling, is it Anna?"

"Let's move on, please Jonathan," encouraged Kramer.

Morriarty nodded to his assistant, signaling her to begin the briefing.

"We have a first-degree felony with five alleged perpetrators. We have four in custody and one on a slab at the city morgue." Hennessy read from a thick case file. It had four colored indicator tabs protruding from the side. Anna wondered which tab was her man. She hoped it was the thinnest. "Our plan is murder one on three defendants under California Penal Code 187. We have one potentially turning evidence for us in return for a guilty plea of culpable homicide."

The news bothered Anna. If Billy was not part of the prosecution's case, as she now suspected, then who is turning over and why are they coming for him? They must know their case is weak on Billy.

"Hang on a second," interrupted Kramer already attentive to the consequences of the information being read. "What you're saying, if I understand you correctly, you have a prosecuting witness who will turn a plea to give testimony against our guy. Is that right?"

"Got it in one," said Morriarty, snapping his fingers and pointing. "Who is it?"

"We do not want to release that information at this stage," Hennessy said.

Anna wondered why they were summoned if the case was going to be so bad against them. She cast Kramer a bewildered look; he clutched his chin, stroking the stubble trying to fathom why they were there.

Hennessy continued. "Our case will seek the death penalty on all three and we expect the support of the judge and jury." Her demeanor toughened, exhibiting a certain resolve.

"So why are we here, Jonathan?" asked Anna, troubled by the news. "I want a deal."

Anna and Kramer glanced at each other. Anna considered her options; maybe they don't have the case they say they do.

"What are you after?" asked Kramer, uncertain where all this discussion was heading.

Morriarty cleared his throat, shifted in his seat, pondering a reply. The confidence showing signs of weakness. Anna flicked another quick glance to Kramer with query in her eyes. He raised an eyebrow in surprise. Morriarty rested his elbows on the table and tapped his fingertips together, breathing into his hands. "I need convictions. No loose end acquittals."

There was a long, uneasy pause.

"I can't guarantee my guy will speak against his brothers. I want your guy to turn evidence and guarantee two guilty convictions for murder one. I am happy to accept two lighter sentences for the other two."

Morriarty needed convictions. This case would guarantee the notoriety he needed to make a run for governor. Any scandal through non-performance and he could forget about a political career.

"I am prepared to offer your client a twenty-year culpable murder conviction, in return for his life. All he has to do, is move our way and give positive testimony against the other two."

"You've got to be kidding," said Anna.

"No, I'm not, I am afraid. That's the deal. If your man doesn't want it, then so be it."

"He'll need to respond before tomorrow's preliminary hearing," added Hennessy. "If he doesn't, he will go all the way."

"Why?" a perplexed Kramer asked.

"Yours is not to understand why, but to consider the offer and put it to your client," Morriarty said. "Death or life is all you need to consider."

"Wait a minute here," said Anna. "You're prepared to deal a guilty for a testimony? I must miss something here. You say an open and shut case on three, which includes Billy Humphries. You say you are going all the way and Billy will be on death row as soon as he can whistle Dixie." She paused for a moment. "You know what I think? I think your case is looking rocky."

There was no response from either of the prosecutors, both avoiding eye contact. Morriarty, uneasy, squirmed in his chair.

"You must be missing something."

Anna suspected Morriarty was on shaky ground.

"The worst crime ever to hit this city and you have trouble putting a case together. This will threaten your careers if you don't get convictions. And we all know what your career track is Jonathan, don't we dear?"

"Anna, take this deal." There was threat in Morriarty's tone.

"You've got nothing on my guy, have you?"

"Humphries will go all the way," Hennessy said.

"Bullshit, lady. You have a weak case on him, and you want me to deal."

"Anna," Jonathan declared, leaving her open-mouthed, distracted by his tone. "We have your guy, and he'll go all the way if you don't take this deal. I am asking you… no, I'm pleading with you, take the deal."

It must have taken an awful lot for Jonathan to offer the deal and then almost beg for it to be accepted. Anna scratched her head. "I'll put it to my client," she said, rising from her seat collecting her files. "I'll offer it to Humphries, but I don't fancy your chances."

"You must think long and hard about this offer, Anna," Morriarty said as she walked to the door with Kramer in tow. "Convince him to take it. You must."

"We'll call you." Was the reply over her shoulder as she strode from the room.

"See you in court counselor." Was all Kramer could think of saying as he scurried out behind her.

"What do you think?" asked Hennessy.

"For their own sake I hope they take the deal," replied a glum Morriarty.

Kramer caught up with Anna at the reception. It wasn't until they were alone in the elevator they spoke.

"What the hell was all that about?" Anna asked.

"Well, as Morriarty said, they want to make certain of two convictions from the testimony of the other two. Two bad guys for long jail terms and the other two face the chamber," Kramer surmised. "It's called pragmatic law."

"I don't understand."

"They jab two to pacify the executionists in government who want revenge. And jail the other two to quell the right to lifers."

"Do they have enough to convict Humphries?"

"Most likely." Kramer jangled coins in his pocket.

"Then what do we do?"

The elevator reached the ground floor, and the doors slid open.

"We do the deal

CHAPTER
30

Anna fidgeted in the interview room, waiting for Billy. Still not used to visiting the miserable place she felt a chill. The stink, the isolation, the intimidation was enough to send another shiver through her. She doubted whether jail was a place of rehabilitation.

Anna shuffled her feet, trying to get warm, wiping her nose, trying to lessen the stench. The stench was like that of a well-used, rarely cleaned public washroom. Nothing could compare with the smell of death. The population of Donovan is the living dead. No prospects, no future, and comatose to the gift of living.

The door swung open. Billy shuffled in, shackled and pathetic in his orange prison garb. He hoped for good news as he took his place at the table. His eyes flicked to Anna, seeking a sign. Any sign. Her silence was unbearable. Anna needed to urge Billy to save his life and spend the next twenty years in jail. Billy wanted to learn when he could go home.

"Billy," Anna started, choosing her words with care. Billy alerted himself, seeking eye contact. She did not glance up from her gaze at the table. "You say you did not take part in the assault on Mrs. Moroni. You said you tried to save her, didn't you?"

"Yeah, like I told you."

Turned off by his denial, she got up and moved behind him to hide from his gaze, freeing herself of suspicious, disbelieving facial gestures. "You realize, I'm required to defend you to the best of my ability and my feelings about what happened have no impact on my work for you, don't you?" Billy bounced his head around, confused. "So, it's with reluctance I seek your advice and instruction how you wish me to go ahead."

"What does all that mean, ma'am?"

Anna raised a hand to the bridge of her nose and pushed her thumb and forefinger into her closed eyes, rubbing back and forward. She breathed through her nose and let out an almost silent sigh.

"Today I met with the District Attorney. He is prepared to do a deal if you turn testimony against the others. This means, if you admit your guilt, you will not die. You will get twenty years to reflect on it."

"But I didn't do nothin'."

"Yeah, I know." Anna now irritated by his bleating of denial. "You can save yourself. You have a slender chance to live, and you can only do this if you agree to the deal. If you don't, well, they will execute you. It's as simple and as complicated as that."

"I'm innocent."

"Oh, for Christ's sake, Billy, wake up to yourself. I know. You know... Christ, the entire city knows you're guilty. All I get from you is this weak, hopeless cry '*I'm innocent*'. Don't you have any pride left?"

He didn't grasp any of her words, wondering why his defense counsel was keen for him to accept the guilty proposition. He was innocent, yet she wanted him to plead guilty. Twenty years in a jail. There was no choice.

"I'm innocent," Billy repeated. "I didn't touch her."

"What answer do you want me to give?" Anna now curt and tired. "Do you want me to plead guilty? Do you want me to accept the D.A.'s offer or do you prefer to take a chance with death? You choose."

Billy sunk into his body. "I am innocent."

Anna circled the room. "What's it going to be boy?" she asked, losing patience and keen to move onto more positive things.

Billy was quiet. He scuffed his feet across the floor, jangling the chains about him. His head hung low. "No deals," he whispered. "I'm innocent."

It didn't surprise Anna. The small mind of her client couldn't figure out the consequences. He thought he was innocent, and he wanted to tell his story. The court would hear his version of what happened and release him.

"Billy, I must tell you, as your counsel, the course you are taking will test your nerve and those who support you." Anna said. "I say to you, your case will be difficult to win. The evidence against you implicates you. Please consider your instruction to me. You must understand what will happen if the jury does not accept your plea of innocence. They will find you guilty and the only alternative is death."

She hesitated to see if the information registered.

"Based on the evidence, I suspect you are culpable but, I give you this promise. I'll defend you as if you weren't. And if I do, then you may get lucky... but I doubt it." She began collecting her things. "The preliminary hearing is tomorrow at ten. I'll see you then and don't talk to anyone." Anna collected her case and left, leaving a reflective Billy staring at nothing in particular.

"It was the Capellis. I did nothin'," he muttered to no one. "They did it, not me."

"Come on, son." The guard kicked himself off the wall by the door and ambled over to a despondent Billy. "Let's get you back to your cell and you can think about telling them all about it in court tomorrow."

Billy shuffled off with his guardian, returning to the lifelessness of his cell. He fantasized about ending the pain, but suicide was too easy. He needed to be heard, not buried. He needed to tell his story. He was innocent of the crime.

As he passed through the remand section, he looked at the future. Innocence would have him home. A life without his pal Max. A life of petty crime. No hope, no future, no life. A shroud of darkness crept through him, and he shrugged his shoulders. Perhaps twenty years inside was a realistic choice and not so bad.

Relieved of his chains, Billy curled up tight on his cot and disappeared into his world of uncertainty. Tomorrow will be better.

CHAPTER
31

The hustle and bustle along the corridors of the courts can be a lonely affair. Unattached people brush past without the common courtesy of civilized acknowledgement. Lawyers, with dogged zeal, rush to meet clients for a last briefing. No hellos or good mornings, no smiles in this place. People rush about, concerned about their day in court, when they put their faith in the justice system.

Suits and denims flashed past each other. Floral dresses adding occasional color to the dark scene, as citizens went about their day. Busy focused people trying to make sense of the law. Guilt and innocence standing together on the precipice of an unknown future, only the law to prevail, justice left to seek alternative arrangements.

Anna waited for Kramer to appear from a courtroom so she could receive his final briefing. A public defender never had the luxury of an office tower to discuss cases. Today Kramer would appear in five cases, all before lunch. Anna knew their briefing would be a simple hello and good luck, but she wished for affirmation. It had been a long time since she came close to advocating before a judge, and she was nervous.

Though not as anxious as the man, stubbing out a cigarette before lighting another by the marble stairs. She studied him as she waited. Men come and go. You bump into them in cafes, on buses and court-houses. Only a few excites the imagination, as this man did for Anna.

"Who are you looking at?" Kramer startled her, almost dropping her papers.

"Christ, Kramer. If it's not the telephone, you're creeping up on people. Where the hell have you been?"

"Oh, saving clients from themselves. You ready?"

"As ever I will be, I suppose."

"Anna, you'll be okay. It's only a preliminary and nothing will happen. You'll be in there five minutes, max."

"Yeah, I know. But I'm still confused by our meeting yesterday, and Humphries is getting to me a bit. I don't know whether I'm fit for the job."

"You are, and I'll tell you why. You are a brilliant advocate, Anna, and this case will give you the confidence to come back. You're wasting your time in escrow, so today is the first day of the rest of your life. Suck it in and enjoy."

"I hope you're right."

"I am, you'll see. Gotta go. Call me when you're done." He merged into the bustling crowd and gone. Anna checked to see if she could catch another glimpse of her mystery man. He too had disappeared.

The boys slumped at the defendant's table, entwined with lawyers. Arnie appeared smug, arrogant, whilst his brothers watched, uneasy about their fate. Billy's demeanor faded to a shadow of his normal self, as if he wasn't even there. Perhaps, in his mind, he wasn't.

Anna sat at the end of the table, toward the center of the room, still perplexed by Morriarty's offer the previous day. Perhaps he thought the brothers wouldn't give a convincing testimony against each other. Maybe Morriarty needed another witness?

The prosecutors worked their files at an adjacent table. Hennessy waited for the nominal procedure to begin. She hoped the charade of feigned work hid her nerves. Beside her worked Lawrence Jordan, a tall, young African American, scrutinizing papers.

Support staff sat in the public gallery, behind the prosecutors and behind them sat impatient arresting police officers. Garcia, glum and concerned sat with Gayle Martinez. Family and friends, interested reporters, and voyeurs attracted to the addictive legal process filled the room. In a back corner sat an attentive Alice and Bernie Johnston.

"All rise."

O'Brien took her position under a sign attached to the back wall, *In*

God We Trust, starting a flurry of activity, attendants rushing about and lawyers gathering papers in preparation.

"Clerk." Commanded O'Brien, peering over her glasses at the assembled throng. It surprised her how many people were in attendance for the hearing, suspecting the notoriety was the reason.

A slender man stood, his uniform of the Court gaining attention and silencing the humming chatter of the gallery. "State of California versus Arnold Reginald, Brett Wilbur and Joseph Patrick Capelli and William Hubert Humphries. Court identification W 287." He sat and silence overwhelmed the room, except for the tic-toc of an enormous clock above the entry doors.

It seemed forever before O'Brien peered up from studying papers. The lawyers waited, Anna drumming her nails against her file.

"This is a preliminary hearing to decide whether the accused have a case to answer before Grand Jury deliberations. It is a procedural process and the likely motion to be heard today is the separation of the cases to individual hearings."

Anna did not want to go to trial with the others. They were guilty, and any association with the Capellis would be a certain death knell for Billy.

No one moved and waited for her. It was real life drama and the judge the director. She peered at the defense table. "Counsel, are you ready?" Silent affirmation from the table. "Counsel?"

Hennessy stood and carried her brief folder to the lectern between the two tables. "Your Honor. We have signed statements from each of the accused admitting participation in this horrendous crime. We have forty-five evidence exhibits, implicating the accused of the crime. Crime scene evidence is damning for each of the arrested."

"Charges Mrs. Hennessy?"

"We are proceeding on murder one, deprivation of liberty, assault, robbery and rape charges against Brett and Joseph Capelli and William Humphries your Honor."

"Arnold Capelli?"

Hennessy faulted slightly. "Mr. Capelli has cooperated with authorities and is prepared to offer testimony against the other three implicating them in the crime."

It surprised Anna. Morriarty said it would happen. It surprised her which Capelli would turn. The older brother was the most notorious, and this action was out of character to his hardened reputation.

"I see. What will Mr. Capelli's charge be?" O'Brien asked.

"He agreed to plead guilty to culpable murder, robbery and deprivation of liberty charges. The State believes a fifteen-year incarceration will result from his plea. We also expect the process to be completed within three weeks, given your ascendancy today Your Honor."

"Another scar to the justice system which we could have done without Mrs. Hennessy. No doubt you wish me to grant your expected motion today, without further discussion?"

"If it pleases Your Honor, yes."

"It doesn't please me, but I have no choice other than to grant you your request." The court flared up into a buzz of noise, with a multitude of conversations going on at once. Only the Johnstons didn't react. O'Brien bashed her gavel a few times and regained the order of her court.

"Defending counsel for Mr. Capelli, do you have any comment on this procedure?" asked O'Brien.

Slovak, a suburban lawyer, who appeared to be more interested in sleep than the proceedings rose in his place and agreed. "Your Honor. It is our intention to follow the path as described by prosecutors."

"Why am I not surprised?" responded O'Brien.

The brothers couldn't grasp the relevance of what happened. This was the first time they had been together since the arrest, and no one said anything to them. Billy knew someone was providing testimony, so the procedure did not surprise him. It troubled him it was Arnie when it was he and Max who murdered Mrs. Moroni. He pleaded guilty. So what? He was guilty.

"What's going on Arnie?" asked a fretting Bo.

"Why are you d-d-doing this, you b-b-bastard?" sneered Joe.

Arnie remained calm and raised a finger to his lips, giving a wink. The brothers quietened, trusting their older brother had everything under control. Capellis never squeal.

O'Brien bashed her gavel again to regain order. As the noise subsided, she ordered, "If this is the will of the parties involved, I have no choice other than to grant the request. Please remove Mr. Arnold

Capelli from the court to be dealt with on another day. And may that day be soon."

The court security officers escorted Arnie to the holding cells. He turned as he passed through the door, giving his brothers a reassuring smile.

Anna speculated about what might have been. Could she have lost her opportunity for a deal with the District Attorney, now they had a prosecuting witness against Billy? She would weaken Capelli's testimony. The D.A.'s Office must know that. She wondered whether they might approach her again before Grand Jury. If they did, she would make sure Billy did the deal.

"In summary Your Honor," Hennessy continued. "We seek the charges as outlined to be agreed, so the matter against the Capellis and Humphries can proceed to Grand Jury for further indictment."

"Yes, counselor, thank you. Before doing so, I shall seek submissions from defense counsel."

Anna waved her hand, showing another time and place for these submissions. She wanted to get out of the place. O'Brien was about to close and announce moving to Grand Jury. Before she could, the defense counsel for the Capellis stood, moving to the lectern to address the judge.

"Your Honor?"

"Yes, Mr. Brunswick."

A prominent lawyer for wanting the exactness of the law to be applied, Anthony Brunswick prepared himself for his request. "Your Honor, I beg your indulgence for just a few moments."

"Yes, Mr. Brunswick," O'Brien sighed.

"Your Honor, this is a most heinous crime. A crime that has influenced all the good citizens of the City of San Diego, my clients included. My clients feel very concerned about the outcomes of any future trial. They both wish the perpetrators of the terrible assault upon the victim..." Brunswick searched his papers for a name. "The victim, a Mrs... a Mrs..." He continued his search, scratching through the papers.

Anna speculated whether he was deliberate with his choice of words and fumbling.

"Umm... sorry Your Honor. Ah yes... here we are. Mrs. Sandra Moroni, be brought to justice."

"He can't be for real?" Anna whispered to no one in particular.

"My clients reaffirm their lack of knowledge with anything associated with her unfortunate and tragic demise."

"Bullshit." Garcia coughed into his hand, just loud enough for O'Brien to hear, and cast a severe expression in his direction.

"Order."

Anna began feeling uneasy. This is not the court to go through this type of submission. He can't be delaying for anything other than a bail application, but they would never grant this in a capital offence. She glanced toward Hennessy, who remained stoic, staring straight ahead.

"Your Honor, the state believes they associate my clients with this crime. They say they have implicated my clients in this crime due to evidence gathered during an investigation. My clients contend the evidence does not support the state's accusations and we seek your ruling on the investigative officers' lack of due process associated with the later arrest of my clients."

"Mr. Brunswick? Are you suggesting your clients are before me without due process followed by the arresting officers?"

Brunswick now baffled Anna. Nowhere in the release of evidence was there any sign of process not being followed. Where was her colleague heading? She wondered how this would impact Billy. It could be his way out.

"Exactly, Your Honor. Given your indulgence, I will put before you proof the arresting officers neglected their duty and got evidence and statements by not following due process requirements. If you agree, Your Honor, I will move a motion of dismissal for my clients to be released without further delay."

"Objection." Jordan surged to his feet. "Your Honor this is irrelevant to this hearing. We completed all arrest procedures and I submit this issue does not belong in this court."

"Your Honor," Brunswick over spoke Jordan. "The key evidence against my clients are articles of clothing bearing alleged blood samples of the deceased. The state also has an alleged personal item of the deceased found in my clients' possession. They also have alleged incriminating confessions."

"Is that about it Mr. Jordan? Is Mr. Brunswick correct in his analysis of the state's case against his clients?"

The prosecutors conferred. "Yes, Your Honor. We base our case on the evidence and statements as described by defense counsel. We also have a witness willing to testify. That of Arnold Capelli who is pleading guilty, having processed earlier."

"Well then counselor what is he talking about?"

"Your Honor. We have statements from arresting officers confirming all necessary procedures followed. We have a video record of Miranda being given prior to questioning. I don't know where defense counsel is going with this. I think he is blowing into the wind hoping to stop the storm building against his clients."

"Let's hope Mr. Brunswick doesn't rain on your parade, Mr. Jordan."

O'Brien was an experienced judge who had been at the bench for thirty years. She witnessed the diminishing and virtual destruction of the system of justice by the manipulation of the law to suit the defendants' needs.

"Mr. Brunswick, normally this court would not be engaged in this type of motion. However, I will allow it until I believe you are stepping over the line. Please continue and support your claim."

"Thank you, Your Honor. Can I lead Your Honor to the case of State versus Hilmer? Reference 85634. In this case, it was determined that..."

"What was that number again?" O'Brien asked, ensuring the clerk of the court could access the judgement.

'85634.'

"Proceed."

"They found the arresting officers did not complete warrants prior to the arrest of Hilmer and the subsequent seizure of incriminating evidence. In the case, the prosecutors based their entire case on the evidence seized and relied on supporting statements made by Hilmer when faced in a police interview with the evidence. He cooperated with police once they confronted him with the evidence. Without the evidence, he would not have given a statement implicating himself. The prosecution also secured a confirming witness, who they identified from the alleged evidence collected during the arrest of Hilmer."

"Your Honor," interrupted Jordan. "This lesson in California case law is remarkable, but it has nothing to do with the case before you. They followed the procedure of arrest for the Capellis. If required, I have in court the arresting officer to confirm the police action."

Garcia glanced at Martinez. She smiled and nodded, showing there was nothing to worry about.

"Mr. Brunswick, please get to your point. You are trying the court's patience at the moment."

The clerk flicked through references on the computer, trying to locate the Hilmer case and its judgement. The prosecutors were doing the same on an iPad. Anna sat bemused about the proceedings, hoping this motion helped her man. O'Brien was not aware of the case and needed to read it to prepare herself for a response.

"Your Honor, the presiding officer in Hilmer reviewed the submission of the defense counsel and found it to have a substantial influence on the bearing of the case before him. As you can see by the judgement, may I approach?"

"Please." O'Brien was keen to get a copy.

Brunswick approached the bench, passing a copy of the judgement made by the presiding officer, Judge Waylan Jones. O'Brien took her time to study it. After a brief delay she raised her head and removed her spectacles, putting one arm of the glasses into her mouth deep in thought, pondering the judgement and how it affected upon the case before her.

"You'll need more than this Mr. Brunswick."

"Your Honor," Brunswick said. "The judge in the Hilmer decided all evidence gathered from unlawful police conduct was inadmissible. Any statements or evidence given..." Brunswick now read from the judgement. 'After unlawful police process were invalid contravening the Constitution and its clear direction on the rights of the individual." Brunswick paused. "Judge Jones dismissed the case, citing no case to answer."

"Your Honor, with deep respect to my colleague, where are we heading with this? This is a preliminary hearing; we should not be moving motions like this." Jordon asked.

"Oh, I quite agree, Mr. Jordan," said O'Brien, placing her spectacles down and sitting forward in her chair. "The point Mr. Brunswick has not made, and I will, is that they dismissed the case he cites at preliminary. Please continue Mr. Brunswick."

Jordan resumed his seat, engaging Hennessy in muffled discussion.

Anna felt anxious.

Garcia concerned with the conversation.

The Johnstons did not know what was going on but remained attentive.

"It is my submission, Your Honor; based on allegation alone, not fact; not confirmed suspicion; not even assumed guilt; just cause principles for the arrest and seizure did not exist. Just on allegation alone, the police officers sought a warrant to arrest my clients and then search my clients' residence. They then found alleged damaging evidence, which the state has based its entire case against my clients."

Jordan interrupted again. "Your Honor this is becoming tiresome. We can confirm the procedure. All is relevant, the systems have complied and followed as procedure requires. The defense has nothing, and I ask you to finish this charade so that we may move onto more important things in our day."

"I hear you Mr. Jordan, and I am sympathetic, but I overrule. Mr. Brunswick, are you going anywhere with this?"

"I do not dispute my colleague's statement Your Honor. In fact, I welcome it, as it confirms my submission."

"How so? Please explain."

"Your Honor, unfortunate for the prosecution, the warrants police used for the arrests were signed four hours after they made arrests, thus rendering all earlier action and statements illegal."

The court burst into noisy discussion.

Both prosecutors now on their feet shouting objections as Brunswick resumed his seat. Spectators in the gallery, ignoring protocol, raised their voices in disbelief. Garcia remained seated with his head is his hands. "Oh, Christ Richard what have we done?" Martinez slumped back on the bench, remembering her last words as she stormed out of the squad room. They assigned the completed paperwork to Sylvester.

He didn't get it done.

Anna sat bewildered, oblivious to the bedlam about her. It puzzled her at what was happening. Her entire defense strategy had just blown apart, and it now she faced the awful prospect of the full weight of the legal system falling down on Billy. Rightly or wrongly, it was not fair this could happen. Her incredulity toward the justice system continued as she understood what was to follow.

"Order," O'Brien shouted, bashing her gavel even harder and louder. "Order! Order! Order, or I shall be forced to clear the court. Order!"

Brunswick waited, anticipating a return to silence.

As the hullabaloo subsided, he rose to deliver his final and most telling statement. A statement which would no doubt bring him notoriety for the rest of his career. "Your Honor, based upon precedence and the clear evidence now before you of unlawful arrest procedure, I ask all charges against my clients to be dismissed forthwith. I ask they be given leave to join their loved ones."

Brunswick resumed his seat.

The silent tension of his words hung in the air. The pressure of anticipation could not withstand much more as the gallery waited for the response. Spectators moved to the edge of their seats, craning for a view of the judge. O'Brien knew what the law compelled her to do. She delayed her response as she considered alternatives open for her to follow. There were none.

"Mr. Brunswick, there is no doubt in my mind as to the guilt or otherwise of your clients. A heinous crime committed, and it's clear from the detail before me your clients were involved. No amount of bleating or cries of innocence will convince me otherwise. They need to be punished and justice needs to be seen to be done."

Her declaration startled Brunswick, and he stirred to object to the judge's statement. He considered it overstepping judicial freedom. Before he could do so, O'Brien continued.

"I order the case of the State versus Humphries to be referred to Grand Jury. I also order, that both cases referring to Brett and Joseph Capelli be dismissed. Sadly, you are both free to go. May God forgive all of us who have had a hand in this miscarriage of justice."

O'Brien smashed her gavel and left for chambers, allowing little time for those in attendance to rise in their place.

Fuss and confusion erupted in the court. Hennessy stunned, turned to Jordan alarm in her eyes. The confident prosecutor had just had the biggest case to hit the city overturned before it moved to Grand Jury. A mistake from an arresting officer, minor in its significance to the case but absolute in its impact. The prosecutors packed their files, beginning the slow chore of preparing their minds for the buzzing media pack waiting to ask them questions.

"What does it mean, Bernie?" a weeping Alice Johnston asked, her ashen faced husband.

"No justice for Sandi. The bastards will never come to court for murdering our baby."

Anna could say nothing as she remained at her place at the table. Her feelings now askew as she mulled over how the justice system could become so ramshackle where murderers could be let free and never face court. Guards led Billy off with no acknowledgement from her. Her view of justice had taken a backward step and well trampled.

She rose, collecting her files and papers. As she left the court, her breath gave a quick gasp. Before her sat the rugged man she had seen earlier. His tousled hair entwined with his fingers. She walked past him without gaining eye contact.

CHAPTER
32

Six months after a Grand Jury hearing, a three-week trial considered all the evidence in the Moroni case. None of it implicated Billy, and the jury agreed. They knew he didn't do it but could not agree on his absolute innocence. So, they declared it a mistrial with a further date for re-trial listed twelve months later, reducing the media hype.

The San Diego Tribune began taking Billy's side in the case, contrary to its editorials at the time of the crime. The evidence convinced the editorial staff of Billy's non-participation in the crime and advocated an innocent verdict. Yes, Humphries was there; and yes, guilty of witnessing the crime, but he wasn't guilty of the murder charges.

The Tribune did not support Morriarty's aspirations for political office, considering this case an opportunity to bring him to heel. Their aggressive position against him allowed the City Mayor, Gerard Wilton, to begin a campaign toward his own higher political goals.

Another court found Arnie Capelli guilty and sentenced him to fifteen years, as agreed with the District Attorney. It satisfied Bernie Johnston, although Capelli would not face the death penalty. Someone needed to pay.

Joey Capelli may have walked from the court a free man after it dismissed his case. It wasn't long before he was again before the court. Three months after the Moroni preliminary hearing, he received a seven-year sentence for armed robbery.

Bo also fell afoul of the law. His simple mind never grasping the difference between a consenting adult and a non-consenting teenager. Found guilty almost a year after the murder for raping a fifteen-year-old schoolgirl and sentenced to ten years' jail.

Anna was even more determined in the second trial. Hennessy had not changed her approach to the case, and it was almost as if she read from the same case notes. Because of this predictable presentation, Anna could expect the evidence and present a good enough case to return a not guilty verdict. Anna remained confident the jury would acquit.

The jury again remained deadlocked.

After three days of deliberation, they returned to deliver a statement to the court. The foreman advised his fellow jurors could not and would not decide. He then went onto criticize the prosecution and the case for the defense. The jury remained unconvinced with the arguments, thus forcing it into an untenable position of not being able to decide for or against the accused. The foreman believed the evidence sloppy and witnesses for the defense irrelevant.

Morriarty's career waited in the balance and needed a conviction to make sure it did not sully his reputation forever. Another hung jury would mean Humphries walks free, leaving no one to be convicted of the murder. He could then kiss his political plans goodbye. He decided to prosecute the case himself when it appeared before the court again. All this placed stress on his future, and the one person standing between him and political success was none other than Anna Booth. What irony, to be foiled by the very person who may have once guaranteed his greater success.

"Mr. Johnston, I can assure you we will convict." Morriarty was sitting at his desk in another meeting with Sandi's father. "I will prosecute, and I can promise you, I do not intend to let you down."

"Yes, yes." Bernie remained impatient. "I have heard all of this before, and I am not convinced. It was you who did the deal with Capelli in the first place, and now all we can look forward to is his fifteen years. Is that fair?" He remained angry and frustrated with the system for letting his daughter down. He wanted justice and needed to make those who murdered Sandi suffer. He would not rest until he achieved retribution.

"I can understand how you feel Mr. Johnston, but you..."

"No, you don't Morriarty." Bernie slapped the desk. "You do not know how I feel. If you don't get a result with this murderer, I will start action against you and your department."

"What?"

"Oh yes. I have already sought legal advice. Unless you secure a conviction, I am taking civil litigation against you, citing negligence. You have a duty of care to do your job and you haven't."

"You can't do that."

"Oh yes, I can. If I don't succeed, then neither will you. I think the publicity will kill your career. Mister, you'll never see the Governor's office."

"Don't threaten me." Morriarty waved him away.

"Don't you let Sandi down." He left, slamming the door, leaving Morriarty with his open files. He must win.

CHAPTER
33

"We're going to win, aren't we?" Billy listened to Anna advising him of the options about the next trial. "I have two chances of getting off and only one chance of being found guilty."

"Now Billy, we still have a long way to go."

"Yeah, but I can see the end. A jury can't convict me with what the D.A. has. I mean twice they tried and failed. So, they will either find me not guilty, or it'll be a hung jury. I get off anyway."

"They could find you guilty."

"Yeah, that's true. If they found me guilty, I would never get the jab, not after all the trials." He grasped Anna's advice but remained confident a murder conviction did not mean a death sentence.

"As far as the public thinks, they consider you guilty and demand a conviction." Anna said, hopeful of securing an acquittal but remaining anxious. She hovered in an emotional bind about the case. Keen to offer an adequate defense, she remained concerned about absence of justice for Sandi.

"What do you expect the District Attorney will do differently this time? Do you think we should try anything new?" asked Billy.

"Oh, I suspect the big guns will come out. No doubt Morriarty will prosecute. Too much riding on the result for him. It wouldn't surprise me if they dig up further evidence against you."

"What could they have?"

"They need a link with you taking part in the crime, so maybe they will get more evidence. They haven't advised of anything new; and anyway, they have to declare pre-trial. They are changing the police investigation witness."

"Who to?"

"Gayle Martinez transferred, and she is unavailable to take the stand. They plan to use a Detective Nicolas Garcia as their witness. Do you know him?"

"Yeah, he was the guy who killed Max. He bashed me."

"No wonder he hasn't been on the witness list. They didn't want other issues to cloud the case against you." Anna decided a visit to Detective Garcia to find out if his evidence would differ from the other detective. "No matter. We know their evidence and we can answer any claims. Too much doubt and the only result can be acquittal."

"I hope you're right."

Anna left Donovan reflecting on Billy's chances of acquittal; he had matured so much since they first met. Gone the sniveling little boy, who would whine about his innocence, to be replaced by a young man looking forward to the future confident of being given another opportunity; but she remained uncertain.

It had just gone midday as Anna parked outside the station house in La Jolla. She collected her briefcase and made her way into the building, tracking her way to the detective squad room's reception.

"Can I help y'all?" asked a chirpy Bonnie.

"Yes, I am here to see Detective Nicolas Garcia, if he is available." Anna scanned the room, checking the detectives working at their desks.

"He is in. Who shall I say is calling?"

"My name is Anna Booth. I am defense counsel in the Moroni case."

Bonnie's cheerful smile evaporated. She sauntered off, searching for Garcia, finding him by the vendor machine, picking up cigarettes. "Nicolas, a woman wants to see you."

"Are you sure? Women don't want to see me. What does she want?"

"She's the attorney for the scumbag who killed Richard."

"Oh Booth. I thought it wouldn't be long before she appeared."

"How can you be so easy about it?"

"Bonnie honey, no one feels more badly about Rich than I do, but her guy didn't do it. He didn't do the other one either, but they'll find him guilty, mark my words."

"Why does she want to see you?"

"Gayle's not giving evidence in the next trial. The D.A. thinks I should do it this time."

"You watch yourself, Nicolas. Her skirt is too short for my liking."

"You have no worries honey; I'm waiting for you."

Bonnie walked off, smiling, throwing him an extra wiggle as she strolled back to her desk. She enjoyed teasing him and appreciated the compliments. A little flirting didn't hurt.

Garcia took his time. He didn't want to see Booth. The picture of his partner laying in his arms lingered with him most nights. No matter how much he cleaned them, his hands still carried the memory of his friend. Richard's mistake was his mistake, and he battled not to blame himself. He took a heavy drag on a cigarette and sauntered back to the squad room.

Anna sat on a bench, waiting. The receptionist came back, smiling, giving her a curt direction to wait.

"Hello Miss Booth, how are you?"

The tousled hair was a dead giveaway. The fellow who made her gasp a few years back was now before her, extending a hand of welcome. The man who seemed so lost and troubled in the hallways of the courthouse was now trying to touch her. She gazed open-eyed unaware her mouth was agape.

Anna struggled to smile and stood to accept his handshake. Her knee buckled and as she righted herself, her brief case thumped to the floor, bursting open, spewing papers across the tiles.

They both collapsed to recover the sheets, clashing heads sending Anna sprawling leaving very few secrets.

Now on her knees, Anna held the briefcase under one bent arm, rubbing her head, retrieving papers with the other free hand.

"Oh, I'm sorry. Clumsy me."

"Are you okay? I'm sorry, how is your head? You had better sit down."

"No, I'm okay. Just a little out of control at the moment."

This man was taking her back to the days when she was a teenager. She got herself together and stood, thrusting out her hand.

"Let's start again. Hi, my name is Anna Booth. Detective Garcia, I want to talk to you about the upcoming trial. How are you?" She wasn't in control just yet.

Her anxiety bemused Garcia. He took her hand, trying to give reassurance and having the opposite effect; he knew it and remained charmed by it. Could this woman be a defense attorney? If she was, then heaven help her clients.

Anna was feeling her knees about to buckle again as Garcia held her hand. She couldn't understand how easily her poise disappeared. *Get out.* That was what her head was shouting to her. It was loud and clear. Get out before she embarrassed herself even further. Make another time when she could speak. Smile and get out. Get out and come back later.

"Would you mind if we had lunch together? I don't know about you, but I'm starved. I'd prefer to talk with you over a coffee," Garcia said.

Anna frowned, then grinned. "I'd love to."

CHAPTER
34

The State of California versus Humphries came to Court 17. The room overflowed with spectators, including media representatives from most national organizations. Billy had become a cause celebre for a group of right to life advocates supporting him. No one doubted his guilt; many doubted whether he should face a mandatory death sentence if found guilty. Victims of major crime had been vocal during the trials demanding greater respect from lawmakers, and many attended the courthouse.

Judge Ryan King was not looking forward to presiding in the Humphries case. He shied from taking a high profile within the legal system; always ruing the increased publicity trials received. Court was not a circus, yet it had become an entertainment vehicle.

After comprehensive opening statements by counsel, Judge King invited Morriarty to call his first witness.

"Your Honor, The People call, Detective Inspector Nicolas Garcia."

The call from the clerk rang out; the drama opened. Anna felt uneasy as Garcia walked to the witness stand. She hadn't spoken to him about the case during the occasions they shared since their first luncheon. She was very aware of the potential impropriety. Nic, ever the pragmatist, reassured her they would not share a thought, let alone a word about the case until concluded. And they never did. She understood he would fight hard for a guilty verdict to account for the death of his partner.

Anna concentrated on her notes, doodling as Garcia completed swearing-in formalities. She took pains not to glimpse at him, trying to display a picture of professional efficiency. Her short, panting breath the only sign of discomfort.

"You okay Anna?" Billy asked.

"Yeah." She flicked her pen away and glanced at the witness.

Morriarty began. "Detective Garcia could you please lead us through the process of discovery, investigation and the arrest procedure with the murder of Mrs. Sandra Moroni."

His words were deliberate, wanting the jury to understand the magnitude of the case very early in the trial. His job was to make sure they never forget they were in a murder trial.

A victim suffered at the hands of a murderer; it was their job to convict.

Over the next two hours, Garcia worked through the entire investigation. He highlighted the assault at the West Coast Lagoon, implying Billy had been an active participant.

Anna objected to much of the evidence, often overruled. She knew she was in for a tough battle, as Garcia introduced each of the prosecution exhibits with more detail than in earlier trials. Jury members seemed persuaded by the tale Garcia constructed, much more than Martinez in the earlier trials. He was convincing. Her work would be tough.

Garcia described the forensic evidence implicating Billy. He followed the questions and probing of Morriarty to complete a picture of Billy belonging to a wild gang who cared little for humanity, taking their animal savagery out on an innocent woman. Not content with having their savage way with her, they then murdered her in a most brutal and sadistic way.

"Your witness, counselor," Morriarty said, finalizing his questions.

Anna paused before standing, nervous about what she must do.

"Detective, you state that... um." She tried hard to avoid eye contact. "You... ah..." She glanced through her papers and there was a long pause.

The gallery became restless, embarrassed by Anna's delay. She readied herself, gaining control as Garcia waited for battle. He was a professional who put business ahead of any personal feelings.

"Detective, you say you are an experienced homicide investigator."

"Yes, ma'am."

"You also say you can track a killer. And like our Canadian Mountie friends, you always get your man, is this correct?" Anna asked in a disarming tone.

"Yes, ma'am."

"And in this case Detective, you are positive you have your man? Just like all your cases?"

"Yes, ma'am."

"You always succeed don't you Detective? In fact, you have an arrest record better than most, don't you?"

"Better than most, yes ma'am."

"You are a detective of repute and the prosecution base this entire case on your team's investigation, doesn't it? I mean, you say you have your killer, and we should believe you based upon your reputation."

"Yes, ma'am." He wondered where she was leading. "And the evidence."

"Detective, do you recall Harvey Schulman?"

"Ma'am?"

Morriarty's frenetic clicking of his pen betrayed him.

"Harvey Schulman. Do you remember him?"

"I'm uncertain ma'am." Garcia felt a sharp, stressful tightening of his abdomen. An uneasy dryness overcame his mouth, and he cleared his throat, shifted in his seat, and wiped his upper lip.

"You're uncertain? Surely not, detective?" Anna mocked him with a belittling hand gesture. "A record trumpeted, and you can't remember Harvey Schulman?"

"Objection. Relevance?"

"I'm interested in the answer counselor, objection overruled," Judge King said. "I caution defense counsel to lead us to a result soon."

"Thank you, Your Honor." Anna moved closer to Garcia, placing a reassuring hand on the rail in front of him. Garcia knew what was coming and couldn't stop it. Her gesture adding to his discomfort.

"Let me remind you, if I may detective." She moved to face the jury. "Harvey Schulman convicted of rape and sentenced to twenty-five years, before an appeal overturned the decision. He ended up serving ten years in a prison and yet he was an innocent man. Once released, Mr. Schulman litigated against the State of California. In fact, he settled out of court for a reported five million dollars. Do you recall this at all?"

"Maybe."

"Maybe?" Anna reeled back to her desk in mock astonishment. "Just maybe Detective?"

"I may have a small recollection of a case, as you described. But I can't be certain."

"Oh, I am sure you can do better than that. Were you not the investigating officer?"

After a long pause, Garcia softly said, "Yes ma'am, I was."

"Were you not arraigned after the civil action? Were you not charged with manufacturing evidence and witness tampering? Quite serious charges are they not?"

"They cleared me of all charges." Garcia clutched his hands, twisting them.

"Yes, you were cleared, weren't you?"

"The facts were, that Schulman was a member of a gang which perpetrated a crime against a fifteen-year-old girl. We had three witnesses and solid evidence implicating him and a jury found him guilty."

"And in your mind, he was guilty?"

"The jury thought so."

"But Detective, you forget, don't you? The prosecution withheld evidence which would have cleared Mr. Schulman from the trial."

"It was not relevant to the case against Schulman."

"Not relevant? Who decided that position?"

"I did."

"You decided important evidence was not relevant?"

"It wasn't supported and was circumstantial."

"Circumstantial?" Anna raised her voice almost shouting. "Evidence withheld placing Schulman elsewhere, because you thought it circumstantial?"

Silence.

"Detective you stuffed that investigation. Who's to say you haven't stuffed this one?"

"Objection. Your Honor, this has nothing to do with the case before you." Morriarty wanted an end to the line of questioning.

"Your Honor, the investigative officer has a history of poor police procedures in a similar case. I want to test the veracity of his testimony." Anna sounded convincing.

"Overruled."

"Well Detective," Anna approached the witness. "Who's to say you haven't got it wrong this time?"

"I haven't."

"Not got the wrong man?"

"The evidence supports the arrest."

"But you even got that wrong, didn't you?" Anna knew it wounded him but pressed on. "Two dead; one a suspect and the other your partner."

Silence. Garcia's face winced.

"You have incomplete arrest warrants, allowing the principals of the gang, prime suspects, to walk free. You have..."

"Objection."

"Overruled."

"Now you sit before me trying to convince the jury you have the man that did the murder. Did my client kill Sandi Moroni?"

"He was there, and he took part."

"Did he use the knife on Mrs. Moroni?"

"No."

"Objection. Badgering."

"Overruled."

"The fact is detective; you have no facts or evidence to support your assertion my client was even at the crime scene. You got it wrong before, didn't you?" Anna paused for a moment. "Detective are you sure this time?"

"Yes."

"You are convinced? You believe the accused is the murderer?"

"Yes."

"No evidence, and you're convinced?"

"Yes."

"Not left something off the paperwork?"

"No."

"Objection! Your Honor, please?"

"Move on counselor," King advised Anna.

"Detective Garcia, did William Humphries murder Sandi Moroni?"

"He was there."

"Is he guilty of murdering her? Did he take the knife and cut her throat? Did he end her life?"

Garcia paused. Looked at Judge King but received no guidance. Turned to the jury and said, "He may not have used the knife, but he was there. He's guilty."

"So, you cannot point to solid evidence to convince the jury Billy Humphries committed the murder? If you can, please do so?"

"He was there."

"Evidence?"

"He was there counselor."

"You cannot say whether he even assaulted Mrs. Moroni, can you?"

Garcia didn't respond.

"Detective, have you tried to cut Billy Humphries from the investigation? Innocent until proven guilty?"

"No."

"Why not?"

"He was part of a gang; he was there. He was part of it."

"Do you have evidence, concrete evidence, he was at the crime site?"

"No."

"And you still think he is guilty?"

"Yes."

"You're convinced?"

"Yes."

"Based upon what evidence?"

"He was there."

"Do you have any evidence at all? Anything that will support your claims?"

"We have witnesses confirming he was with the gang and at the scene."

"He may have been there detective, but are you convinced he murdered Sandi Moroni?"

"Yes."

"You were convinced in the Schulman case too, weren't you? No further questions."

"Detective Garcia," queried Morriarty in redirect. "Does the evidence you presented today; support your assertion the accused is guilty."

Garcia paused, his head dropped, then he raised it and gazed at Anna. "No doubt in my mind, sir."

"Thank you. Nothing further."

"Witness is excused. Next witness, Mr. Morriarty."

"The People call Thomas Moroni."

Anna quivered as Garcia left the witness box, stalking past her without acknowledgement. She needed to cast doubt on the investigation process and their confrontation had been unfortunate; if the arresting officer places doubt on the guilt of the accused, then the jury must acquit.

Any hope of a not guilty verdict depended on reasonable doubt and Anna's skill in bringing as much doubt as she could to the jury of seven women and five men.

There had been no alternative.

She had to discredit him, and she felt troubled at having done so. Her client must come first, before any personal feelings.

As she tried to concentrate on the emotional testimony of Sandi's husband, she felt her phone buzz with a text in her jacket. She couldn't think what it was about, covertly withdrawing it onto her lap under the table and peeked at the screen.

Congratulations Counselor on a solid cross examination.
I am very proud of you. Nicolas X.

She smiled, slipping the phone into her leather compendium. Perhaps she had underestimated Nicolas Garcia.

"Counselor, are you with us?" King's booming voice came into Anna's consciousness. "Your witness, for the third time."

A startled Anna regained her composure. "No questions, Your Honor."

The prosecution's case set about establishing Billy's involvement in all gang activities on the evening of the attack and established a solid case. Witness after witness provided a compelling argument for finding Billy guilty. Anna discredited much of the testimony by raising doubt through circumstantial evidence; but the graphic image of a young woman coming to a brutal end remained paramount throughout much of the testimony.

Rudi Curtis' evidence was damning on this occasion; more than the earlier trials because he added more color to his testimony. He described Billy, when in other trials he was unsure. No amount of prying, doubting, or probing from Anna could change his view of what he thought he had seen. He embellished enough to suggest Billy had a leading role. The reality was, he hadn't seen him. The image of Sandi running from the bar in distress lingered with the jury after the Curtis testimony.

Morriarty establishing a solid case against Billy with witnesses by painstaking questions and introducing exhibits. Barbara Smethers through her tears blamed herself for what had happened. Subtle dabbing of eyes by several jurors during her evidence showed sentiment favoring the prosecution.

Judge King adjourned for the day after Smethers left the stand. Anna considered day one had been an equal contest considering the number of witnesses testifying against Billy, but she worried she needed a breakthrough to move the testimony back, favoring Billy. Malaxos was the key.

CHAPTER
35

A confident Dr. Charles Malaxos settled into the witness chair, preparing himself for his testimony, hoping it would seal a conviction. He did not doubt the evidence and knew Humphries to be guilty. In his mind, science was never wrong.

"I arrived at the crime scene and sealed the area. I discovered a naked female body displaying severe injuries and a large quantity of discharged blood. Insect activity was prevalent, developing into tertiary stages. From this insect activity, and the greenish red skin color of the head and chest plus the advanced stage of skin blisters, I estimated time of death between eleven thirty and twelve midnight the previous Saturday evening. Rigor was well advanced; the body swollen and facial features diminishing."

No matter how many times Anna had heard it, it upset her. Those listening to the testimony for the first time would find it harrowing.

Malaxos was a good prosecution witness working the jury well by reinforcing particular points. He often removed his glasses and looked straight at them, emphasizing important information.

"After approval from the investigating officers, I removed the deceased, transferring her to the city morgue. Twenty-four hours later I performed the autopsy."

"What were your findings doctor?" asked Morriarty.

"The deceased had extensive injuries to most parts of her body. Bruising was consistent with an extensive, prolonged, physical attack.

She had various contusions to the head, face, breasts, groin, shoulders, buttocks, and legs. These varied in size, wound lesion and severity of infliction. There was evidence of skin burning, consistent with cigarette burns, to her breasts, chest, abdomen and groin."

A woman scurried from the gallery.

"I recorded lacerations on her back and hips. The most significant, a 15-inch laceration stretching from her shoulder to her hip. Dragging the body by the feet across rough ground, consistent with the terrain they found the body, may have caused this. It is my estimate they dragged her twenty yards.

"Eyes had major bruising around each socket, suggesting a heavy beating. There was evidence of jewelry indentations found on the skin at the edge of the left socket. This would most likely show a signet ring mark, from a considerable punch. Her right eye had a detached retina. Heavy bruising about the temples and ears consistent with a frenzied and sustained physical abuse. Her right eardrum perforated."

"The deceased carried heavy bruising to her legs, buttocks, trunk and arms. There was evidence of teeth marks in both buttocks from distinct different bite profiles. Her anus lacerated, consistent with forced penetration.

"The body had multiple fractures. Her nose smashed and split. She had a hairline fracture of the skull. Two fractured ribs, consistent with an injury caused by severe kicking. One of the fractured ribs punctured her left lung. She suffered a fractured cheekbone with contusions consistent with the heel of a boot or heavy-duty shoe. Someone stomped on her head. She had bruised kidneys, a split spleen and comprehensive internal bleeding. Her heart was showing signs of ventricle damage."

A juror became distressed, and Judge King signaled to an attendant to pass a glass of water to her. The man accepted with grateful appreciation.

The medical examiner continued. "We detected evidence of recent sexual acts. I made an assumption about rape; we found four fresh semen samples. We could confirm semen samples from her vagina, anus, mouth, and hair. Although the mouth and hair samples are inconclusive, we can confirm DNA from at least four assailants.

"We also took skin scrapings from under her nails. The amount of sample shows the deceased fought hard and scratched an assailant. We also found evidence of foreign pubic hair on the body confirming multiple sexual contact." Malaxos looked up, waiting for the next question, then remembered. "Oh yes, she was seven weeks pregnant." This news more emotionally devastating than other testimony.

"Can you describe for us, the cause of death?" a somber Morriarty asked. The gallery didn't want to know.

"It is my opinion the deceased would have died within hours of the attack if immediate medical attention was not available. No one could have survived a brutal attack like that without immediate medical help. Although internal and respiratory injuries were severe, she did not die from them. Cause of death came from massive blood loss, caused by extensive lacerations to the throat and neck.

"These wounds were terrible and should be considered at the same time as the severe lacerations to her hands, in particular her fingers. These injuries were deep wounds, in two cases almost severing a finger. They are defense wounds, warding off the attack to her throat."

"She fought her killer?" Morriarty asked.

"She fought for her life. She put up a good fight by the evidence of these wounds. The tragedy of this crime, was that although injured, and she would not have lived for much longer, she fought hard for her life during the killing act."

"Can you describe how she would have died?"

With the support of graphic crime scene photographs, first passed to Judge King and then to the jury, Malaxos described the death sequence.

"I suspect the killer sat or kneeled on the deceased's back and pulled her head back by the hair, exposing the throat. There were no hesitation marks, which show a deliberate act. There were four major lacerations, the combination almost severing her head. One laceration cut from behind the left ear, down and across, to the right side of her throat. The longest laceration was eleven inches."

"Four slashes in total?" Morriarty asked.

"Yes. One laceration cut all tissue, an artery, and severed the spinal cord exposing the vertebrae. At one point there was no further skin to slice."

The court fell silent. A soft whimper, the only sound.

After a pause, which seemed to take forever, Morriarty said, "Was Mrs. Moroni conscious when the fatal wounds came?"

Malaxos as bland as his previous evidence replied. "I would have expected death within two minutes. From the defensive wounds and position of the lacerations, I would be almost certain to say she was alive and also conscious during and after the fatal laceration. In fact, they left her to die. She knew what was happening to her. She realized she was dying."

"Oh no," a juror whispered, sinking his shaking head into his hands.

"How long did she sustain the assault?"

"Difficult to say. I would estimate from bruising analysis and the quantity of dried blood. They attacked her for a good ninety minutes before they killed her. Perhaps two hours."

Without warning, Judge King called a five-minute recess and rushed from the court, holding a handkerchief to his mouth. Jurors wiped their eyes and blew heavy sighs of relief as they filed from the room.

Anna turned to Billy. She had heard and read the evidence many times, and should be used to it, but she wasn't. Casting an eye over the jury, she told Billy, "I suspect you are in deep shit, my friend."

Billy replied. "Hey counselor, how many times do I have to tell you, I didn't touch her?"

After five minutes, the judge, with more color in his face, resumed his position and motioned the clerk to return the jury.

Morriarty continued. "The accused claims no link to this crime. He says he is an innocent bystander. What do you think Doctor Malaxos?"

"Objection. The witness is not qualified to give that opinion Your Honor."

"Sustained."

"Okay. Doctor Malaxos, is there any evidence that can link the accused to the crime?"

"Oh yes, there is plenty. Based upon this evidence, I consider the accused took part in the crime." Malaxos had given Morriarty what he had wanted. "Can I direct you to exhibit thirty-two, the accused's jeans."

Morriarty lifted them high from the exhibit table in front of the judge's bench, ensuring the jury could see them.

"Police arrested the defendant wearing them and they had blood-stains on each leg, below the knee. After testing, we found the blood matched that of the deceased although DNA testing was inconclusive as the samples were inconsistent."

"Any other incriminating evidence linking the accused, Billy

Humphries, to the crime, doctor? DNA perhaps?" Morriarty worked the jury through the evidence.

"In the vehicle he was driving, when arrested, the police found a bowie knife, exhibit twenty-eight."

"This one?" Morriarty picked up the knife, slashing the air in wild motions, as if it was a sword. "Doctor, was this the murder weapon?"

"Yes."

"Objection. The exhibit is not a sword, Your Honor. Counsel is intimidating the jury with his flamboyant use."

"It's big enough to be a sword Your Honor, but if defense counsel wishes me to conceal the size of the murder weapon, then so be it." Morriarty replaced the knife back on the table. "You say they found it in the accused's vehicle. How do you know it was the murder weapon?"

"We tested it on animal cadavers, giving a 98% accuracy of the same slashing and tearing wounds as those from the deceased. Plus, we detected residue of blood and DNA samples matching the deceased on the blade, the hilt and the handle."

"So, we have the deceased's blood on the accused's jeans. We also have a knife with the deceased's blood and DNA ingrained upon it, found in possession of the accused. Did you find any other evidence implicating the accused?"

"Yes. The police found a credit card in the name of the deceased amongst personal effects of the accused, beside his bed. I believe that is item sixteen on the exhibit listing."

"Clear evidence linking the accused, Billy Humphries, with Mrs. Sandi Moroni?"

"Direct evidence. It was last used at the Brewery Restaurant on the evening of the attack. I deduced they have taken the card from her that night."

"Billy Humphries could not have gotten the card elsewhere?"

"He may have, but the complimentary evidence implies he would have taken the card from Mrs. Moroni."

"Doctor, how many years have you been the medical examiner?"

"Almost twenty-eight years."

"Based upon your experience and the evidence implicating the accused, would you say Billy Humphries took part in the murder of Sandi Moroni?"

"I would go further than that, and say, he was a major participant."

"Thank you, doctor. Your witness."

Anna jumped to her feet, hastening to a position in front of the doctor, facing the jury. "Doctor, you say my client is the murderer because of three damning pieces of evidence, is that right?"

"Yes, that's right, counselor," Malaxos said. He had given the same evidence in early trials and was yet to be ruffled by any of the defense's questioning. He knew what he had to say to get a conviction and expected defense counsel questions.

"In fact, you could say the prosecution has based the case on your evidence and your exhibits, can't you?"

"Well, not the entire case. But much of the evidence comes from my observations."

"If this case did not link the evidence to my client, what then?"

"It does counselor."

"But if it didn't, what then?"

"Objection. It is not for the medical examiner to make judgements upon his evidence. He has already stated he believes the evidence to be enough to convict the accused."

"Your Honor, I want this expert witness to draw upon his twenty-eight years of experience to tell me, and the jury, what the state of evidence is, if they did not link it to the accused."

"I'll allow it."

"Thank you, Your Honor. Now Dr. Malaxos, if your evidence could not link to my client, what then?"

"If it didn't have any direct connection, and that is a big if, because it does, and this is speculation, but if it didn't, then I suppose there could be reasonable doubt placed on the evidence."

"Doubt?" Anna heard the word she didn't get during early trials. "If the evidence did not link my client to the murder, then there would be enough doubt to call for an acquittal." She was looking straight at the forewoman. "If the evidence does not link Billy Humphries to the murder of Sandi Moroni, then there is reasonable doubt, and the jury must acquit." The woman noted the message Anna was giving her, nodding her head.

"Well then doctor, let us look at the evidence before us."

Anna returned to her table and picked up a notepad of writings. She read her way through it before replacing it and turning to the doctor. "You say there were four samples of semen residue found at the crime scene. Was any residue identified as coming from Billy Humphries?"

"Inconclusive. We couldn't detect any, one way or the other."

"So, no clear evidence of Billy Humphries, did you find residue from others?"

"Yes, we identified two others."

"Who might they be?"

"Objection. Miss Booth is entering others into the trial process. It is Billy Humphries on trial."

"Your Honor, it is already in evidence there were others present during the murder. I am trying to test the veracity of the medical examiner's evidence."

"Overruled. Please answer the question, doctor."

"I found semen samples consistent with samples taken from Arnold and Brett Capelli."

"So, you identified two assailants, but not Billy Humphries?"

"That's correct."

"You have no semen residue implicating Billy Humphries at all, do you doctor?"

"No, but that doesn't mean he didn't leave any residue. It just means the testing was inconclusive."

"You have no evidence of my client having raped Mrs. Moroni, do you?"

"No clear evidence. No."

"DNA?"

"No." Malaxos wiped his mouth.

"Doubt?"

"No. It just means we can't say for sure he raped her."

"You have identified only two assailants from semen residue, and not my client. I would call that doubt doctor. Was there any residue or evidence such as DNA linking my client at the crime scene?"

"There was evidence he was at the murder scene."

"I'll come to that, doctor. In the meantime, did you find anything to suggest my client was even at the park?"

"He was there."

"You are not listening doctor. Do you have hard solid evidence, not conjecture, but solid evidence he was even at the crime scene?"

"No, but I have other..."

"No evidence." Anna was loud in admonishing the doctor. "You have no evidence to say Billy Humphries was at the crime scene. Surely this is doubt, doctor?"

Malaxos didn't answer. He lamented his confidence and stupidity in saying the word. He hadn't used the word in the earlier trials and now he may be more thoroughly cross-examined.

"Doctor?" Anna pressed her point for an answer, looking to Judge King for support.

"Please respond, doctor," King directed.

"I suppose you could see it that way. But he was there."

"There's no forensic evidence to say he was there though doctor, is there?"

"No."

"You said in testimony doctor, the most damning evidence against my client were the three pieces of evidence which are provided as exhibits. Three pieces of evidence so crucial to the prosecution case that they implicate Billy Humphries in the murder of Mrs. Moroni."

"That's correct."

"What if the evidence... this vital evidence, is discredited?"

"It won't be."

"What would you say doctor, if you were the one to discredit the evidence?"

"I don't understand."

"Would the prosecution case be so solid if you were to withdraw your evidence?"

"Your Honor where is counsel going with this merry-go-round of questions?" Morriarty asked.

"Prosecution counsel has a point. Where is this leading?"

"Your Honor if you could bear with me for just a few more questions on this line I am sure you will see for yourself where this is going."

"Alright but get moving or I'll call a stop to it."

"Doctor, could we convict Billy Humphries without your evidence?"

"He will be."

"Doctor, would the jury convict without your evidence?"

"He will be."

"Your Honor I need direction from you for the witness to answer."

"Doctor, please answer the questions defense counsel puts to you."

"Your Honor my evidence proves beyond doubt it implicated the accused. Counsel is trying to trip me with words."

"No, I'm not a doctor. All I want to show is whether Billy Humphries could be convicted if you discredited your own evidence."

"Okay counselor, I'll play your game. If my evidence was not included, then it would be very difficult to convict. But I can assure you the defendant is guilty, and my evidence proves it."

Anna now directed the jury's attention to the doctor's earlier testimony as she prepared to discredit him.

"Is it reasonable to suggest Billy Humphries lived in a household which had transient accommodation for whoever wanted it? In fact, as Detective Garcia told us in evidence earlier, it would be reasonable to say people were coming and going from the house, wouldn't it?"

"Yes, I suppose so, but..."

"In fact, a deceased accused, one Maxwell Roberts was often sleeping over, wasn't he?"

"I don't know about that."

"Can I suggest to you, Detective Garcia gave earlier evidence confirming this?"

"If Detective Garcia said that in evidence, then yes."

"If this is the case, is it fair to say my client checked every little thing that happened in the house?"

"Of course not."

"It would be silly to say so, wouldn't it?"

"I suppose so." Malaxos realized where she was heading.

"Really?" Anna sounded surprised. "But you say you found a credit card owned by the deceased beside the bed of my client?"

"Yes."

"Were his fingerprints found on the card?"

"It is always difficult to find fingerprints on credit cards. They smudge and we can't get a good exact impression."

"Were they found?"

"No."

"Were any found?"

"Yes."

"But not my client's?"

"No."

"So, Billy may not even have touched it?"

"It was by his bed, he must have."

"What evidence do you have it was his bed?" Malaxos couldn't respond. "In fact, you can't say who slept in the bed, let alone say who put the credit card beside it with any great certainty can you?"

After a long pause, "No."

"So please help me here, does that constitute doubt?"

"I suppose so."

"Strike one against your solid evidence doctor."

Malaxos fumbled for the nearby water and took a long drink. Anna noticed his trembling hand.

"Now, let us consider the alleged murder weapon. You say the police found it in Billy Humphries' possession, is that correct?"

"Yes, in his vehicle. Yes."

"His vehicle?"

"The one he was driving when arrested."

"Were there two alleged felons in the vehicle at the time of arrest?"

"Yes, there were. One had a gun and killed an officer during the arrest. The other had the knife, your client, Miss Booth."

"You know that for certain, do you?"

"His fingerprints were on it."

"Yes, you say that. Does this mean ownership?"

"Yes."

"You saw the District Attorney pick up the knife earlier, didn't you?"

"Yes."

"His fingerprints would be on it now, wouldn't they?"

"Of course."

"But doctor, he doesn't own the knife, does he? He didn't use it as a murder weapon, did he?"

"No. Of course not."

"Then how can you be so certain my client, Billy Humphries owned the knife? Have you any evidence, other than his fingerprints to confirm he owns the knife?"

Malaxos groped for another drink.

"In fact, you can't confirm my client owned that knife, any more than you can say the District Attorney doesn't own it, can you?"

"No."

"Is this what you might call circumstantial evidence Doctor Malaxos?"

The doctor shifted in his chair.

"Strike two, against your rock-solid evidence doctor." Anna walked to the table. "Now the jeans."

Malaxos brightened, knowing no further trouble lay ahead.

"You say they were bloodied. Can you again confirm whose blood it is?"

"The deceased's, Mrs. Sandi Moroni."

"Are you sure, doctor? You have no DNA."

"Yes, absolutely."

"No doubt?"

"None. Mrs. Moroni was Type A. The blood from the jeans matches hers."

Anna plucked a thick sheath of papers from her briefcase and approached the witness box, flicking through the stapled wad. She found what she was looking for and passed it to Malaxos.

"Doctor, I present you the medical records of Billy Humphries and ask you to read to the jury the highlighted section."

Malaxos scanned the section and looked up with alarm at Morriarty. His demeanor changed and his complexion almost turning white. Morriarty frowned.

"Dr. Malaxos, could you please read it out?" Anna repeated. He mumbled a response. "I'm sorry doctor. The jury didn't quite hear you."

"A positive."

"A positive? You are saying the medical report of my client, which I just asked you to read from, states he has a blood Type A positive?"

Why Anna hadn't seen this information in the past confused her. Perhaps she too thought he was guilty and didn't bother to look.

"Is it conceivable that Billy Humphries had injured himself and the blood on his jeans could be his blood?"

"It could also be Mrs. Moroni's."

"Yes, doctor you have said that. But could it be blood of the accused?"

Silence.

"Doctor?"

"Yes, it is possible." Malaxos felt beaten.

"Strike three to your damning evidence, Dr. Malaxos. Only circumstantial evidence, and we know that constitutes doubt, don't we? No further questions Your Honor." Anna resumed her place.

"Mr. Morriarty?" Judge King inquired for a redirect.

"Yes, Your Honor." Morriarty tapped his pen as he gazed at his witness, feeling he had lost the advantage, and he didn't like it. "Dr. Malaxos, based on your twenty-eight years' experience, the evidence before you and the evidence supported by other witnesses, do you consider Billy Humphries as the likely murderer of Sandi Moroni?"

"Yes. There is no doubt in my mind." He didn't sound convincing.

"Thank you, no further questions." Morriarty was keen to see the back of him.

"Thank you, doctor. You may step down. Mr. Morriarty you can call your next witness.

"The people call Arnold Capelli."

The Malaxos testimony had gone better than expected, as Anna did not break his testimony during the early trials. She considered the most damning evidence against Billy was the graphic photographs of Sandi. The images of her injuries would be hard to wipe from the minds of jurors.

When Capelli entered the courtroom, Billy shifted in his chair, restless. The loathing obvious to any observer. Billy fidgeted, muttering to himself. He knew the testimony he was about to hear was a lie; he could do nothing other than listen.

"Do you swear to tell the truth, the whole truth and nothing but the truth. So help you, God," the attendant asked.

Arnie placed his hand on a Bible. "I sure do."

Billy hoped he would burn in hell.

"Please state your full name," Judge King directed.

"Arnold Reginald Capelli."

"Please be seated Mr. Capelli. Your witness Mr. Morriarty."

"Mr. Capelli did you mercilessly and brutally murder Mrs. Sandra Moroni?" Morriarty's voice boomed, and the bluntness of the question brought everyone's attention to the answer.

"Man, you don't mess about, do you? No, I did not."

"Were you present when Mrs. Moroni was murdered?"

"Yes, I was."

"Do you know who murdered Mrs. Moroni?"

"Yes sir, I do."

"Please tell the court Mr. Capelli. Who did you witness slaughter Mrs. Moroni?"

Arnie paused, stared straight at Billy and, displaying a slight, devious smile, pointed straight at him.

"Billy Humphries killed her."

"Liar!" Billy shouted, standing, and banging his fist onto the table. Anna stood and put her arm around his shoulders, trying to pacify him, encouraging him to sit.

The gallery responded with mutterings and comments. Judge King bashed his gavel to regain order. "Order! Order! Miss Booth? Please restrain your client. Order."

Morriarty continued. "Mr. Capelli, has the State punished you for your role in the crime?"

"Yes sir. I am serving a fifteen-year sentence at Donovan," Arnie said. "It's hell out there."

"Your witness, counselor."

Anna moved from her table and stood in front of the jury, glaring at Arnie. "Mr. Capelli. You have stated you were involved in the murder of Mrs. Moroni. I'm thinking one of the semen residues might be yours. The medical examiner just confirmed it."

Arnie scoffed a laugh.

"And if you raped her, then I reckon that maybe, it proves you took part in killing her." She paused for effect, as the jury took in the smiling, self-absorbed evil sitting before them. "I'm also thinking that you are a smart dude. Did you do a deal with the District Attorney's office to give evidence for a lighter sentence?"

"Objection. Inadmissible."

"Sustained. The jurors will ignore the question of defense counsel."

Anna knew the judge would overrule her question but wanted the jury to know about the deal. They would see one bad guy doing a deal to snitch on another bad guy.

"Mr. Capelli, is it fair to say you don't hold my client in high esteem?"

"I don't understand. Please explain."

"You aren't friends, are you?"

"No, we're not friends. No."

"In fact, on the night of the murder you fought with him, didn't you?"

"Yeah."

"Why?"

"Well, he ah..." Arnie was struggling. Morriarty hadn't counseled him on this line of questioning, and he didn't know what to say. He glanced at Morriarty for help.

Morriarty didn't let him down. "Objection. Relevance?"

"Your Honor, I am trying to link the witness's testimony with the earlier events of that tragic night. He was part of the sorry mess and I want to place doubt on his testimony."

"No doubt you do counselor," Judge King smiled. "I'll allow it."

Arnie regained his composure and answered Anna's question when she asked it again.

"Billy called me a pencil dick for not having a go at the bimbo in the bar. I didn't think it right that we should attack women, and I told him. He didn't like me telling him, so he hit me. I gave him a few back."

"Wasn't it the case you were angry because Billy had intervened on you, when it was you who was attempting to rape Mrs. Moroni in the West Coast Lagoon?"

"No, ma'am."

"Liar," Billy mumbled.

"Mr. Capelli, isn't it the case that you started the first assault? That it was you who fought with my client after he intervened? That it was you who encouraged the gang to snatch an innocent woman from the street?"

"Nope."

"That it was you who was the first to rape and assault Mrs. Moroni? That it was you who brutalized her, and it was you who reeked your pleasure upon her for two hours?"

"Nope."

"You bit her."

"No."

"You slapped her."

"Nope."

"You punched and kicked her."

"No."

"You had your wicked, evil way with her. And when you had enough of her, you willfully and callously slashed her throat. And as she struggled for her life, you cut her from ear to ear. Not once. Not twice."

"No."

"Not even three times. You did it four times."

"No, it wasn't me."

"And when it was over, you suggested covering up the crime. You burned her clothes. It is you, Mr. Capelli…'

"No."

"Who is guilty of murder and not Billy Humphries?"

"No. It was not me. It was Humphries."

"And is it not true, when it comes to courage, you have none?"

"Objection. Badgering."

"Overruled."

"When it comes to supporting your pals, you have no courage. For isn't it true Mr. Capelli, that although you are guilty of murder, you like a skunk, like the lowest form of life there is on this earth, like the lowlife you are, you did a deal to save your own neck?"

"Objection."

"Sustained."

"No. It was Humphries and his pal Roberts. I didn't do nothin'. It was Billy."

Morriarty winced. Anna paused, then glanced at the jury, then back to Capelli.

"Who is this Roberts person?"

"Max Roberts."

"Did Max Roberts rape her?"

"Yeah."

"Did he hurt her?"

"Yeah."

"Does Roberts own a knife?"

"Yeah."

"Did he use it on Mrs. Moroni?"

"I don't know."

"You said it was Billy Humphries, now you say you don't know who did it."

"So what?"

"So what? First you say it was Humphries, then you say it was Roberts, now you say you don't know."

"Yeah... so?"

"Well, Mr. Capelli, your ruse has exposed you. You have come in here to implicate Billy Humphries and now you say it might have been Max Roberts... you just don't know what to say, do you?"

"I don't know what you're talking about."

"I've no further questions for this trash, Your Honor."

Anna sat down still trembling from her questioning and attack on Capelli. She got it. The very thing she was after, a statement implicating Roberts. Capelli revolted her, and she remained angry with herself as she had lost control during questioning, but she got what she wanted. It was not Billy, but this creature in front of her who murdered Sandi. Although Billy was part of the gang, he was no guiltier than this creature and should not have to die for it.

"Counselor, you should be more careful with your language," admonished King.

"I'm sorry Your Honor. I withdraw the word trash."

"Is that your case, District Attorney?" asked Judge King, as they led away Capelli.

"It is Your Honor," said Morriarty, confident forty-two exhibits and weight of evidence from twenty-six witnesses would deliver a conviction.

"We will take this opportunity to adjourn. The court will reconvene at ten tomorrow morning."

"Well, Billy," Anna said, turning to her client as she collected her papers. "We have had a good and a dreadful day. Tomorrow will be your day."

CHAPTER
36

The shrill of the telephone startled Anna from dozing. Intense courtroom drama forced her to succumb to much needed sleep. She intended to prepare papers and notes for the following day's court appearance, but a mixture of fatigue and Jameson's whiskey meant her body had given in to the need for rest.

Anna hadn't spoken to Garcia since his testimony. She felt dreadful, but his text soothed her concerns.

"Hello, Anna Booth."

"Hey. It's me."

"Oh, Nicky." Garcia surprised her. "I'm sorry for bringing up the past like that the other day. Please forgive me. I'm sorry, but I had to. I couldn't tell you; you realize that don't you hon?"

"It's okay, babe."

"I feel so terrible about it all. If I had any other choice, I would have taken it. You know how I feel, and you know I wouldn't do anything to jeopardize us."

"You were wonderful. You did what you had to do. You were doing the job of a defense counsel and I'm proud of you."

"You can't be serious?"

"I am. I want this guy to get what he deserves, but he deserves a solid defense and you're providing that for him."

"Nic, I'm sorry..."

"Anna, forget it. I will not lie and say it didn't hurt, that's my problem, not yours. No matter what we think about each other, you placed that kid ahead of us and I reckon that is damn terrific."

"Geezus, you're such a gorgeous man."

"Now buck up, you're doing well, probably too well. I'm afraid to say, you may get what you want."

"I've trampled over you in court, and you ring to tell me I'm going to win. I think I love you."

"Whoa there, girl. I thought we would not get into lovey-dovey?"

"Can't blame a girl for trying." Anna chuckled. "I'm not ashamed to say it. In fact, I have been wanting to tell you for a long time. I think I'm falling for you, Nicolas Garcia."

No response.

"Nic, are you there?"

"Yeah, I'm here."

"What's wrong?"

"You scare me a bit."

"How?"

"Well... it's just... well, I feel the same way... and I don't know what to do about it." He paused for a moment. "I suppose, if we just keep doing the things we are doing then... maybe... we will know what to do."

"You make me happy."

"One thing's for sure."

"What's that?"

"I'll have to get you to stop swearing profanities."

"Not even."

"Well then, don't start using them when I tell you my news." His tone changed.

"What is it?"

"Anna, you know I want your client to go down. He's as guilty as hell."

"Yeah. Yeah. What have you got?"

"Boy, you get tense when we talk about this, don't you?"

"To be frank, we shouldn't even be talking about it," said Anna.

"Yeah, maybe. Anyway, I reckon you agree with me."

"You understand all my clients are innocent," Anna replied with a touch of mischief in her tone. "Anyhow, I can't express my feelings about the guilt or otherwise of Billy. I must admit his story is becoming a little more compelling."

"He's guilty; you know it." Garcia paused for a moment. "I may have something which could help with your case."

"Why do you want to help him, if you think he's guilty?"

"Well, as you suggested the other day, I owe it to the victim to make sure of a complete investigation. If there is something you should know, then so be it."

"What have you got?"

"James Liberatore."

"Never heard of him. Who's he?"

"Jimmy the Snake is not someone I would expect you to know. He's a snitch. A scumbag of the highest order. I have sent him inside a few times and over the years we have got to know each other."

"What does that mean?"

"He gives me information and I give him a blind eye sometimes."

"Doesn't sound like solid police work. Are you sure you are in the right game?"

"It worked in the past. If he goes over the line, then he gets busted. He knows that and that's how we work."

"He has information?"

"Yeah. He rang about an hour ago and said he might have favorable information for you. He didn't know how to find you, so he rang."

"He doesn't know, does he?"

"I don't think anyone does."

"Good. Then what's he got for me?"

"I don't know. He wouldn't tell me. He wants a meeting. I would say, if he's asking for a talk, it might be worth your while listening to what he has to say."

"How much?"

"I don't know. You'll have to negotiate that yourself."

"What do you expect? Should I meet with him?"

"I think we should," Garcia said.

"Hang on. What's this we business? I thought he wanted to meet me?"

"He does, but he won't without me. Does it concern you?"

"No, I don't think so. I'm just conscious of your position with the case."

"It could be a risk, but I don't assume it will be a problem."

"When?"

"Do you know the Irish Pub on Coronado Island?"

"Yeah, I think I do."

"I'll see you there at ten."

"I'll be there." They announced their goodbyes, ending the call.

Anna sat for a few moments, pondering the call. What could Liberatore have that could interest her? Maybe a witness, or maybe he knows something she hadn't considered? She knew she needed more doubt to help her case; maybe this would help? She collected her papers, tossed them into her briefcase, and readied herself for meeting a snake.

Anna scampered across the street from her parked car to Paddy O'Reilly's. A cozy establishment, well-known for its live Irish music and jolly character. She moved to the counter, searching for Nic, and saw him in a booth toward the back of the lounge. He stood as she approached, and she stepped into his arms for a reassuring hug. It was strong and the affection it generated heartened her. They kissed before sitting opposite. Anna reached for his hand. They gawked at each other, musing about their feelings.

"What?" Garcia asked, laughing, a little self-conscious about the touchy closeness.

"You're a great cop. Why are you doing this?"

"Oh, I don't know," he said. "I have a duty to serve the community. This means I apply the law to catch the bad guys; ensuring innocent rogues don't get caught up in it all. Your guy is as guilty as hell. He was there when they murdered Sandi. If he took part, then he should go to death row. If he didn't, then the truth should come out. My job is truth, your job is justice."

"What is this guy going to tell me?"

"Jimmy has just finished four years in Donovan. He is a bad guy with no brains, like most of them. He can't seem to stay out of trouble."

"What's he got?"

"Beats me." Garcia shrugged, keeping his eye on the door checking each new entry. "He didn't say. But I said earlier, he never meets unless he has something worthwhile, so, it may be helpful."

"What could he have that I would want?"

"Who knows? Fancy a drink?"

"Yeah, a Keoke Coffee would hit the spot, thanks."

Garcia moved to the bar to order drinks. Anna pondered what to expect from her meeting. Would she be able to use the information and how could she introduce it? She had already submitted her witness program and wondered whether she could alter it.

Garcia returned to the booth with a beer and a Kaluha and coffee for Anna. "Do you think Humphries will get off?" he asked.

"Who knows? The last two trials were looking good for him. If I can have the same result, then he walks. This jury worries me. They seem more emotionally invested than the other two. There's enough doubt to get him off, but the brutality of the murder may sway them to a guilty verdict." They sat, sipping their drinks. "What will happen if they find him guilty?"

"It's up to the judge." Garcia shrugged. "Because it's a capital offence, he will have no alternative but to send him to execution. The method will be up to him. It normally is the gas chamber or lethal injection. They haven't used the chair for a long while. He could choose to hang him, which is still on the statutes. Christ, that would be gruesome. There hasn't been one of those since the sixties."

"Surely they won't. There's too much doubt."

"Look Anna, it seems to me politics has taken over. Morriarty wants to use the case as a stepping-stone for politics. If he loses, then he may as well retire. Mayor Wilton wants to be seen to be tough on crime, and I reckon he'll push for execution if they find him guilty. We have two ambitious men wanting an execution."

"The public won't agree?" Anna said. "I know there are those who would love an electric chair, or maybe even a lynching, but we can't be that barbaric anymore."

"Here he is," Garcia interrupted. He jumped up and waved to the weird little guy. Anna thought he looked like a weasel. Bulging, shifty eyes, lean unshaven facial features and protruding teeth, sucking on a toothpick. He slipped into the booth next to Garcia.

"Saaay, Garcia baby. You didn't tell me she was a honey. Oh, to be a bee and suck on her honeycomb."

"Just relax Jimmy, or the lady might swat you."

"Oooo Garcia, you're touchy. Methinks you've found a queen bee," Liberatore sneered, twirling his toothpick.

"Cut the crap. What have you got, or I am out of here?" snapped Anna.

"Shit lady. Don't you believe in foreplay, or do you get straight down to it?"

"That's it, I'm out of here." Anna began squeezing out of the booth.

"Easy lady. Easy." Liberatore reassured.

"I haven't got time for this crap. Either you've come here to dance, or you can drink by yourself."

"Sit down, honey and I'll tell you how your boy can walk free."

Anna slowed her exit, and Garcia motioned her to sit. "What have you got?" he asked.

"What I have got is worth ten big ones."

"You must be a joker, Mr. Liberatore," Anna said. "What I have, is a bad guy with no money, who will die if found guilty. If he walks free, based on what you tell me, then a payday might come. It won't be ten. It won't even be five. It could be one. But that depends if you help him walk. Now what have you got?"

"Christ lady. Do you eat nails? I bet your momma fed you molasses every day and put you to bed on thumb tacks."

"Look, you little weasel. I ain't got time for you or your kind. You want to talk? Then sing like a freakin' canary. But if you choose to play stupid word games, go join the Padres."

"Alright," a defeated Liberatore exclaimed. "Damn Garcia, I bet she goes on top as well."

"Shut up, Jimmy and give the lady what she wants."

Playing tough with a wise guy was an unfamiliar experience for Anna. Her heart pumped. She was relishing it and found it hard not to laugh out loud to relieve tension.

"Your boy is innocent," Jimmy the snake sighed.

"How do you know?" asked Garcia.

"I've just come out of Donovan and spent the last six months sharing a cell with that dirt bag Joey Capelli."

"So what?" asked a skeptical Garcia.

"I know what took place on the night the broad got sliced up."

Anna faced the truth for the first time in four years. Garcia seemed just as anxious. No one spoke for a moment as they waited for Liberatore to continue. "What happened?" Anna asked.

"Roberts slashed her. He and the Capellis did her. Humphries was wasted. Totally out of his tree and did nothing, just sat in the car."

"So, he is telling the truth," Anna said.

"Your boy was there in body only. His mind was off with the fairies. He didn't lay a finger on her."

"Who told you this? Joey?" Garcia asked.

"No. His brother Arnie told me. The freakin' psycho bragged about it. He told me about his deal with the D.A.. He knew the cops stuffed up the arrests of his brothers before he did his deal."

Garcia shifted not liking what he was hearing.

"He knew they would do him for the murder if he didn't deal. When he learned Roberts was dead, he shifted the blame to your guy." The others stared at the snake. "Smart boy, Arnie. He gets fifteen years and maybe gets out in ten. His brothers get off and your schmuck becomes the dead man walking."

"Are you willing to testify?" Anna asked.

"Maybe."

"What do you want?"

"I agree with your miserable cash deal if he walks. It ain't fair, but I guess it's better than nothing."

"What else?"

"I want my friend Garcia here to do me a favor."

"Like what?" he asked.

"I got picked up humping a bimbo in a truck out at Pacific Beach. She's only sixteen, and I'm looking at indecent exposure charges. They might move to stat rape, and I don't want that around my neck."

"I don't know, Jimmy," Garcia said, shaking his head. "It's a big ask to drop sex charges."

"Come on Garcia. She might have been underage, but I couldn't teach her a damn thing. She had me doing things no hooker even suggested. As it was, she left me high and dry."

"I'll talk to my boss."

"You saying that means I can relax. Okay lady, you want me to sing like a canary, where and when?"

"Tomorrow at ten, Central Law Courts."

"See you there." And the snake slithered away.

They both sat for a few moments, reflecting on the news. Garcia somber, biting his lip. Anna somewhat bewildered. The weird little man had given her renewed hope of getting Billy acquitted.

"Another drink?" Garcia asked.

"Yeah, I'll get it." Anna tossed a few bills on the table. When Garcia returned, she sipped her coffee. "What do you make of all that?"

"I always suspected we let Capelli off too easy. The D.A. insisted we get help from someone. He just happened to be the first to put his hand up."

"It seems Billy might have been telling the truth."

"Didn't you believe him?"

"As his lawyer of course I did, otherwise I couldn't advocate for him. But was Anna Booth? I had my doubts."

"He was there, Anna. Stoned or not, he was there. And as he was, he is as guilty as the others."

"Yeah, maybe, but he's not guilty of murder. Execution should be out of the question."

"Yes, but he'll walk if they find him not guilty."

"He's done his time. Heavens, four years is long enough for doing nothing."

"It's not long enough. He and the Capellis are vermin. If he gets off, then no-one is held accountable."

"That's the law."

"Well, the law sucks." Garcia grimaced.

The prospect of no one paying the price for the murder was bad enough, but no one being punished for Richard's death was even worse.

"Sandi Moroni was going about her business, and a group of lowlife thugs treat her to a nightmare for two hours. Who stands up for her? When will she get her day in court? Where is her eye for and eye?"

"The law says the accused must have a fair and open trial. Billy has been through the wringer three times without one person believing him."

"Oh, I feel real bad about that." His tone oozed sarcasm.

"Now we have someone who can confirm he didn't take part."

"And he walks?"

"Well, shoot Nic. If he's innocent, he must. It's the law."

"Tell that to Sandi and Richard."

"You sound as if you only want vengeance, no matter who."

Garcia stood to leave. "No. I just want justice. For once, I just want a little justice for the victim."

"Where are you going?"

"Home. I'll see you tomorrow."

"Hang on." His sudden exit alarmed Anna. "I thought we might..."

"Might what?" Garcia snapped, not in the mood for company.

"You know... spend time together."

"Not tonight, counselor. Adios."

Anna remained puzzled, disappointed, a little shocked, and somewhat angry with the first man she had been keen on for quite some time. Confused by her mix of emotions, she yawned once and turned grumpy by the second. Nic was wrong about Billy; she hoped he would come to terms with it. Otherwise, if Billy went free, it may be the catalyst to end what was proving to be the start of a wonderful romance.

A man who had a little too much to drink disturbed her, fancying his chances with a woman sitting by herself. "Hey lady, what say I buy you a drink and we can talk about breakfast. Your place or mine?"

"Aw go blow yourself." She went home.

CHAPTER
37

"I call William Humphries," Anna's voice echoed through the courtroom. She had mulled over the need for placing Billy on the witness stand, considering he might damage his case. She figured that to not put him on the stand would give an even greater negative to the case, providing a perception of wanting to hide. She considered the risk too great not to have him give testimony.

Billy shuffled to the witness box and stood ready for swearing-in. This did not differ from his other court appearances, except for one minor issue. This time he was much closer to freedom.

"Billy, did you murder Mrs. Sandra Moroni?"

"No ma'am, I did not."

"Do you know who committed this shocking crime?"

"Yes ma'am. Max Roberts, killed Mrs. Moroni."

"How do you know this to be a fact?"

"He told me."

"Objection. Hearsay from a dead suspect, Your Honor."

"Sustained."

"Other than telling you, how do you know your friend murdered Sandra Moroni?"

"I can remember him walking back to the car, covered in blood. He bragged to the Capellis about it. And he showed me his knife which was covered in blood."

"Did you rape and assault Mrs. Moroni?"

"No ma'am, I did not."

"Did you hit or hurt her in any way?"

"No ma'am, I did not. I tried to protect her."

"How?"

"When we were at the bar, I tried to stop the others from attacking her. They wanted to hurt her, and I tried to stop them."

"Were you in company with those who hurt her?"

"Yes ma'am. It was Max Roberts and the Capelli brothers. They hurt her."

"Who raped her, Billy?"

"The Capellis and Max."

"Why didn't you? What were you doing when this was going on?"

"I was stoned. It all seems pretty weird to me now, being spaced out and all. Once we picked her up, I was out of it. I can't remember much; all's I know is I didn't touch her."

"Let me ask you again. And remember you are under oath. Did you murder Sandi Moroni?"

"No, ma'am."

"Your witness." Anna had asked enough. No point in covering anymore, as it could come back to haunt her under cross-examination.

Morriarty was to his feet, almost bouncing toward the witness box. Here was his chance to get at his man and bring the focus of the gruesome murder back to the jury. He must convince them to hold this man responsible. He needed to diminish the homeboy image.

"Have you ever told a lie Mr. Humphries?"

"Pardon?" Billy squirmed a little.

"Have you ever told a lie?"

"I don't understand. What do you mean?"

"Which part don't you understand?" Morriarty mocked. "Have you ever told a lie?" He asked a little more sternly.

"Oh yeah. But I'm not lying now." Billy's palms were clammy, and he wiped them along his thighs.

"So, you have told a lie."

"Yeah."

"Have you ever hit anyone?"

"What do you mean?" The line of questioning bothered Billy. It was different questioning from when he faced the prosecutors during earlier trials. He didn't know where these questions were heading.

"What do I mean? Let's see now. Have you ever hit, slapped, bashed, punched, kicked perhaps, elbowed or even pinched anyone?"

"Yeah, of course."

"Of course you have, haven't you, Mr. Humphries? A regular pugilist you are, aren't you?"

"Objection."

"Withdrawn. So, you admit to lying, and now you admit to using violence against other people."

"Only when they needed it."

Anna winced.

"When they need it? I see. You use physical violence against someone when they need it? I wonder whether Sandi Moroni needed it?"

"Objection, rhetorical."

"Withdrawn. Now reflect carefully on your answer to this question Mr. Humphries, have you ever raped anyone?"

"No, sir."

"Never raped?"

"No, sir."

"You've lied. You've assaulted, but you have never raped?"

"No, sir."

"No sir. You say, no sir. Strange you should say such a thing. You must remember Mr. Humphries; you are under oath and must tell the truth."

"Yes, sir." Billy glanced at Anna for help. She sat steely eyed toward Morriarty.

"Do you remember a girl by the name of Conchita Morealas? A girl you and your dead pal, Max Roberts, met one night."

"Objection. Permission to approach."

"They found me not guilty."

"Permission granted." The lawyers moved to the front of the Judge's bench for a private conversation. Anna was livid with Morriarty's tactics.

"Your Honor, the prosecution is introducing more evidence irrelevant to this case. In precedence, he should not be raising the record of the accused before the jury."

"Not true Your Honor. This event of which I speak never came to court. Humphries has a history of violence against the opposite sex. We based this case around this earlier incident, and I am trying to show the jury he can do what we accuse him of."

"Jonathan, you are skating on thin ice. But as the case of which you speak never came to court, then it is not previous record, and so admissible. I'm sorry Anna. Step back... objection overruled."

A king hit. Anna didn't know about it. She checked Billy's record, but there were no charges of any significance. This case was not listed. She questioned Billy; he never mentioned it. What a mistake. A certifiable mistake and Billy may pay for it.

"Mr. Humphries, is it not true, you and your pal Max Roberts had sex with an illegal immigrant by the name of Conchita Morealas." Billy didn't respond. "There were witnesses were there not? In fact, five citizens, who saw you rape a girl of fifteen."

"I was not guilty."

"No, that's not right, is it? You never came to court, did you? Because she was an illegal immigrant, the Department of Immigration deported her before they tried the case, and they dropped the charges against you."

"She was Mexican and said yes."

Anna could see her client's credibility flying out the window.

"She said yes?" Morriarty placed heavy emphasis on his mocking words. "Your Honor let me present photographs taken of the girl, Miss Morealas, just an hour after the attack from Mr. Humphries and his pal."

He placed before the judge graphic photographs of a Mexican girl bruised with a swollen face and bruising to her arms and back.

"Objection." Anna canvassed as soon as she received copies of the damaging photographs. She wanted to stop the jury from seeing them.

"Objection noted, but I will allow them to be presented."

As they passed the photographs through the jury, Morriarty continued. "I put it to you Mr. Humphries, that Miss Morealas did not say yes, as you say she did, and that you raped her."

"She consented."

"She had it coming, perhaps?"

Billy sunk into his chair wiping his upper lip of perspiration.

"You admit to being a liar. You confess to hurting people. Now I present you with evidence that suggests you are a rapist. Why should we believe you when you say you didn't murder Sandi Moroni?"

Anna realized the point was crushing.

"I didn't touch her."

"Yes, you did. You and your pals snatched an innocent woman from the street. A woman going about her business and your gang had your evil way with her. You abused her. You kicked her..."

"No, sir."

"You punched her. You sodomized her and then you raped her..."

"No, sir."

"And when you had your way with her. When you had satisfied your animal lust. When you had grown tired of her, you coldly and viciously killed her."

"No!"

"Yes!" Morriarty shouted. "Yes, Mr. Humphries, you took her life. You snuffed out the life of an innocent person." Morriarty reaching a climax. "You, sir, are a murderer, and you will pay the penalty. No further questions."

Anna sat stunned. She thought her case good enough to get Billy acquitted, but now, after that cross-examination, she was unsure.

"Billy, did you kill Mrs. Moroni?"

"No ma'am, I did not."

"No further questions, Your Honor."

"You may stand down, your next witness counselor."

"Your Honor, I need your guidance. I wish to call a witness who is not listed."

"Objection Your Honor. This motion is unprecedented, and you should not allow it and I seek your disallowance."

"Counselors please approach," sighed Judge King, and both came before him again.

"Okay counselor, please explain why you need this change."

"This new witness will strengthen my case Your Honor. It will transfer the element of guilt from my client to others already mentioned in testimony. It will also strengthen the defense concept: it was the Capellis, rather than my client, who perpetrated the crime."

"This cannot happen, Your Honor. A stunt like this will only belittle the court..."

"It's no stunt, Your Honor."

"It can't help the defense and is only going to turn the trial into a farce. Defense counsel has run out of ideas, and they want a mistrial," Morriarty said.

"There will be no justice if there is a mistrial Your Honor," Anna said. "My client seeks justice. He has had three attempts at trying to get it. The District Attorney is tired. I'm tired, and the court must be tired of this crippling case. Let's get a resolution this time and end it. This witness will help us do that."

"It is an unusual request." Judge King wanted an end to the trial, which he felt was becoming a media driven event. The community wanted a result one-way or the other, and he needed a conclusion. "But it's not unprecedented. I'll grant you your witness. Now move back and get on with it."

"Thank you, judge." Anna resumed her place. "I call James Liberatore."

Jimmy slinked into the witness box and blasphemed by swearing on the Bible to tell the truth. He identified himself and settled back in his chair with a knowing smirk. Easy dollars in the making.

"Mr. Liberatore, you are a former inmate of Donavon Correctional facility, are you not?"

"I am that. But I am reformed counselor, and I won't be going back." No one believed him.

"In fact, they released you from this institution after serving four years for burglary. Is this correct?"

"I did my time because I did the crime." He was enjoying himself and sniffed. No one laughed.

"What was unique about your last term at Donavon?"

"Nothing much. The food wasn't unique, I can tell you that."

"Did you share a cell with Joseph Capelli?"

"Oh yeah, that was different."

"Did you meet his brothers?"

"Yeah, I met the freakin' psycho, Arnie, and his dumb as a mule, bozo brother."

"Did they ever talk about this murder case?"

"Yeah often. In fact, they laughed and joked about it."

"What did they say about the trial?"

"Oh, Arnie bragged about it. How he stiffed the cops and got off a more serious charge."

"What do you mean, stiffed the police?"

"He reckons he knew Roberts was dead when he did the deal with the D.A.'s office. So, he did the deal, knowing he would get off the more serious charge. He said, he and Roberts killed the broad."

"Objection. Hearsay."

"I understand your reasons Mr. Morriarty, but I will allow this line of questioning and the testimony being given."

"He said, he and Max Roberts killed the girl?" Anna asked.

"Yeah, he said, he would have killed her if he had the knife. It's just that Roberts had it, otherwise he would have done it."

"Did he tell you he raped her?"

"Yeah. He said he raped her. They all did. They laughed and joked about it."

"Was the accused involved?"

"Who Humphries? No. They reckon he was so whacked he couldn't get out of the car. Arnie said Humphries was a real pain in the ass... oh, excuse me... he said, he didn't like him. He said Humphries tried to stop them. He said, the incessant nagging was a real pain."

"Could you repeat that?" It surprised Anna. The best piece of testimony she could ever hear. "You say Arnie Capelli was complaining about how Billy Humphries was nagging the gang to leave Sandi Moroni alone?"

"Yeah."

Anna glanced at the forewoman of the jury, hoping her nonplussed expression confirmed doubt was racing through her mind. Anna couldn't believe her good fortune. By itself, it meant nothing, but combined with other doubtful evidence, this new testimony may swing the jury to Billy's favor.

"No further questions. Your witness."

Morriarty didn't move. He remained seated, tapping fingertips together in front of his face, weighing up the testimony. Attack the witness or stand by his case presented? He knew this revelation could damage his case and pondered what to do. After a few moments, he rose and strolled toward the witness stand.

"Mr. Liberatore is it fair to say you are a man of a criminal background?"

"Stating the obvious. You must have failed common-sense one-oh-one."

"Is it fair to say, you have provided information to the police in the past, in return for a deal against one transgression or another?"

"Yeah, I have done a few."

"Did you do a deal to come here today?"

"Objection."

"I'll allow it."

"Your Honor, with respect, you disallowed similar questioning with Mr. Capelli. I ask you to review your ruling," Anna said.

"I'll allow it."

"Appealed."

"Noted."

"Have you done a deal Mr. Liberatore?"

"Yeah. But it doesn't change the truth."

"Maybe not, but you are here today giving testimony because you did a deal. A deal with whom?"

He pointed toward Anna. "Booth there, and the cops."

"A deal with defense counsel and the police? You are here because you did a deal with these people?"

"Yeah, so what?"

Morriarty moved to the jury and, with a ridiculing gesture said. "You sold your story, and you expect us to believe it. You sold your story, so you could be better off. You traded on the misery of others for your own benefit, and now you expect us to believe you?"

"I couldn't care less whether you believe me. That's your problem. I'm here to tell the truth, and I've done that."

"No further questions." Morriarty knew the testimony of the scumbag would hurt, and there was nothing he could do.

"The defense rests, Your Honor." Anna wasn't certain about the jury, but she remained confident there was enough doubt to acquit Billy.

"Are counsel ready for closing statements?" King asked, checking his watch. Both parties nodded confirmation. "We will adjourn until tomorrow morning; at which time we shall hear them. I adjourn court until ten, tomorrow morning."

CHAPTER
38

Anna struggled through a restless night's sleep, her mind racing over her address to the jury. Billy's future lay in her hands and although she had been in the same circumstances before anxiety coursed through her. Kramer called her to say he would join her in court; she appreciated his support. Her new career progressed, but she longed for an end to this case.

Anna arrived early at the court, taking time to prepare for her presentation. She sat in the quiet courtroom, gazing around the seat of justice, pondering whether they would serve it today. Justice for Billy meant none for Sandi. The dilemma created apprehension, and she hoped justice would survive, no matter the decision.

As Judge King settled into position, Anna's moment had arrived. Her words could motivate the jury to acquit Billy. She could stop a miscarriage of justice and remained confident the jury would agree with her. In her own mind, Billy was innocent. She kept doubts. Now there were none.

When the jury filed in, all was ready for a tense hour of closing arguments. Once they settled, Judge King allowed procedural matters and then called upon closing statements to begin.

Anna rose from her desk, hesitating for a moment before moving toward the jury. Billy sat so tense he almost trembled. She passed him a reassuring glance before commencing her address.

"Ladies and gentlemen of the jury, you've heard a lot of conflicting stories since this trial began. Now comes the time for you to decide who is telling the truth. To decide who is guilty of committing this terrible crime. Who to believe and what to believe. This is the task that you must embrace and decide here today. You must decide about the guilt or innocence of Billy Humphries.

"I don't envy you your job. No thanks, not for me. The decision you have to make could mean the end of a life. No thanks. But it is you who must decide. You must decide whether the accused is guilty. And in doing so, decide who to believe, and what to believe.

"Billy Humphries is innocent. The law of this great nation says so. Billy is innocent until proven guilty. Innocent until... proven... guilty. And guilt has to be judged, beyond reasonable doubt.

"The state would like you to believe Billy coldly and callously brutalized Mrs. Moroni, raped her, then murdered her. The District Attorney believes beyond reasonable doubt, that Billy did it. He would like to see the killer punished, and if you decide him to be guilty, the full wrath of the law should come down on him.

"The community wants... no... demands, justice for Sandi Moroni. We want the truth, and we want the guilty to suffer. This is their cry. This is their cry every night on the television and on social media. Thankfully, you have not been exposed to the proliferation of media on this case, for if you had, you most surely would be confused and bewildered about the innocence or guilt of Billy Humphries. But I must tell you, the people expect justice."

The words resonated through the room. Anna waited for their meaning to sink in. She then added. "And so do I."

She stepped backwards to her desk and stood above Billy, pointing straight into his face. "If my client is guilty. If you have no doubt at all, then let him go to death row to await execution for the terrible things he did. If he is guilty of this gruesome murder, then let him suffer before sending him to be executed. Let him suffer as Sandi Moroni must have suffered... alone... during that terrible night. Let him suffer if you think he is guilty."

Anna paused for effect.

"But if you have doubt." She now whispered. "If you think Billy didn't take part. If you have a doubt about who killed Sandi. If you have doubt who assaulted her, then you must acquit him."

She stepped toward the center of the jury box.

"Not an enormous amount of doubt. No, the law says there doesn't have to be a lot of doubt. The law says, just a reasonable amount of doubt. In fact, the law demands it. If there is doubt, you must find Billy Humphries not guilty."

Anna grew in confidence and felt the jury was with her. They wanted a reason to acquit Billy, and she wanted to give it to them. "Doubt is what the law says. Innocent until proven guilty, beyond reasonable doubt.

"Is there doubt? We heard evidence to suggest Max Roberts killed Mrs. Moroni. We heard he murdered her by using his bowie knife. We have heard he didn't think twice about killing her. It was Max Roberts, not Billy Humphries, who committed the murder. Is there doubt who killed Mrs. Moroni? The state says Billy did it. Testimony says Max Roberts. Doubt? You bet there is.

"We've heard evidence Billy did not take part in the savage attack on Mrs. Moroni. We heard he was an unwilling witness. So stoned from smoking marijuana, he was out to it and incapable of doing anything, like standing, let alone rape and murder. The state says he did, yet on the one hand, we have evidence and testimony saying Billy didn't. The state says he was involved. Who to believe? Doubt perhaps? Is there doubt Billy took part in the assault? The answer is yes.

"We have sworn evidence to implicate the Capellis in the crime. These criminals have never appeared before a court to answer the allegations. Because of the stupid nuances associated with modern day legal procedure, these ugly men have never faced the court to answer the claims of their involvement in the murder. Were they involved? Did they kill Mrs. Moroni? I don't know. I sure know there is enough doubt to suggest Billy Humphries did not kill her; and there is more doubt about his involvement compared to the Capellis.

"The compelling evidence of Doctor Malaxos confirmed this shocking crime was a gang killing, yet out of his own mouth, he confirmed there is doubt implicating Billy Humphries. Doubt about the evidence. Doubt about who did it. Doubt! Doubt! Doubt! Doubt!" Anna emphasized each word to reinforce the term into the consciousness of the jury. She then raised her hand and motioned with her fingers. "If you have the smallest, the tiniest piece of doubt, then you must, you must acquit. The law and the community require it from you."

Anna moved to the jury and leaned on the rail, bringing them into her confidence. "You know, I had my doubts about my client when I first took this case. I thought, how could anyone do this to another human being? The people who brutalized Sandi Moroni were animals and they deserve to die. I tried hard not to be invested in this case and give my client a fair hearing. But how could I?

"Sandi was a woman, a sister. I thrust the fear we women live with every day into my face, and I was angry. I wanted those bastards punished. Not just for Sandi. Lord knows that would be justification enough. No! I wanted retribution for all women. How dare they do this to a woman? An innocent woman going about her business, just like me and every other woman in this room. It could happen to anyone of us. How dare these criminal thugs place even more uncertainty in the minds of other women? They are animals and need to be punished… hard.

"Frankly, I thought my client did it." It charged the room.

"But over the years, and with the presentation of evidence, I had my doubts. I now have a huge doubt about who murdered Sandi. In fact, I suspect Billy is an unfortunate victim of circumstance. Sandi Moroni was a victim, a tragic victim, and so is Billy. Both are victims in the hands of others. Both innocent victims. Both deserve justice, but a guilty verdict for Billy is not the way.

"I now believe Billy Humphries to be innocent. I don't think he did it. I don't think he had anything to do with this crime. He was there, of that there is no question. Being there is not guilt, beyond a reasonable doubt.

"You know what turned it around for me? The two things, which convinced me, he was innocent? Do you know what they were?" Everyone wanted to know.

"It was the testimony of Arnold Capelli. The boastful and obnoxious Arnie. The other, was the testimony of James Liberatore."

Anna couldn't believe her luck. Jurors were nodding.

"These two powerful moments convinced me. Remember Arnie? The man who said he did nothing, then later we find he would have committed the murder if he had the knife. Arnie! The man who said Max Roberts might have done it. The man, who says he cannot remember his own involvement. The man implicated in this murder.

"And then Liberatore said, Billy tried to stop them and was nagging them about letting her go. He wanted them to let her go. Now he is the one facing a guilty verdict. The very person, who wanted to let her go home, is facing execution, unless you acknowledge there is doubt. He wanted to let her go. Surely this must say to you, doubt.

"The state has to prove guilt beyond a reasonable doubt. I don't consider they have. Therefore, you must acquit. Thank you."

As Anna resumed her place, Kramer leaned across and squeezed her wrist.

Morriarty was quick to his feet, considering it vital to focus the jury on the victim and change the somber mood toward acquittal.

"William Humphries, confessed liar, confessed violent criminal and admitted rapist; this man stands trial for his part in the despicable, brutal murder of Mrs. Sandra Moroni. A woman terrorized, beaten, raped, and then murdered; conscious when her throat was slashed. A woman who can't speak for herself asks you to bring justice for her.

"We have confirmed William Humphries was a member of the gang who snatched Mrs. Moroni from the street. He was part of the gang which murdered her. We have a witness who stated, under oath, Humphries took part in all aspects of the attack. Let me repeat that.

"William Humphries took part in all aspects of the savage attack against Sandi Moroni. We have forensic evidence confirming the accused handled the murder weapon, found in his possession. We have Mrs. Moroni's blood detected on his clothes and we found her belongings amongst his gear. Items of evidence pointing to William Humphries taking part in the murder. What more can the state do to prove guilt?"

Morriarty was gaining momentum as he worked to swing the decision pendulum back toward a preference for guilty. His dramatic presentation riveting to all, except Billy, who sat head bowed.

"Ladies and gentlemen, you have an obvious choice. Guilty or not guilty. Yes or no. Nothing could be simpler. Humphries is guilty, or he is not. There are no ifs or maybes. He is guilty, or he walks. And as you think about your decision today, think about the one person we should never ever forget… Sandi Moroni.

"Mrs. Moroni was one of nature's beautiful creatures. She was a charitable person who sacrificed her own life and all its pleasures to help the needy. She was out there most weekends, doing the things we always take for granted. We always suspected others did these things, like collect money for charities. Someone else was always available to do the things we thought should be done… that someone else was Sandi Moroni.

"She walked into a bar, going about her business, when she came upon a group of hoodlums, who would prove they had nothing to do with human charity. They attacked her. They attacked her in a public place. These thugs didn't care, they just wanted to destroy a beautiful thing and have their selfish way with her.

"Mr. Curtis happened by and rescued her from a terrible assault. Mr. Curtis described Humphries as being a participant. Let me repeat that, to overcome any doubt you may have. Under oath, Mr. Curtis said Humphries took part in the attack on Sandi Moroni. Humphries tried to have his willful way with an innocent woman, again. Sandi escaped, finding sanctuary with her friend and together they enjoyed dinner and she calmed down. After they had a quiet meal, they traveled home, and Sandi, wanting fresh air, walked the few extra yards to her house. Then the same gang, including Billy Humphries, snatched her from the street.

"Within moments she had a broken nose. Her hair almost torn from her scalp and stripped naked. The gang raped this woman. This pregnant woman. When she spoke, they beat her. When she pleaded, they beat her. When she cried for help, they beat her. They beat her so badly she was hardly recognizable… well… you saw the photographs."

Morriarty took a mouthful of water to allow the jury to consider his words.

"The gang then went to a private spot, dragging her from the car and subjecting her to repeated attacks. They raped her. They sodomized her. They forced oral sex upon her. They burned her and if she dares speak, they beat her. They treated her like a piece of meat, and when they had enough of her, they murdered her. They subjected her to such brutal physical violence no other human being could have withstood it, nor ever have to bear witness. They broke her bones, they tore her body, and they took from her, her spirit… well, almost.

"They tried to take her spirit but could not. When they finished with her, they killed her. Her spirit enabled her to keep fighting for her life, but she could do nothing more than raise a defensive hand to protect herself. She tried to protect herself as they hacked into her, almost severing her fingers.

"When these animals finished with her, they climbed onto her back and wrenched her head back by the hair, exposing her throat." Morriarty's voice broke ever so slightly.

"And then they hacked into her neck so much, her head was almost cut clean off. And when they had hacked into... into..." Moriarty gulped. "Into her neck. They left her to die.

"She remained conscious and with no help. Sandi Moroni, with her head almost severed, took two minutes to die." He paused to regain composure.

The silence in the courtroom remained uncomfortable.

"The accused and his pals took from this world a beautiful thing in the most brutal way. Humphries was there, we know he was there... and he took part.

"Billy Humphries says he tells lies. He admits to hurting people when they need it. He admits to having sex with girls who say no. Now he says, no. I bet Sandi said no. I bet she screamed no. I bet when the knife was being drawn across her throat, almost cutting off her fingers, she was saying no. Yet, this confessed liar says he didn't do it, he says no.

"Ladies and gentlemen, yes... you have a logical choice. Only one choice, and that choice is guilty.

"Sandi Moroni asks you to help her gain justice. She says, help me gain justice and choose guilty. Humphries is guilty based on the evidence. He is guilty based on the witnesses and their powerful testimony. Billy Humphries is guilty. I ask you to choose a guilty verdict."

It was a powerful close, and Anna knew it could create a challenge for the jury. So powerful, it may also create enough doubt for another hung jury.

After the judge directed the jury and they filed out to consider their verdict, Anna sought to reassure Billy before they took him to the holding cells. "Don't worry; they can't convict you based upon the evidence. There will either be a not guilty or another hung jury, which means you will walk."

"Oh, I hope you're right."

"Go get some rest. It may be a long wait."

"Rest? You're kidding me. My life is in the hands of twelve individuals, and you expect me to rest? Mission impossible, I'm afraid."

Anna suggested to Kramer they go for coffee and a snack at a local diner. She remained anxious about the decision and wanted a friend nearby as she waited. The first trial jury took five days, with the second jury taking three days. It could be over in an hour on the first vote, meaning acquittal or another couple of days leading to any decision.

As they walked into Easy-Eat Diner, she saw Garcia sitting at a booth by himself, sipping on a coffee with a half-eaten donut. The man needs to get a grip on his diet, but she felt pleased to see him. A tingle ran through her, and she felt good about it. He glanced up and beckoned them over with a smile. He kissed her on the cheek as she and Kramer settled in for a chat.

"What do you think?" asked Anna.

"Oh, I don't know," said Garcia. "I don't think they'll be undecided. I can't say which way it will go. If you pushed me for a decision, I would favor guilty. The D.A. made a powerful close."

"Maybe," said Kramer, scanning a menu. "Anna would have put a fair amount of doubt into their minds, and I suspect they may acquit." Coffee arrived, and he thanked the server. "If I was a betting man, I would say Morriarty's career in politics is over, thank Christ. Could you imagine that pompous man as governor?"

They all smiled into their coffee and gulped a little relief into their bodies.

"You were great," Garcia said. "Did you stay up all night working on your close?"

"I wished I had other plans, but no one rang."

Garcia smiled. Kramer seemed unaware of their friendly banter. Another server took their order of light snacks and they set about reviewing the trial. Pleased it was over, as it had dominated their lives for too many years. They joked and laughed their way through the details of the case's lighter moments, releasing tension and preparing them for whatever the future held, all relieved to be free of it.

Anna was biting into a ham and cheese bagel when a court officer rushed over to them and announced the jury was back. An astonished Anna, chewing agape a mouthful of food, couldn't believe the news. "They can't be."

Garcia was undeterred at finishing his donut and appeared disinterested.

"Gee, they were quick," Kramer said, wiping mayo off his mouth.

"Let's go," Anna said, keen to make a move and hurry back.

"Settle down Anna," Kramer advised. "We're five minutes from the courthouse and they won't come back until the hour, so we have fifteen minutes, relax."

"Christ, I can't believe you, Kramer. How many cases do I have to do before I get as relaxed as you?"

"If they're back early, it may mean they have voted before any discussion, which suggests a unanimous vote. They couldn't get a guilty vote after everything you put before them. So..."

"Sooooo?" Anna nervously asked.

"Well, if I was a betting man, I would buy champagne expecting a celebration."

"You're too confident," a somber Garcia said.

"Garcia, you are a worrywart," said Anna, trying hard to contain her glee. "You, more than anyone, tried your best to get a conviction. But you know in your heart there is doubt about Billy's participation in the crime."

"If he walks, then no one will be brought to book. Who gives Sandi justice?" It quietened the celebration.

"It's the law," Anna said.

"Well, the law sucks."

"Maybe," said Kramer. "But who will fix it? The politicians won't. The justice system won't. We just have to live with it."

"You might. I don't think I will."

"What do you mean?" Anna asked, frowning.

"Oh, I don't know. I might just call it quits."

"Well, if you ever go private..." Kramer plucked a business card from his shirt pocket and tossed it on the table. "Come see me. I could do with a talented investigator like you. See you back there." He left, leaving them in silence.

Anna took Garcia's hand and gazed into his eyes. "Nic, no matter what happens now, I want to plan a future together."

"I hear what you say, Anna, and I must admit, I feel the same. If you knew my past, that would be a major turnaround. This case has gotten to me. I still dream of Richard; I can't help thinking it was my fault. I need to purge my guilt somehow. I was hoping for a guilty verdict to do that for me." He squeezed her hand. "I know there is doubt. Big doubt, and perhaps he should walk, but there are too many victims in this case and not enough justice."

Anna drew his hand to her and kissed his fingers. She knew, even after all this time, he was hurting. Her tenderness touched Garcia. He stroked her face, wishing it were another time and place. "We'd better go."

"Can I see you tonight?" Anna asked.

"Yeah, okay. What about dinner?" He paid the tab, and they walked out onto the sidewalk. As they reached outside, he spun her into his arms and kissed her. Softly at first and then as Anna responded. The warmth of their embrace eased the tensions between them. "Come on, we'll be late." They rushed off hand in hand, back to the court.

Billy was waiting at the defense table as Anna resumed her place. His uncertainty diminished as he saw his beaming attorney. "What's happened?"

"A prompt return may mean a not guilty, you could be home tonight."

"Oh, thank you, Anna."

"Don't thank me too soon. Let's just wait and see what the jury has to say."

Judge King took his seat, and everyone settled. The jury filed in and after an appropriate pause. "Will the defendant please stand?" Then turning to the jury. "Have you come to a decision?"

The forewoman stood. After all her positive body language and acknowledging head nods during the trial, Anna remained confident she was on Billy's side. "We have Your Honor."

A clerk took the judgement from her and transferred it to the judge, who opened the slip of paper and read it. There was no sign of the likely verdict through his expression. He folded it again, passing it back to the clerk, who returned it to the forewoman. Billy watched the exaggerated movement, hoping for a sign.

"Forewoman? So say you one, so say you all?"

"Yes, Your Honor."

"Very well, in the Case of the State of California versus William

Hubert Humphries on the charge of capital murder, how do you find the defendant, guilty or not guilty?"

"Guilty."

CHAPTER
39

Two weeks after the verdict, Anna appeared before Judge King. The verdict a surprise to many case watchers, believing an acquittal a more sensible outcome. The community reaction varied, with an even split of opinion as to guilt or otherwise.

Morriarty was, of course, delighted with the verdict and sought the death penalty.

In her submission to Judge King, Anna raised Billy's dysfunctional behavior. She spoke of his reckless nature, caring less of himself than he should. Living a life of intoxication with aggressive attitudes to authority; drugs playing a major part of his story. She wanted the judge to accept Billy's life was worth saving.

Anna argued against a harsh penalty. Her strategy was to offer a picture of a victim society dismissed and could not help. His involvement in crime was as much the fault of the community for its lack of intervention. It wasn't only his fault; it was the community's, and it should accept part of that responsibility.

Judge King entered the court and took his place. There was a prolonged silence and little activity as he reviewed papers. Everyone waiting for him to look up and address the court. Morriarty not in the courtroom, leaving procedural matters to Jennifer Hennessy.

"The case before me has had a significant impact upon the community and it is my melancholy duty to apply the law as determined."

"Under section 187 PC of the State of California penal code, I retain authority to make judgement upon the case before me. I have jurisdiction to direct sentencing following the penal code set out under capital murder provisions as determined by state legislature."

"A unanimous verdict found William Hubert Humphries guilty of the capital felony of murder. The maximum penalty for this crime is execution."

Billy squeezed his hands. Anna dropped her head.

"I have the authority to decide if this penalty is adequate and can reduce the sentence to a jail term based upon submissions placed before me."

"The evidence presented found William Hubert Humphries being part of a gang that snatched Sandra Emily Moroni from a public place. He is found to be the major perpetrator of criminal actions against her. In company, the state maintains Humphries deliberately and maliciously murdered Sandra Emily Moroni with callous intent. It is also the assertion in the case against prisoner Humphries that he engaged in sexual attacks against Sandra Emily Moroni, and inflicted actual bodily harm in performing these degrading acts.

"The state also asserts William Hubert Humphries knew before the act of murder, that such willful murder was to be committed, conspiring with others to make sure they executed this act.

"These allegations placed before the court, supported by witnesses and evidence, and after due consideration by an empaneled jury, a guilty verdict determined.

"The state has proven its case against prisoner Humphries. First, the prisoner had sexual intercourse with the victim against her will, and then agreed to kill her. Second, the prisoner knew before the death of the deceased there was a conspiracy to end her life, adding intent to the crime. This warrants the capital nature of the felony.

"Sandra Emily Moroni was a victim of savage assault, becoming the prisoner's plaything for a prolonged period. He abused her, he assaulted her, he repeated anal, oral, and vaginal sadistic assaults against her and then, like a wild animal, he killed her. The prisoner humiliated the victim and when this humiliation was complete, the prisoner sadistically, willfully took her life.

"William Humphries was a member of a gang, which hunted for the sole purpose of satisfying their perverted lust. He killed premeditatedly.

The crime was deliberate and horrendous for the victim and so requires the full gravity of the law.

"A gang set upon a young woman walking home after a day of working for a charity. This should not happen in a civilized society, yet it did. Citizens should have confidence moving within the community without fearing a stranger in the dark. We base our society upon civility and the need for all citizens to respect the rights of others.

"I have sat on this bench for many years, having to deal with all forms of people appearing before me over various crimes. I find criminals guilty, and others leave here after being treated fairly by the judicial system. The law of this great country requires we live together as one people. Not as a society divided between good versus evil.

"Yet this case has disturbed me by its evil. The prisoner, not content to satisfy his lust, went about rendering the victim an indistinguishable object of personal lasciviousness. The prisoner and his gang took all humanity from her. He has shown little remorse, and still professes his innocence when clear evidence suggests otherwise. It is the worst crime to have appeared before me and I regret only one of the gang brought to account.

"Would the prisoner please stand?"

Both Billy and Anna stood for the impending sentencing. There was complete silence; only distant traffic noise heard as the court waited for the judgement.

"William Hubert Humphries, a jury has found you guilty of murder. The state has given me authority to apply a sentence in keeping with the capital nature of the crime. There are two options, prison, or execution.

"Execution under the State of California's statutes allows a choice of three methods. These being death by lethal gas, lethal injection, or hanging. In the United States of America, a fourth and fifth form of execution is death by electrocution and firing squad employed in other states.

"The State of California has the preferred method of execution as lethal injection overriding earlier preference for execution by lethal gas for the guilty. The last hanging was 1942 and the Supreme Court barred cyanide in 1994. We should note lethal gas and hanging survive on the statute books, although not prescribed; nevertheless, these methods of execution remain if the presiding judge so rules.

"Because of the horrendous and brutal nature of your crime, I intend to use the power vested in me by the state to make sure you also recognize the barbarism in your sentence. As you await execution, I want you to reflect upon the barbaric, tragic death of your victim for which the state has found you guilty.

"Therefore, in the case of the State of California versus William Hubert Humphries, I condemn you to death by hanging at a time and place to be determined. May God have mercy upon your soul."

CHAPTER
40

A fter nine years and six appeals, Billy kept a healthy attitude toward bad news. He already resigned himself to prepare for death; it held no fears for him. The isolation and negative life on death row could do nothing other than prepare for death. Thoughts in solitude can link many ideas, but never anything about the future. There is no future. Life passed by every day, and each day was not a start. It meant a day closer to the end.

Acceptance of this hopelessness as early as possible allowed the condemned a more balanced mind. Good news was always encouraging, and bad news would never be a problem; nothing was ever a problem. Death brings with it an end to the future.

When Anna sat opposite, trying to smile, he knew the news was not good.

"Billy, the Court of Appeals of the Supreme Court has rejected your motion for reconsideration. They cannot agree your trial judge erred at law in his summation and sentencing. They do not agree a retrial is necessary."

"When?"

"Thirty days."

When the sentence was first administered, Governor Braun supported commuting the sentence to life imprisonment. Humphries would be the first execution in California after many decades and the

Governor wanted no part of it. He remained committed to the view execution was not punishment; rather, it was an act of hate.

"Humanity must have a greater value for life than the State taking a life as punishment."

He wanted to end the barbarism of death row. He ran on the issue for another term as governor and lost.

Governor Braun's nemesis was Gerard Wilton, the former mayor of San Diego, campaigning on law and order, citing the improvement in crime figures in his city as his greatest achievement. He promised to get tough and re-introduce executions. His first act as governor ensured those prisoners condemned on death row had their sentences executed.

"We waste too much money housing the killers of our community," he said during his campaign speeches.

Billy had fallen foul of a unique "Catch 22' quirk of politics. The mayor of the city where the most horrendous of murders for many decades committed was now the governor of California. He had the power to overturn the execution and commute the sentence to one of life in jail. The politician, so outraged by the murder of Sandi Moroni and promised a huge reward for the capture of the perpetrators, was now the only person with the power to stop the execution.

Billy knew there would be no late telephone calls from Capitol Hill.

A growing band of supporters lobbied to stop his execution and have the case reopened. They structured a two-pronged attack: the first application was for a commuting of the sentence to a prison term; their second approach, assuming their first appeal failure, to change the form of the execution. Judge King had directed, with the worst retributive justice for a crime; and this is what so horrified the public.

"Thirty days? Hey that's just... yeah, it is... that's just two days before my birthday."

"I'm sorry," Anna said, turning away wiping her mouth.

"Do you think I could bring it forward?"

"What? The... ah..."

"No Anna. Goodness no... my birthday."

"Oh, sorry," she said, confused.

"It would be a splendid party. What presents could I expect?" Billy asked, playing with her. "Mom could send me a subscription to National Geographic. No doubt, someone would give me slippers."

"Stop it, Billy, it's not funny."

"Oh, I don't know. It could be fun. We could toast the future."

"Maybe, the governor will commute," a circumspect Anna replied.

"I wouldn't waste your time, my dear."

"It's worth a chance."

"No, it's gone. My time has come. Seeking more delay with another appeal will only reduce the dignity of my journey."

"Billy, we still must try."

"Why? Why bother? To be disappointed again? To be kept hoping and reduce the pleasure from what's left of my life? No, I'd rather prepare myself by placing my soul in the hands of God."

"Sounds marvelous, Billy, but that's bullshit," she said. "The fact is you die in thirty days. We can either fight, or we can give up. I prefer to fight."

"Look, Anna, I admire everything you have done over the years. No one could have fought harder for my cause than you. I appreciate it, I really do. But it's over. I know it. You do what you think is best. I won't hold my breath hoping for a change of heart from the authorities who want me dead. If nothing happens, I won't blame you. It's over."

"You have taken too much of my life for me to give up now, Billy Humphries. Thirteen years is a long time, and I am not prepared to walk away. I will prepare a submission for the governor to consider."

"That sounds like a pain in the neck to me, excuse my pun."

Anna chuckled. She admired him, just a boy when he first went to prison.

"Billy, you do what you have to do, and I'll do what I have to do."

"Anna, thank you for your efforts. I appreciate everything you have done. We almost got the result we wanted; I mean, we were close, weren't we?" Billy reached out for her hand. "I have learned much here, and I can understand what it means to live a life beyond crime. I have grasped you can get out of the hole of no hope, and that starts with education."

Anna squeezed his hand.

"My only regret in life, and I should have many," he said. "I just wish I realized how important school was to me, but I never did. So many things are achievable with knowledge, yet so many people just let it go. The opportunities over the last ten years to learn... well, this education thing has given me a whole insight into life. Maybe, I'll be an example for others, what not to do."

"I suppose that's a plus for the last few years of effort; but it all means nothing. Unless I can convince the governor to review your case."

CHAPTER
41

As the countdown to execution continued, media played a higher profile, bringing so-called experts forward to advocate points of view. The letters to the editor pages filled with arguments for and against Billy's execution. Social media streamed with crazy trolls, especially on twitter where hashtags where being used to promote hate for both sides. Facebook pages were set up promoting both sides of the debate. No one could have missed the issue and failed to form an opinion.

With fourteen days to the execution, a small group of abolitionists assembled outside Donovan. The prison developed almost twenty miles east of San Diego, in a remote region of southern California. The location did not stop thirty people from setting up a vigil camp. They brought their campers and tents, a site worthy of any holiday camp. Only this was not Conchita.

Amongst the growing debate, two aged citizens kept their own counsel as they waited for judgement day. The Johnstons hoped justice for their beautiful Sandi would come, bringing peace to their lives. They called for an eye for an eye, hoping they would ease their grief once the state took Humphries' life.

Vengeance would then be theirs, and justice served.

The community pressure on politicians increased, with many Republicans getting nervous. They issued sympathetic media releases, encouraging the governor to reconsider. These statements had more to do with voter backlash than a genuine request to see justice done.

During this last week, they transferred Billy to a holding unit in the execution wing of the prison. His new cell was not as homely as his other cell of nine years. This was different. This section of the jail was not a place many viewed. Those who did had a sense of dread.

He stood in the doorway and sniffed at the fresh smells. The authorities must repaint and clean before a new resident enters, perhaps to take the stench of death away for the next visitor.

Billy's new cell was a mere twenty feet from the death chamber in the execution block. The entire wing a structural masterpiece, serving three death chambers with no conflict of use. Lethal injection replaced gas as the official method of execution. The sight of a solid chair with heavy leather restraining straps was no longer possible. These artefacts now only seen at the ghoulish museums of former prisons, such as Alcatraz.

Modern prisons were more clinical. Donovan's execution chambers fashioned more like day surgery rooms than killing rooms. Although within the same building, each chamber had its own separate access and privacy and associated holding cells.

Billy's home for the next few days would be a square room of fifteen feet. A cot, John, an open shower section with a basin and a desk shelf with a chair, the only fixtures in the room. Ceramic floor tiles and painted green walls completed a sterile picture. Cold and rigorous was the likely trip to eternity for Billy, and he likened his new home to that of the cells of priests in training.

"No wonder they always have icy hands," he said, blowing into his as he tried to make himself comfortable.

Over the years, Billy drew closer to Christianity, gaining great peace of mind from his readings of the Bible. He prayed twice a day and wrote to Christian groups seeking guidance and advice. He became a celebrity for many groups. The irony in supporting a convicted killer of a Christian girl did not seem to worry these God-fearing groups.

Visitors came and went during count down. Friends coming to say goodbye and others trying to purge themselves of their own implied guilt for not getting the sentence commuted. The visits were a miserable time for the participants, with Billy having to console many of his well-wishers.

His mother visited every day and sat with her boy in the visitors' room, watching as others showed up and left. She still believed him innocent, standing by her son, hoping a last reprieve would save him. She remained confused by the justice system which allowed her baby to face the death penalty when those more guilty walked free. They paroled Arnie Capelli the previous year, and the other brothers continued to move in and out of jail on minor offences. Guilt would never be part of their lives.

Billy appreciated his mom coming every day and wondered what life may have been like for her. Beatings, too many drugs and alcohol, and not enough money filled his memory of his mother. He tried not to blame her but couldn't help reflecting. If she had not married her last husband, his behavior may have been very different.

He gained strength during the last days from the prison chaplain, Father Joseph Carlton, who became impressed with Billy's knowledge of the Bible, more than his own interpretations of the ancient writings. They spent many hours discussing theological theory, challenging each other in tough tests of knowledge. They prayed together every day, and Billy wanted Father Joe to be with him as he shuffled toward the gallows.

"You know, Father, you have helped me realize the influence of the Lord God and His very necessary presence in our lives. It's a pity we never learn these things until it's too late."

"It is never too late to ask forgiveness."

"Do you think, if I did, He would have a word with the governor?" Billy said, still the joker.

As the days counted down, public debate grew.

CNN, the cable television news broadcaster, picked up on the growing dilemma and debated the issue daily on many of its current affair programs. The evening before the execution, they brought together eminent commentators to debate the issue.

Jeffrey Monarch, an outspoken advocate for capital punishment, anchored the program. He had his own forthright program aired each day and called for increased discipline, such as corporal punishment, including whipping, to be introduced to the prison system.

"Too often, these thugs think doing time is a luxury. I say, let them rot after a good beating with the cat-o-nine-tails."

He didn't mess with too many niceties when discussing crime and justice.

At eight thirty, the Jeffrey Monarch Tonight program opened with a photograph collation reviewing the most recent executions as background for the debate.

"In a little over three hours, we will execute William Humphries for the willful murder of Sandra Moroni," Monarch began. "Tonight, we have four eminent commentators to discuss the merits of capital punishment. People who can put their point of view about the rights or wrongs of capital punishment. My view is the bastard should hang. What do you think Dwight Kasprowicz?"

The sudden introduction stunned him. "Well, I'm of the view hanging Billy Humphries is not only against our moral standing within the community, but it also infringes on the Eighth Amendment." said Kasprowicz, the executive officer of a leading Right to Life policy group, campaigning against abortion and euthanasia laws. Capital punishment was no different to these other life issues.

"Well," Monarch guffawed. "What else would you say. Nothing new from this side of the debate. What about you Mary Baja?"

"The person we forget in these types of discussion is the victim," said Baja, a respected academic in social reform and a well-known feminist. "A person is murdered. We find this man Humphries guilty of her murder. He appeals six times and his appeals overturned six times. The legal system says there is no doubt about his guilt. Therefore, the system must carry through with the trial judge's decision. The victim needs justice and if that means the death penalty, then so be it."

"Sounds like a tough woman there," continued Monarch. "Let us turn to the judicial aspects of the death penalty. Ted Welsh, is the law diminished if we abolish the death penalty?"

"Jeffrey, I first have to respond to Dwight's assertion the death penalty was against the constitutional rights of Humphries. The fact is, it's not. Amendment Eight deals with cruel and unusual punishments, and I don't think this is valid in relation to the death penalty. The Fifth Amendment allows the death penalty if due process of the law applies. Clearly, in this case, they have followed due process. Humphries has no appeal processes left, so tomorrow's execution is in keeping with the law," the retired judged said.

"That makes sense to me." The wincing face Monarch made to the camera gave a different interpretation. "And Phillip Messenger, what are your reasons for abolition of the death penalty, when most of the community is demanding greater truth in sentencing?"

Messenger, a noted author, had many published writings about the barbaric nature of the death penalty. "Before writing my book about the Gilmore case, I was like most people, I suppose. I didn't give a toss about the death penalty. If someone asked me to give my opinion, I would have said I was not in favor. I thought that emotions about revenge were dangerous, and our heads should rule our hearts on issues about taking a life. I have changed. I have become even more anti-execution than I have ever thought I would." He looked around the panel. "I no longer consider there is ever enough evidence to justify taking someone's life. We play fast and loose with people's lives, and no amount of formula will ever convince me we have it right. Why should we execute someone in Kansas for a murder, yet in Georgia that same person would live?"

"What say you, Mary? Do we have it right?" Monarch now hoped to take a lower profile on the set and let the guests battle it out.

"I'm sure we do, Jeffrey. I think Phillip is wrong. As Ted said, the constitution allows the death penalty after, and this is an important point… after due process. What Phillip fails to mention in the Gilmore case, was that there was no appeal. Whereas, in our country, it is the right of the convicted prisoner to appeal as many times as necessary to achieve the right judicial decision. The fact is, Humphries has had many days in court, and he will hang for the dreadful crime he committed."

"But that's the point, Mary," Kasprowicz interrupted. "Humphries did not commit the crime. He was there, but he did not commit it."

"Rubbish." Mary responded. "He was there; he could have tried to stop it. He could have informed the police afterwards, he didn't. We have found him guilty as if he did the actual deed itself. Therefore, we must punish him, as the trial judge said we must."

"No doubt?" asked Messenger.

"There is none," Mary said. "The jury determined there was none and later appeals have judged there was none. Why is it so difficult not to remember Sandi Moroni? A gang of five men butchered her. She had no say whether she lived or died. They executed her without appeal."

"This is the entire problem with the debate," Messenger responded. "Dogma rules."

"No, it's not just dogma," said Kasprowicz. "The emotion of the debate has turned. Perhaps abolitionists are emotional about the issue, not taking a life etcetera. But it's the retentionists who are emotionally out of control. This eye for an eye theory has just got to be seen for what it is, emotional clap-trap."

"Are you suggesting, Dwight, that we who want the death penalty are the emotional ones?" Monarch joined the conversation.

"Yes."

"All this sounds a little lightweight," Messenger said. "It's the dogma of the retentionists which any thinking person would reject."

"Like what?" asked Monarch.

"It seems people like yourself would argue one murder needs to be punished with another murder. It seems it is only the punishment that would compensate for the crime. Most would say it is the only just penalty."

"Damn right." Monarch didn't hold back.

"I suppose Phillip would have us all think life imprisonment was a proper punishment, when life imprisonment does not exist." Welsh joined the discussion. "Most states just don't have a set number of years and murderers can walk free under the parole provisions."

"If you want to punish someone, why would you pick the death penalty?" Kasprowicz asked. "It lasts but a moment. So why not boil them in oil or burn them at the stake?"

"That's stupid, Dwight. Barbaric methods have long gone," Mary said, with a sense of disdain.

"All forms of the death penalty are barbaric, that's the point," Kasprowicz replied.

"Why should soldiers have the constitutional, moral and community approval to kill or murder? I mean, the military legitimately murder people. In fact, we train people to do it. If it is good enough for that part of our lives, why shouldn't we be able to take the life of someone who has taken the life of another?" Welsh added.

"Oh, that's just crazy stuff." Messenger said. "How can you equate war to the death penalty? That's a ridiculous notion. The fact is, if you love the thought of killing someone, you are in favor of the death penalty. If you hate it, then you are against it."

"Phillip, if the killer can kill, why can't the state?" Monarch asked.

"I would hate to think a state thinks and acts the same as a murderer."

"As humanity softens, as we civilize so should punishment we meter out. The death penalty is not the punishment for a modern world." Kasprowicz said. "It just is not a deterrent."

"Swift and certain punishment is a deterrent," Baja said. "But only if the punishment is fitting. A five-day detention for a rapist, if given the day after the rape would not be a deterrent. The death penalty would if it was swift. The Humphries Case is an example of it not being swift at all. Nine years is too long to be on death row."

"You have said we should follow due process." Kasprowicz queried.

"Yes, but he is guilty. We all know that. He should have gone to the gallows years ago."

"Well, there you are," Monarch said, calling a halt to the program and addressing the camera. "We have heard the death penalty is a deterrent, and we have heard we should leave barbarism behind. What do you think? Should we execute Billy Humphries tomorrow?"

CHAPTER
42

Leading up to midnight, when Billy would face the hangman, spontaneous singing erupted. He was due to be hanged on Wednesday, the seventh of September. Warden Jeffries intended to carry out the sentence as soon after midnight on Tuesday night as he could. If a day starts at midnight, then one minute past would be the moment.

The crowd increased to almost ten thousand in the hours leading up to midnight. Respected community leaders took their turn in addressing the hushed audience. The media broadcast from the gathering, with news crosses from other units outside the governor's residence, hoping to capture a response to the last pleas to commute the execution.

Billy started preparing for his last hours by saying goodbye to his family. They spent the last day with him, reflecting on earlier years and laughing about the memories.

Their goodbyes were emotional, and Billy felt a brief twinge of regret for the first time. He thought how unfair it all was to be ending his life in a few hours. His morbid feelings becoming deeper as he hugged each; each hug powerful with emotion, lingering for what seemed to be minutes.

The last meal menu was one of outstanding culinary delights. Billy ordered big, like a kid in a candy store. He hadn't been able to access such food whilst he was in custody and looked forward to sitting down to a grand banquet. When he received his order, he found he didn't have the appetite for any food. He wasn't hungry. Who would be when there was no point?

Anna spent an hour with him, discussing the probability of Governor Wilton changing his mind. The governor spent the last three days in New York, expecting to be back in California that evening. When she left at eight, there had been no news. Billy didn't hold out much hope for a late reprieve.

After Anna left, there were no further visitors expected. They delivered an execution suit; the clothes were a white starched one piece, manufactured in such a way to reduce unexpected soiling during and after execution. He pondered how he had taken for granted his drab clothes of the last twelve years, as he now treated them with a sad reflection, folding them and placing them at the end of the bed. He kept his socks on as he slipped on special loafers. He placed his shoes together under his bed.

At nine o'clock, a distressed Father Carlton came to visit to stay with him until the end. He had spent the day in the crowd outside and brought with him many messages of support. Although impressed by people supporting him, Billy couldn't stop thinking they were, perhaps, misguided in what they are doing. He wasn't an idol, one to be adored like a martyr. He was nothing, but a criminal found guilty of a crime he did not commit. Now he was going to pay the ultimate price for his misadventure.

"Father, it seems too many people are praying for me."

"Yes, there are many who are, Billy."

"Do you think they are praying for a reprieve or for my soul?"

Similar questions confounded Father Carlton. He took great solace from Billy's strength of character; he had displayed no tears, no regrets, and no last hopes for a reprieve. His family goodbyes stung him, but he was a resigned man who had prepared himself for death.

"I hope it's for my soul, Father, otherwise I might disappoint them."

"Oh, I don't know. It seems to me, if so many people can come and pray for you, they have a strength of belief, your soul will be safe and welcomed in Heaven."

"Heaven Father? It will be hell for me. I think you have been sipping the communion wine a little too much. Evil men like me aren't welcome in Heaven."

"You aren't evil my son, misfortunate maybe, but not evil."

"No, Father, that's not right. I knew what I was doing. I could have done things differently, but I chose not to. Life is all about the choices we make."

"You are innocent in the eyes of God. Your belief and your acceptance of Jesus will allow you to pass and sit at the hand of the Father. Redemption will be yours."

"I only hope God gives me the strength of dignity to pass from this life to His with grace and nobility. I wish no further shame."

"My son, you have the strength of many. The strongest I have had the privilege to know. They will line your journey with those who ask for peace for your soul."

"Amen to that Father."

They prayed together until eleven o'clock, when Billy asked to be left alone to write one last letter. Father Carlton blessed him and moved out to leave Billy with his thoughts.

Once alone, he sat at his table, knowing time was not on his side to let his mother know his last thoughts. He felt it was right for the person who gave him life to be with him in the end.

Dearest Momma,

After so many years of not talking to you, I am now faced with the significant challenge of doing so now, my last time. Oh, how I wish it could have been different.

Mom, I have had a rotten life.

I don't blame you for that. You did your best, and it wasn't your fault for the things I did. You showed me incredible love, and you tried to give me a life of hope. But in the end, I was not good enough to know the value of what you offered. I wanted more.

Did I care about the rest of the family? I did not, and perhaps never did.

I was selfish to the extreme. I demanded love from you and then took it with no thanks. I demanded everything from you and took it all with no thought for you. In return, I abused your trust, your compassion, and your hope for me.

Most wickedly, momma, I abused your love. I never rejected your uncompromising gift of love for me. I enjoyed it, but I never ever reciprocated and even during these last few days, I have had difficulty in expressing how I feel about you and what you mean to me.

And for this I ask for your forgiveness.

As I sit here contemplating what will happen to me in less than an hour, I wonder how things may have been different. If only I had listened to you more often.

Who knows? Mom knows.

Why was I so stupid not to realize your wisdom? What drives a boy to reject the wisdom of a parent and at such a young age?

Was it the money, or lack of it, which drove me away from you into the arms of crime? Did it turn me against you and your husband? Maybe it was. But each time I tried to get it, it just caused me too much aggravation.

I have been a bad boy, yet I leave knowing my sins of the past will be forgiven as I enter the Kingdom of God, where we are all welcome. I am an example of evil. I did not set out to be bad, but I chose its easy benefits.

Evil remains in all of us, and we have to stand constant vigil against the darkness coming out. We are only different from the rest of the animal kingdom because of civility. Lessen the morals we have gathered and passed down through the ages, or strip away humanity, and it leaves us with nothing other than animal instinct which has deep within its roots an evil base.

Evil exists because we sometimes let it back into our souls. I let it in, and it engulfed me. I embraced it with all the enthusiasm I could muster, and the evil within enjoyed it, no matter how brief it may have been.

Momma, I knew it was wrong to kidnap and murder that girl. I knew it and I should have stopped the others, but I didn't. Her life, so precious to so many, was nothing to us and we took her life from her.

Am I guilty?

Yes, maybe I am.

I am guilty of neglecting moral ethics and walking onto the highway of anti-establishment. Never satisfied, always complaining, never seeing the good in life.

I am guilty of not recognizing the Lord's beauty and his devotion to his children, and I will stand before him and ask his forgiveness for taking one of his most precious.

I am guilty of not rejecting evil with its many forms, especially its disciples, the ones who drew me into it all, the Capellis.

I am guilty of ignoring the love you gave me.

And I am guilty...

"It's almost time, my son." Father Carlton re-entered the cell.

"Just a few moments, Father."

of not realizing life is for living, not existing.

Momma, they have come for me, and I am ready. I love you so much and I apologize for not saying it enough. You have been a great strength to me over my time in here and I have appreciated your dedication.

Please believe me when I say I did not do what they say. I was there and did nothing. That is why I am now about to be killed by them. Hold no grudges against these people, they are but the tools of the system.

Give my love to the others and remember me from time to time. The image I will have with me when I close my eyes to life will be your sweet, smiling face.

Your loving son,

Billy. XX

He folded the letter, sealing it in an envelope, passing it to Father Carlton.

"Please make sure my mom gets this tonight, will you please, Father?"

"I will, Billy," Carlton said, head bowed.

Billy opened up his arms to hug his religious confidant, who responded with similar affection. As they embraced, Warden Jeffries and four officers joined them in the cell, crowding the room.

They parted and considered each other.

"Billy, you must have more hugs like that waiting for those in Heaven. They have something to look forward to."

"No, I think not, Father. I just want to thank you for all you have done for me. Love is all I have left." Looking about as he wiped his eyes; Billy noticed the glum faces. "Boy, time flies when you're having fun, doesn't it guys."

It was five minutes to midnight, and the Warden read aloud an official statement.

"William Hubert Humphries, by order of the Supreme Court of the State of California, it is my solemn duty to summon you, to be taken from this place to another where the sentence as determined by the Court will be carried out. Your peers have found you to be guilty of capital murder and the penalty determined is death by hanging. The Governor of the State of California has signed a compliance notice, and it is my intention to carry out the sentence. So, help me God."

"Warden, you are so serious." Billy smiled.

"Billy, this is not a time for jokes. Is there anything you would like to do before my officers truss you?"

A dry mouthed Billy responded in the negative, shaking his head.

The officers responded, knowing a fast response to the order welcome by all concerned. Billy's arms secured behind his back at the wrist and elbows with leather straps, which slipped through loops on his sleeves. A large leather strap tethered above his knees restricted his legs, only allowing him to shuffle, pivoting at the knees.

They placed a gray hood on his head, revealing only his face, with a tightened cord under his chin. A flap, which would drop over his face as a mask, attached to a velcro strip above his forehead and then laid back over his head.

He was now ready to go wherever they wanted to take him. He had no power left. Tears welled in his eyes. He tried to control them by stretching his lips over his teeth, grimacing. He wanted dignity in his last moments.

"Billy, it has been a pleasure knowing you." The Warden touched his shoulder. "If it was in my power, I would choose something else to do tonight."

"Thanks Warden. You've helped me and I appreciate it. Father, will you come with me?"

"As far as I can, my son."

"It's time," an officer interjected.

"Oh, come on you guys!" One last joke. "Why the sour faces? Anybody would think it was you taking the big plunge and getting rope burn. Lighten up, will you?" Billy, trussed, tiptoed out of the cell toward the chamber.

"Dead man walking."

"You really say that?" Billy scoffed. "I thought that was only in the movies."

CHAPTER
43

A nna was uncertain how to respond to the invitation card received in the mail two days before Billy's execution. It seemed like being invited to an official state social event. The card was gold embossed, and the language official.

YOU ARE INVITED TO ATTEND AS AN OFFICIAL
WITNESS OF THE SUPREME COURT OF CALIFORNIA
THE DIRECTED SENTENCE OF
WILLIAM HUBERT HUMPHRIES
AT DONOVAN CORRECTIONAL FACILITY
7TH SEPTEMBER.
YOUR ATTENDANCE BEFORE 11.30 PM PROMPT
TUESDAY 6TH SEPTEMBER IS APPRECIATED.

They required official guests to confirm their participation, and pre-event refreshment would be available.

An invitation to an execution Anna tried hard to stop over the thirteen years since Billy's arrest. She knew in her heart he had nothing to do with the brutal murder, yet it seemed the doors of justice were closed. The state judicial system wanted him to be executed. Now she faced the choice of witnessing his death.

She considered whether she would attend. It wasn't until she left him, after expressing their last goodbyes, she accepted the invitation. He needed support, and her presence might help. She didn't think it would be so bad. She would close her eyes and there would be a screen.

Fate had played its part in the whole sorry story of Billy Humphries, and there were only victims strewn across its history. He was yet another victim society would like to forget. They would sacrifice his wretched life to make sure the law and justice prevailed. The legal system had let the guilty abdicate responsibility, and all they had left to apply justice and retribution in this case was Billy Humphries.

Anna was just about to leave her home when a telephone call from Kramer advising her of Governor Wilton's decision interrupted her. She asked Kramer to read the outcome. This was Billy's last chance, and the good news she was expecting could not wait another moment.

"The justice system in the State of California has developed a richness of quality, whereby all citizens can seek justice for themselves." Kramer was reading from the message. "A jury of his peers has found William Humphries guilty. He appealed this decision and his sentencing many times. On each occasion, they found there was no cause to change those decisions. This is the will of the people through the law of the state."

"Doesn't sound good, Kramer," Anna interrupted.

Kramer continued. "I am a servant of the people. I cannot alter their will based on slim argument. I cannot intervene and commute the sentence as prescribed and indeed will not do so."

Silence. Anna almost dropped the phone.

"Are you there Anna?"

"Yeah," she said, wiping a tear from her cheek.

"I'm sorry. You worked so damn hard. The system is just so unbelievable that it can let an innocent man die."

"Yeah, well, shit happens," Anna replied, as a sense of dread flowed, tightening her abdomen. She verged on panic, controlling herself until she placed her phone on the counter. So devastating was her distress. She curled into a fetal position on the floor and sobbed, crying out the years of frustration. She exorcised her demons and after thirty minutes felt more capable of completing the next stage of her agony and left for the prison.

She gathered with official witnesses at eleven-thirty in a room decorated with patriotic paraphernalia. Photographs of important persons littered the walls. Anna wondered who they might be with no wish to know. She shared the room with twenty others. Recognizing a few journalists, most of the others unknown quiet in their own thoughts. She couldn't image anyone volunteering for such an event.

The refreshments on a table remained untouched. Anna's stomach was still giving her trouble, and she asked an official for directions to the washroom. As she entered a cubicle, she felt flushed and clammy, forcing her to dry wretch over the bowl.

She moved to the washbasins to sluice cleansing water onto her face. She gazed into the mirror and did not recognize the face before her. It was pale, confused, perhaps bordering on unkempt crazy. She stared deep into her eyes.

"Christ, you look terrible," she mumbled to herself. More water helped, but she knew time was running out.

On returning to the waiting room, she noticed a familiar figure sitting in a corner, hoping not to draw too much attention. Anna would have none of that and strode over to Bernie Johnston.

Retribution was one thing, yet forgiveness was more proper than a gloating campaigner. Bernie had sunk into a lost world of hate as he campaigned for the death penalty to apply to Billy Humphries. He was at every appeal, every court appearance to plead the case for application of the penalty. He blamed Billy for losing his daughter. His actions and language were not those of grief, rather those of the starry-eyed looking for vengeance.

"I suppose you're proud of yourself," Anna said.

"I forgive you, for trying to save him. You were just doing your job and I respect that. This scum needs to die."

"It won't bring your daughter back."

"No, it won't." Bernie shook his bowed head. "The point you miss, dear, is no one has stood up for Sandi. No one did when they murdered her; when those animals had their way with her."

"You know he didn't do it."

"Where was he when his pals hacked into her? He was there, I wasn't. If I had been there, it would not have happened." He wiped a tear from the corner of his eye. "I let her down, then. I won't let her down now. He could have stopped them and didn't. He's as guilty as the others."

"I feel sad for you Mr. Johnston. Sandi would not have wanted an innocent man to be punished for what others had done."

"Don't kid yourself, honey, she is waiting for this guy, as she is the others, no matter how long it takes. They took her life, and they all deserve to lose theirs, starting with Humphries."

A solemn, quiet announcement broke their glare.

"Please gather round," a uniformed official said from the doorway.

The group shuffled closer.

"In a few moments, we leave this room and enter the execution chamber. It is a stark room. The configuration, and apparatus may distress you."

Anna wondered whether she should pull out.

"There are no seats in the chamber. You will only be there for about five, maybe ten minutes."

Heavens, is that all?

"We ask you not to smoke, and if you have a cell phone, or a tape recorder, then I would ask you to leave them on the table now."

The journalists put their small dictaphones on the table, other witnesses placing phones. As Anna left her phone, she realized she was the only woman in the group.

"I hope none of you are carrying cameras. This is a fierce, violent process and you may consider it barbarous. The prisoner cannot see you, although you will not be in total darkness. The prisoner will see you, but only in silhouette. We ask you to say nothing during the procedure. Do not respond to anything the prisoner might say. I must stress, you are official silent witnesses."

The officer paused. "If any of you wish to retire, then now is the time to say so."

An opportunity to opt out.

Silence

"Okay, if you are all in, are there questions?"

"Yes. What time is the execution?" A voice behind Anna asked.

Why didn't she say she wanted out?

"The prisoner will appear at midnight. I would consider the process would then be over in sixty seconds."

Nothing! A life ends in just sixty seconds.

"What happens after the execution?" a voice asked.

"The body falls behind a screen and a doctor will declare death when it takes place, then..."

"What do you mean when it takes place? Surely death is instantaneous?" the voice asked.

"It is, but the heart continues to beat. Medical advice suggests it could take up to twenty minutes for actual death to be declared."

Anna quivered. Her hands were clammy, and she felt a high temperature rush. The air in the room abruptly too stuffy.

"The hangman knows what to do and we do not expect any problems."

This news did not lessen her anxiety.

There were no other questions, so the official led the group out of the area. It was three minutes to twelve.

The witnesses filed through a darkened corridor. The sweaty rasping of a fat old man behind her was all Anna could hear as they waited in the dark. Her heart was pounding, and she clenched her hands to relieve tension. They entered a low ceiling alcove of a larger room with much higher cathedral ceilings. Everything dimly lit, and the group settled into places, along the walls, within their own space. No one was keen to share the experience.

Before Anna towered a massive structure of piping and platforms. Above this construction was a heavy wooden girder, which traversed the room about twelve feet above the highest platform. This execution platform was twenty feet above her with nothing other than a metal lever to one side. Immediately below was a canvas screen draping to the floor.

A heavy, stiffened rope hung from the girder. They had wound it around four neat times, and it dangled to almost touching the platform before snaking back on itself with the noose tethered by a black ribbon six feet back up the rope. The blue metal structure, gleaming eerily in dim light, a startling reminder of what was about to happen.

Anna scanned her colleagues who were quiet, some dabbing their faces. Others stood eyes closed, not wanting to absorb too much into memory. A journalist took notes.

She quivered. Anna was not cold, but her skin erupted into goose bumps. She whisked her forearms, trying to get warmth into them.

A sudden shaft of brilliant light and an echoing noise of a metal door snapping open startled Anna, taking her breath away. She gulped in air as breathing became tense and erratic; she was not alone. The panting from the man in front became much louder. Anna clawed hair from her face and squinted into the bright light, trying to recognize anything. She tightly crossed her arms.

A group of uniformed men entered and parted, leaving Billy to tiptoe to the foot of the stairs. Sorrow overtook Anna as she barely recognized him, dressed as he was in starched garb. He seemed to be a helpless creature stuck in the spotlight of fear, as rabbits are when faced with a gun. A priest stood behind him, reading from a Bible, a hand resting on Billy's left shoulder.

Before she could recover from the impact of seeing Billy, two guards began helping him in the slow process of climbing the metal stairs at the side. The loud noise of intense lights sparking into action panicked her. Could he see her?

"Boy, if I knew it was going to be this bright, I would have worn my sunglasses," Billy joked as he completed the first of four six-step stages. The tiptoeing shuffle was slow. The guards almost having to lift him onto each step.

Anna shivered as she stared at her wretched client, who wanted dignity at the end, but was getting none.

When he reached the top of the stairs, they positioned him in the center of the platform above the canvas screen. Anna put her hand to her face, cupping her mouth and nose, compelled to watch.

Billy glared beyond the glare of the lights, squinting into the darkness, assuming people were watching. He continued a stare into the group, his eyes flicking about, straining to see someone. He focused on Anna. It may have been coincidence because she knew he couldn't see her. He smiled as his eyes kept her gaze, then he turned away when he heard a portly figure, the shape of a man, move into the room, padding up the stairs.

Presumably the hangman, dressed from head to toe in a black, skin-tight lycra suit, like a cat suit. He was also wearing large goggles. There was no way anyone could recognize him. The only part of him visible was the roughened gray stubble around his mouth and chin. It was bizarre, almost surreal, as this figure went about his work, checking the leather straps and strapping Billy's ankles. The executioner nodded to the Warden, who gestured to the guards and the priest to leave the platform.

"Any last words, Billy?" the Warden asked.

"Such is life." No one laughed.

The executioner came from behind and draped the cloth mask over Billy's face. It looked pale and frightened. Anna panted a whimper. He then tore the tethered noose from its flimsy ties and with unbelievable haste, fastened and adjusted it around Billy's head.

"God bless you and make it fast," whispered Billy.

The executioner lunged back, and a savage crack echoed through the room as the trapdoor swung away and Billy's trussed body dropped from sight with a thud.

Terror gripped Anna as she twitched, watching the strained rope whirling.

Billy Humphries was dead.

CHAPTER
44

Within a month of the execution, a mother and her five-year-old daughter visited El Camino Memorial Park in La Jolla.

Sally hadn't visited a cemetery. Her mommy thought it might be nice to visit someone special and pay their respects.

When they came upon the grave, Sally realized it was special. Fresh flowers decorated the headstone. Although the person died years earlier, it was obvious the grave was much revered. "Who is it mommy?"

"Well, today is her birthday, if she was still with us. She was an extraordinary lady, and she helped many people."

"What did she do?"

"Oh, nothing outstanding or anything like that. She worked hard and cared for others, and we should never forget her."

"What does the sign say?"

"It's a plaque, honey."

"What do the words say?"

"It says, Sandra Emily Moroni. Loved wife of Thomas. Cherished daughter of Alice and Bernard Johnston."

The mother paused for a moment.

"May life be forever sacred in the hands of others."

"That's nice mommy, isn't it?"

"Yes, it is." Anna Garcia scooped up her daughter and gave her a tight and loving hug. "Yes, it is."

ENJOY THE READ?

Consider leaving a review on Amazon or Goodreads.
I would be very grateful if you did.
If you would like to communicate with me then please do.
I always respond and enjoy chatting about future projects
If you would like to be added to my Advanced Readers list, then please
let me know
readers@richardevans-author.com

AUTHOR'S NOTE

When I was serving as an Australian federal politician, I attended the Republican National Convention in San Diego in 1996. I was on my way to Atlanta to represent the sports minister at several social events at the Para-Olympics. After a busy morning of smiling, hand shaking, listening to speakers, I stumbled into Dobson's Bar and Restaurant for a late lunch.

The bar wasn't overly crowded but seemed to attract various political celebrities. I had a chat with the owner Paul, who it seems was a bullfighter. Go figure. He introduced me to a few lawyers who had positioned themselves in the window. After waxing lyrical about Australia one of their colleagues came back to join the group after shopping for a book.

A first edition of a Norman Mailer.

He was extremely excited by the purchase because the great man was having lunch upstairs and he wanted to have Mailer sign his copy. It was late afternoon when Mailer was wondering out with a group of folks. I was struck by how small in stature he appeared with a weird style of a white hair and enormous ears.

He graciously signed the book, so I took the opportunity of asking him for any tips on writing a first manuscript. He said in his gruff manner, 'Stop talking about it and just do it.' Great advice.

I started to pen Out of My Hands when I returned to Australia using the suburb of La Jolla and the US justice system as themes. Then rewrote the two handwritten notebooks of 40,000 words into a word file, putting it into a bottom draw. Indeed, I misplaced the file. I found it recently and rewrote it for publication.

Funny how things work out.

This edition has been enthusiastically supported by 852 Press who enjoy helping Australians tell their story.

Thanks to my colleagues at Yarraville writers' group for their patience and enthusiasm displayed toward their own writing. It's an absolute pleasure to learn from you all. For anyone who wants to write, I encourage you to join your local writing group. You may be surprised by what you learn.

I would also like to thank the many readers and fans of my work that have contacted me with their positive feedback, and I hope this change of style is welcomed

I thank Julia and my children Anthony, Kaitlyn, and Taylor for providing my life with so much wonder.

ABOUT THE AUTHOR

Richard Evans served as a federal member of the national Australian parliament representing the citizens of Cowan in Western Australia during the turbulent 1990s. He now specializes in writing thrillers; writing about contemporary issues confounding the community and weaving in exotic characters in the mysterious world of politics and those who seek our support and trust. He lives above a pub, opposite a church in the historic bayside village of Williamstown, overlooking the grand international city of Melbourne.

For more information about his other books, or to contact Richard please visit:

www.richardevans-author.com

A plane crash begins a sequence of events which leads corrupt Prime Minister Andrew Gerrard, after a long political career, to rush through legislation designed to secure his ill-gotten gains for his retirement. Stalwart – and soon retired – Clerk of the Parliament, Gordon O'Brien, sets out to foil the Prime Minister's plan with the help of investigative journalist, Anita Devlin.

O'Brien, a stickler for correct parliamentary process is concerned by the rush to legislation and becomes aware of various incidents, which by themselves would mean little but collectively shape a conspiracy to defraud the government.

The Clerk anticipates there is a potential fraud upon the government being enacted, he has run out of time and now must act. He forces the Speaker to resign, and O'Brien takes her place, causing the parliament to prorogue, imposing a general election, preventing the fraud.

For a **FREE COPY** of Deceit and to join the advanced readers team is now available from the following link:
www.richardevans-author.com

The Mercantiles, a long-established, clandestine group of high-tax-paying business owners have grown frustrated by Prime Minister Andrew Gerrard's failure to meet promises, and decide the nation needs a change of government at the upcoming election. They call upon experienced and ruthless political operative Jonathan Wolff to organise their election campaign and defeat the prime minister.

Realising he cannot win the election his way, Wolff initiates an explosive campaign designed to remove the prime minister by defeating him in his own electorate using an independent candidate. Tapping into the communities' latent anxiety over immigration policy, the community is subjected to violent demonstrations, triggering increased racist attacks. Ironically, the candidate Wolff supports – and manipulates to drive the campaign against the prime minister – is Indian immigrant and university professor, Jaya Rukhmani.

Investigative journalist Anita Devlin is appointed by her editor to promote the Stanley campaign as the publishing owner, unknown to her, is a member of the Mercantiles. She discovers the nefarious Wolff strategically working the campaign, and endeavours to expose his influence and manipulation.

For more information and purchasing options visit
852 Press
852Press.com.au

Three years after the change of government, the nation is facing huge social, policy, and environmental-related disasters yet the Australian government seems paralyzed on how to proceed. Two senior ministers resolve that a change of prime minister is essential for Australia's future and begin to lay the foundations for his dismissal.

Meanwhile, the parliament is held in a balance of power by the independent, Jaya Rukhmani, who can decide at any time if government legislation will be approved. Upon hearing the news that former prime minister Andrew Gerrard wishes to re-enter parliament, Jaya turns to Barton Messenger as an ally.

Doomed takes us behind the scenes of a parliament unaware of how their ambitions and political manipulations affect the everyday Australian. When the environment and economy are brought into the mix, which will be the one to flourish, and which one is doomed?

For more information and purchasing options visit
852 Press
852Press.com.au

FIRST NATIONS HAVE NEVER CEDED SOVEREIGNTY...

FORGOTTEN PEOPLE

IS CULTURE WORTHY OF REVOLUTION?

RICHARD EVANS

She wants her culture and country back. Independence was never ceded, and she will do whatever it takes to get it back, including the ultimate sacrifice. When government peace talks stop, revolution begins.

Revolutionary leader, Nellie Millergoorra, campaigns for an aboriginal homeland to preserve indigenous culture by advocating the prohibition of mining in Arnhem Land using a United Nations declaration to convince a disrespectful government to sign a treaty. Nellie will do whatever it takes to finally gain independence and end government regulation over her people.

When there is no agreement, she recruits mercenary special forces to inflame community chaos establishing an explosive aboriginal revolutionary movement. Using high-tech intervention, the mercenaries destabilize the national energy grid starting a fanatical revolution with chaos on the streets. Their secret intent is to embezzle money when security systems are disabled.

In a surprising confrontation with a reluctant prime minister, who is threatened with an ultimatum he can't ignore, Millergoorra negotiates a treaty whilst facing her own battle for survival.

Forgotten People is gripping political thriller featuring surprising plot twists, compelling characters, and a kick-arse female heroine.

For more information and purchasing options visit
852 Press
852Press.com.au

He's the nation's chief law maker. His daughter is fighting for her life in intensive care, a victim of a terrible crime. Will he ignore the prime minister's demands and his own laws to save her? Or will politics and the Catholic Church prevent him from doing his job?

Treasurer, Parker Osborne, initiates a covert plan, in partnership with Vatican emissary, Cardinal Rosseau, to guarantee proposed euthanasia legislation is destined for failure in the national parliament triggering a leadership challenge.

In a surprising development, the prime minister makes a decision which changes everything.

The Kill Bill is a gripping political thriller featuring emotional and surprising plot twists, convincing characters, and exposes the black-art of politics that will have you questioning the ethics of assisted dying. If you like fast-paced, page-turning thrillers that draw you into the story then Richard Evans' fourth book will not disappoint you.

Buy The Kill Bill today and learn how the black arts of politics really works.

www.ingramcontent.com/pod-product-compliance
Lightning Source LLC
Chambersburg PA
CBHW070539120726
47909CB00007B/2181